# DEAD MAN'S CAVE

# DEAD MAN'S CAVE

## JAMES GALLAHAN

Cover design by Marianne Nowicki, https://www.PremadeEbookCoverShop.com
Developmental editing by Shay Siegel, https://www.shaysiegel.com
Copy editing by Brandi Aquino, https://www.Editingdonewrite.com

ISBN-978-1-7354526-0-9 (Paperback)
ISBN-978-1-7354526-1-6 (eBook)

Published by:
JG14 Publishing
www.jg14publishing.com

# DEDICATION

To Mom and Dad,
Thank you for always loving and supporting me.
I miss you more than words can say.
Love you, and mwa.
G

# ACKNOWLEDGEMENTS

Foremost, I wish to thank my beautiful wife, Teresa. *Dead Man's Cave* would not have been written if it weren't for her. She was the first person to read all the drafts of this novel and listen to my different plot twists and ideas. Her support and advice were invaluable. I am grateful for everything she does for me.

Special thanks to my wonderful sons, Jimmy and Joey, whose input made this book much better. Your words of encouragement mean so much to me.

My good friend, Brent Bohn, is a great inspiration regarding my writing. I especially appreciate our lunches discussing story ideas.

There were many aspects to publishing that I had to learn. The award-winning writer, Arjay Lewis, provided exceptional guidance to me with editing, designing the front and back covers and blurb, marketing, and formatting. He also gave outstanding advice on improving the opening chapters.

I thank those who read drafts of my novel. Mary Heisey, Richard Heisey, Brenda Toms, Jorge Rangel, Brent Bohn, Diana Gearhart, Jennifer Schonour, Amanda Sue Creasey, MM Finck, Dennis Doty, and Rachel Thompson all contributed helpful comments and suggestions.

I also want to recognize my editors, Shay Siegel and Brandi Aquino, and book cover designer, Marianne Nowicki. You three are the best in the business.

# DONATIONS

Half of the gross earnings from sales of *Dead Man's Cave* will be donated to All Breed Rescue.

As indicated on their website, https://allbreeddogrescuevt.org, All Breed Rescue is a compassionate, non-profit rescue dedicated to saving highly adoptable dogs from high-kill shelters and placing them in loving homes in the Northeast.

Established in 1996, All Breed Rescue has rescued over 8,000 dogs from overcrowded shelters and has grown a vast network of volunteers, fosters, and supporters in the process. We work within the community through local schools, colleges, and businesses to raise awareness of pet overpopulation and the need for rescue organizations in our country.

# DEAD MAN'S CAVE

# 1

*THE ARABIAN SEA*
*1695 A.D.*

CAPTAIN HENRY AVERY leaned against the rail of the *Fancy* and gazed out at the empty blue sea.

He peered through his spyglass searching for the large treasure ship he was promised would be sailing past his fleet of four ships on its way to Mecca. Two weeks had passed and it was still nowhere to be found. He had told the crew that their next plunder would be the biggest of their lives. Now, their patience was coming to an end.

The pirates onboard the *Fancy* scowled at Avery. He knew from previous experience he'd either be dead or wish he were if these men turned on him.

Avery's goal was to make this his last robbery, then use that fortune and all of the loot he had hidden from previous raids to become a well-respected businessman. But turning that dream into reality was quickly becoming just that—a dream. The men might not wait much longer. Sweat formed on his face. He looked up at eleven-year-old Finn, the ship's cabin boy, standing in the mainmast lookout. "See anything?"

Finn lowered his spyglass and shook his head. "Nothing yet, sir."

Avery cursed, pulled a dagger from his belt, and threw it at the deck. He narrowed his eyes and surveyed the crew. The pirate he wanted was standing partially hidden behind a barrel of water. Avery pointed at the man. "Bring Cornwell here."

Two pirates seized Cornwell and pushed him in front of their captain. Cornwell wiped his brow. His eyes darted from pirate to pirate. "What'd I do?"

Avery picked Cornwell up by his shirt, raised him high over his six-foot-one muscular frame, and carried him toward the railing, pushing him hard against it. Years of hoisting heavy objects on ships made lifting and carrying Cornwell simple for him.

The crew stopped what they were doing. "Give it to him, Captain," the pirates yelled.

Avery pulled a knife out of his boot and held it to Cornwell's throat.

"You said, in Madagascar, that the Emperor of India's 'treasure ship'—the *Ganj-i-Sawai*—would be sailing to Mecca on pilgrimage."

"Yes, sir," Cornwell cried out as he looked over the railing at the sea below. "That's what I heard. They go this time of year."

"Off with his head," the pirates shouted.

Cornwell looked wide-eyed at the pirates and back at Avery. "I'd never lie to you, sir."

Avery clenched his jaw and his face grew red. "You told all of us she'd be carrying a massive amount of treasure onboard. That we would even have a prize hostage if we wanted—Mumtaz, the Grand Mughal's daughter."

"Again, sir, that's what I heard."

Avery smacked Cornwell across the face. "Well, it's been weeks, and we haven't seen that 'treasure ship' yet."

"Sorry, sir. I'm sure it will be coming soon."

Avery glared at Cornwell while yelling up to the lookout. "Anything yet, Finn?"

No answer.

Avery dropped Cornwell and looked up. He could see the boy fidgeting and glancing around. Finn looked down at the captain, eyes wide and a big grin on his face.

"Is it her?" Avery shouted.

"Could be, sir. It's a huge ship. The biggest I've ever seen. But she's about three leagues away, sir. I can't see what flag she's flying. Should be able to tell in a little bit, sir."

Avery shoved Cornwell to the ground. "You'll be shark bait, if it isn't her."

Avery waved over his first mate, Seeds, as he put his boot on Cornwell's throat. "Men…keep an eye on him. Seeds and I are going to my cabin. Come get me when Finn knows that ship's colours."

"Aye, Captain," the pirates yelled as they grabbed Cornwell and tied him to the mainmast.

Avery's cabin was small but ornately decorated. The walls were draped with tapestries looted from his victims. The bedcover was adorned with the beautifully handsewn crest of a rich Spanish family he had robbed earlier that year.

Avery sat at the table and grabbed a bottle of rum and pulled out the cork with his teeth. He took a big swig and handed the bottle over to Seeds. "It's got to be her."

Seeds stroked the blue-and-gold macaw perched on his arm and gave it a sunflower seed. "I sure hope so, sir. The men are getting a little…crabby."

"I know. That's why I thought it best we come to my cabin. Looting the *Fateh Muhammed* was good, but it wasn't the big haul we were looking for." Avery reached out his hand for the bottle.

"Do you believe her captain told us the truth about the rest of the convoy sailing past us at night?" Seeds asked.

"I don't know. I hope so. You were pretty persuasive in getting him to talk."

Seeds laughed. "My specialty, sir. What's your plan if this one's the treasure ship?"

Avery stroked his stubbled chin and grinned. "Our fleet will stay in the cove behind the island, until she's close enough for us to pounce on her. We should be able to come up on the *Ganj-i-Sawai* before she knows what's happening. The sloops and brigantine will take the lead and flank her, clearing the way for us. The *Fancy* will head straight for her. Each captain agrees with the plan."

"Excellent, sir. Our four ships should be no match for one vessel, even if it is as large as expected."

Avery took a big gulp and slammed the bottle down, splashing rum on the table. "I was hoping Captain Gibson would listen to us and we wouldn't have to take over his ship, but he was an idiot. I told him we could make her sail like no other. Clean the hull. Get rid of useless parts. But did he listen? No. Well, she's my ship now, and we're doing things my way. Now she's one of the fastest ships of her class. Her new name suits her well." Avery handed the bottle to Seeds.

Seeds took a gulp. "Yes, sir. And bringing the *Fancy* to sixty-two cannons will make her too tough for any ship to handle."

"The admiral should have made me captain, not Gibson. He said I wasn't ready yet. Can you believe that?"

"Both the admiral and Gibson were fools, sir."

Avery grabbed the bottle and took another mouthful of rum. "Just because I didn't come from money. That's no reason not to make me a captain. If I were rich, I would have been a captain years ago. I'll show those pompous fools. A captain is a captain, no matter if he got the title from the Royal Navy or by mutiny."

Seeds looked at the floor and fidgeted with his shirt. "Yes, sir."

"Look at me when I'm talking to you, Seeds."

"Sorry, sir. It's just…"

"Just what? Don't be so mealymouthed."

"Well, sir, you broke Johnson's nose last time you got upset when talking about the Royal Navy and Captain Gibson."

"Johnson had it coming to him. He's an incompetent boob."

"I'm sorry, sir."

"As I was saying…I was a gentleman when we took over the ship. Did I kill Gibson? No. I should have, but no. Leaving him on that island was extremely kind of me. That's how a man of distinction acts."

"Yes, sir."

Avery stood up and walked back and forth behind his desk. "I deserve to live the life I want."

Seeds sighed. "Yes, Captain. It'll happen."

"I've waited long enough. Robbing the *Ganj-i-Sawai* will give me what I want now, rather than having to rob a bunch of ships for the next who-knows-how-many years. This is a once-in-a-lifetime chance, Seeds. I need that treasure."

"This ship has got to be her, sir. Finn said there was a huge ship sailing our way. The *Fateh Muhammed* was a big ship, and a big haul, sir. This next ship sounds even bigger."

"Give me the bottle," Avery bellowed, and took another gulp of rum. He balled up his right hand and punched the wall. The parrot squawked and jumped onto Seeds' shoulder. "My plans for a better life will happen."

Seeds slid his chair back. "Of course, sir."

Avery looked up at the ceiling and rubbed his temples. He whispered as if he were thinking out loud. "First, I become a captain and save a ton of money. Start a business and become the most respected man in the community." Avery looked at Seeds. "Being a captain is good, but not good enough. I'll show them."

"Sir, trust me. Your plans will happen."

"How can you be so sure, Seeds?"

"Captain, you and I have been fighting side-by-side since we joined the navy together."

"You've saved my life at least twice, Seeds."

"And you've saved mine, Captain. I know the kind of man you are. It will happen, sir."

Avery took another large gulp of rum and slid the bottle across the desk to Seeds. "If Cornwell's wrong…he's a dead man."

THE PIRATE RAN down the steps and stood outside the captain's cabin. He overheard the captain talking. He took a deep breath and knocked on the door. Seeds opened it.

The pirate looked down at the floor. "Umm…sorry to interrupt. Finn said to get the captain. He'll be able to tell us about that ship any time now."

Avery pushed the pirate out of the way and ran up the stairs onto the deck. "Give me good news, Finn."

"I can just about make out her colours, sir. Almost…almost… India, sir. She's from India."

Avery briefly smiled and then scowled at Cornwell. "This ship better be the one. If your information is wrong, I won't leave you on an island like I did Gibson. I'll let the men have at you."

Cornwell, still tied up, stared at the deck, not looking Avery in the eye. "I'm positive I got it right, sir,"

"Now tell Finn what the *Ganj-i-Sawai's* looks like."

Cornwell yelled up to the boy. "It's got a big crown on the bow and the letter 'G' carved in it."

"You got that, Finn?" Avery asked.

"Yes, Captain. I should be able to tell any…second…now." A few moments later, Finn grabbed the railing of the lookout and jumped up and down. "Captain, it's her. It's her."

# 2

AVERY PUFFED OUT his chest and smiled as he looked out at his fleet. The other captains chose him as their leader—their admiral. The *Fancy, two* six-gun sloops, and a six-gun brigantine were all under his command. He called out to Seeds. "Signal the captains and tell them to come aboard. I want to tell them the ship's close."

Once aboard the *Fancy,* the captains gathered around Avery. He grabbed each one by the shoulder and called them out by name. "Faro, Mayes, and Wake…the *Ganj-i-Sawai's* almost here." Avery wiped the sweat from the hot sea off his brow.

"Finally," Faro said.

Wake chimed in. "I was thinking she might never get here."

"I know, but she should be here early tomorrow," Avery said. "We've waited a long time for this day. We've been a fearsome fleet this past year. Robbed some pretty big ships, but nothing of this size. We're going to be rich—very rich. Now go back to your ships and get your crews ready. We'll work this like we planned."

The next morning, as the sun broke over the horizon, Avery yelled up at Finn already in the lookout. "Where is she?"

"She's about a league out, sir."

Avery stood on top of an old barrel and told his crew to gather around him. "She's almost here, gentlemen. Remember what we discussed. No time for sloppiness. We'll be going after her in a few minutes. I'm going down below to change into something more appropriate for the occasion. Now get to your posts."

Avery couldn't help but give a big toothy grin as his crew of pirates cheered and ran to their stations.

In his cabin, Avery changed out of his everyday attire. He threw his baggy trousers onto the floor. He took off his short jacket and simple grey shirt and tossed them on the bed. Whenever they were about to overtake a ship, Avery always put on an indigo-colored jacket and expensive leather boots he had stolen from a captain aboard a vessel he'd looted. He wanted to send a message to his victims that he was a prosperous pirate. Avery looked at himself in the mirror and smiled.

Back on deck, Avery adjusted his jacket, stood up straight, and called out to his fleet's captains. "She's almost here. All ships, keep your British flag flying until I tell you otherwise. She's about an hour away. Get your crews ready."

Avery walked alone to the starboard side of the *Fancy* to go over his plan one more time. He kept the British flags raised, just like his old pirate friend taught him. The spied vessel would think they were another British fleet on the high seas.

Avery shook his head and laughed. *Funny how you remember things at a time like this*, he thought to himself. *Patterson taught me so much. He sure was funny looking without any teeth. Older than dirt but still loved looking at the ladies. Everyone in Madagascar respected Patterson. None more than me. A bottle of rum and he'd tell you everything he'd learned over the years.*

"We're ready, sir," Seeds said as he walked over to Avery.

"Remember Patterson?" Avery asked.

"Sure do. Great pirate."

"He was the one who told me about keeping several flags onboard from different countries so I could fly under false colours. Said that flying a country's flag would allow my ship to get near my target without drawing suspicion. Then, while they were off guard, raise our colours and attack."

"It hasn't failed us yet, sir."

Avery took one last look at the island, turned around, and adjusted his coat and hat. "Let's do this, Seeds."

# 3

AVERY LOOKED UP at Finn. "Where's she now?"

"She's in front of the island, sir."

Avery nodded and shouted to the fleet. "All hands, get to your stations! Remember the battle plan. Clear the way for us, men. Now, let's go get her."

The pirates sent out a resounding cheer as the ships set sail.

Fifteen minutes later, Avery yelled up to Finn. "What's her distance?"

"Captain, she's three hundred yards to our starboard side."

The pirate fleet, flying British colours, came from behind the island. They got within one hundred yards of the gigantic vessel.

As Avery and his fleet got within range, he yelled out orders to Seeds and his captains. "Lower the British flags and hoist our flags." Avery's lips twisted into a grin as he watched the skull and crossbones flag raise overhead. He loved to instill fear in the sailors of the ships he plundered. He nodded, satisfied with his pirate flag blowing in the breeze overhead, loving his reputation as a cunning and prosperous pirate.

Avery saw Finn anxiously going from side to side in the lookout. "She's lighting a cannon, sir," Finn yelled.

The cannon on the *Ganj-i-Sawai* malfunctioned and exploded. Avery's eyes grew wide as shards flew in all directions on the ship.

Twenty men were blown back against the railing and others were thrown into the sea.

Avery yelled at Seeds. "Fire!" The cannonball hit the *Ganj-i-Sawai's* mainmast, snapping it in two.

"Seeds, make sure you don't hit her hull, you old salt," Avery screamed from behind the whip. "I don't want her sunk."

Seeds saluted. "Aye, aye, Captain."

Avery didn't want to damage the magnificent ship in front of him. He merely wanted to stop it so he could loot her and possibly keep her as his own.

"Swarm 'em," Avery ordered his fleet. The sloops and brigantine surged upon the *Ganj-i-Sawai* as it tried to fire off another shot. Avery signaled his fleet's captains to board the ship as more than one hundred pirates stormed their prize. They came swooping upon the massive vessel from all sides, firing their guns and brandishing their swords. The pirates first disabled the *Ganj-i-Sawai's* rudder so it couldn't escape.

"Get ready to board," shouted Avery at the *Fancy's* crew as it came up the starboard side of the ship. "Now!" yelled Avery.

The pirates threw grappling hooks with ropes onto the *Ganj-i-Sawai* and climbed up the side of the ship. Several crewmembers leaned over the side and fired at the pirates. A pirate's boarding axe hit one of the men and he fell into the sea. Several pirates were shot and killed trying to board the *Ganj-i-Sawai*. Smoke and screams filled the air.

Avery looked on as three of his crew covered Seeds as he ran onto the prized vessel. They fired their pistols and swung their cutlasses at any Indian sailor who stood in their way. A sailor snuck up behind Seeds, and as he was about to stab him with a sword, a fellow buccaneer swung his cutlass at the sailor's hand. The sailor grabbed his arm and screamed only to be shot in the chest by another pirate running by.

Seeds nodded thanks and both went about fighting.

Chaos reigned on the deck of the *Ganj-i-Sawai*. Some of the passengers swung swords at the pirates but were no match for men who fought for a living. One pirate laughed as he knocked the sword out of the passenger's hand and pointed his boarding axe at him only to see the man run and jump off the side of the ship into the water below. Another passenger tried to run belowdeck as a pike flew and hit him in the leg, making him tumble down the stairs.

The fight was going in Avery's favor. The crew of the *Ganj-i-Sawai* was being slaughtered as additional crew from the pirate fleet was coming onboard. Avery saw a man, whom he assumed was the ship's captain, climb up a few steps, cup his hands, and yell, "Lay down your arms. Do not resist them any longer."

The besieged crew backed away from the pirates, put down their armaments, and held up their hands. The pirates, still holding their weapons, pointed to the crew to go toward the center of the ship.

As if on cue, Avery slowly and regally climbed aboard the *Ganj-i-Sawai*. He surveyed the ship, and with two heavily muscled men at his side, stomped toward the man who told the *Ganj-i-Sawai's* crew to lay down their weapons. "Are you this ship's captain?" Avery scowled.

"Yes, I am Captain Ibrahim."

Avery walked up to Ibrahim and stood an inch from his face. "Surrender, or I will show no mercy to you, your passengers, nor the crew."

Ibrahim nodded and turned toward his sailors. "Do as they say."

While the pirates held the *Ganj-i-Sawai's* crew at gunpoint, Avery shoved a quivering Ibrahim to the deck. Narrowing his eyes and twisting his lips into a snarl, Avery demanded, "Where are you going, and what and who are on this ship?"

"Sir, you are making a big mistake. This is the Emperor's…the

Grand Mughal's ship. She is no ordinary ship with ordinary passengers. This is the *Ganj-i-Sawai*."

Avery turned toward Seeds and nodded. He snarled at Ibrahim and slapped him across the face. "I will not ask again. Where are you going, and what and who are on this ship?"

"Very well. We were going to Mecca."

"No," yelled one of the sailors. "Tell them nothing."

"Dyson...shut him up," commanded Avery.

"With pleasure, sir," Dyson said. He walked toward the sailor, grabbed him by the shirt and pants, and threw him overboard. The rest of the pirates walked closer to the remaining Indian sailors, pointing their weapons at their heads.

"You were saying," Avery said.

Ibrahim lowered his head and softly spoke. "I beg you, sir. Mumtaz, the emperor's daughter, is onboard. Take all our money and jewelry if you must, but please let her...please let all of us go." Ibrahim trembled as he pleaded with Avery. "What we have is on the second level."

Avery grinned. His smile grew when he saw Ibrahim's crew shaking their heads at their leader. Avery pointed to a group of his crew standing to the side. "Six of you, go bring up the money and jewels."

The men came back with ten bags of coins and two chests loaded with jewelry. "This is all of it, Captain," said one of Avery's crew.

Again, Avery smacked Ibrahim across the face. "Is there any more?"

"You have it all. Now, please let us go."

Avery brought his hand to his face and tapped his chin as he thought about what he'd do next. Avery's men were watching him, and he knew he couldn't show any sign of weakness. But, if the pirates harmed Mumtaz, there'd be no place Avery could hide. The emperor would hunt him down for the rest of his life.

Avery straightened himself and glared at Ibrahim. He looked over at his pirate crew and swiped a finger across his throat.

"No, please don't kill me!" begged Ibrahim. "I'll do whatever you say."

The men understood what the captain meant. Avery didn't like killing unless he absolutely had to. Swiping his finger across his throat was usually enough for the captain of a raided ship to hand over any last bits of hidden treasure in exchange for his life. This was a trick he'd learned from his friend Patterson.

Clearly afraid of being killed, Ibrahim blurted, gasping for breath, "There are two money chests in my cabin. They are to be presented as an offering at the Shrine of Mahomet."

Avery looked at Ibrahim's crew and noticed them once again shaking their heads and spitting on the deck. He grinned, pleased that his hand-across-the-throat ploy had worked again.

Avery pointed to the same six men. "Go get the chests and bring them to me."

The pirates returned carrying two ornate chests adorned with rubies and emeralds and placed them in front of Avery. He glared at Ibrahim. "Give me the keys."

Ibrahim looked down, sighed, and then pulled out two keys and handed them to Avery.

Avery held his breath, unlocked the padlocks, and gradually opened the money chests. His eyes grew wide when he saw they were filled with gold, silver, and jewels.

Avery beamed knowing they had seized the largest prize of their lives. He stood up straight, adjusted his hat and jacket, and walked over to his crew. "Take all the money and jewelry from the passengers but do not harm them. We will let them go without so much as a scratch. Gather their supplies and put them on our fleet. We'll leave them their ship. We don't need this behemoth slowing us down."

He looked at Ibrahim and raised his chin and held back his chest. "As you can see, I have been rather generous. Tell your emperor I have been a true gentleman and spared his daughter's life. Even the passengers and you are still alive. I have also given him back his ship."

Ibrahim bowed slightly.

Avery hoped the emperor would be relieved his daughter was alive and not be quite so eager to hunt him down. But he realized this sentiment wouldn't last long. Avery knew the Grand Mughal would demand retribution for his ship being robbed of his money and jewels. Ibrahim would most likely be executed when he returned to India, if his crew and passengers didn't throw him overboard first for giving up so easily.

The pirates gathered all of the Indian sailors' weapons and loaded them onto their fleet. They went through the entire ship taking off everything that could be useful to them. Avery ordered his men to take the cannons too, in case Ibrahim got brave and decided to sail after them. When the pirates had taken everything they wanted, they disembarked the ship and returned to their own.

Avery told the pirates to return to the small island. There they'd find out exactly what was the extent of their plunder and divide up the spoils.

# 4

SEVERAL HOURS LATER, Avery called his fleet's crew over. He opened a rolled-up scroll he had written notes on and spoke to them in a manner a naval officer would address his sailors. "Men, we lost a number of our crew during our recent battles, including Captain Tew. But, as we all know, being killed is one of the possible perils of our profession."

"Aye," the pirates whispered.

"Now…as we agreed upon before setting sail to the Arabian Sea, I have set aside the approved amount of our newly acquired money and goods for the following: needed repairs; to Doc for fixing up those of us hurt; to our carpenter Thomas; to your captains, and to me as your admiral. We will use the food and supplies taken from the *Ganj-i-Sawai*, so there is no need to save any money from our latest adventure for those things. Doc told me no crew has lost a limb nor eye, so no one needs an extra share for any such misfortune."

To increase suspense, Avery climbed on a boulder and adjusted his jacket. He looked out at the crew and smiled. "We have taken in the greatest haul of our journey so far."

The pirates cheered and patted themselves on the back.

"I have performed the calculations and have determined we have plundered over £600,000 in Pieces of Eight, gold, silver, diamonds, and jewelry from the *Ganj-i-Sawai*."

Many of the pirates shouted for joy and danced around in circles. Some stood wide-eyed in shock at how much they had stolen.

Avery held up his hand to quiet the men. "In addition to the money we took, I have calculated the value of the jewelry and diamonds in determining your shares. After taking out the agreed upon amount, each of you will receive…" He paused for effect. "£1,000 in coins and gems!" Another loud cheer rang up from all the pirates. "Finn, the captains and I have agreed to give you extra for your hard work. You get £500."

The pirates ran around throwing bottles of rum in the air. They had done it. They had captured the Mughal's main treasure ship. It was the most they had ever received from one robbery. Avery kept the larger share, and the two adorned money chests for himself, giving his first mates a greater share, per the pirates' agreement.

AVERY AND HIS pirates drank rum and ate the food stolen from the *Ganj-i-Sawai* for the next several days. They enjoyed being on land for a while and not confined to the tight quarters on ship and breathing the stale air belowdeck. There was no need to stay onboard their ships, waiting for another ship to rob. They could roam the island without bumping into each other, unlike the tight confines of a ship.

Avery lay on the beach smiling with a bottle of rum in his hand. He could walk away from the life of pirating with his share of the bounty stolen from the *Ganj-i-Sawai* and all the ships they'd previously looted. He could now live as a rich gentleman anywhere in the world. Of course, he'd have to keep looking over his shoulder wondering when, not if, the Grand Mughal would come after him, but he supposed that was the price to pay for what he'd done.

He had given a low estimate regarding the worth of the jewelry and diamonds when he spoke to the crew. Now, taking into account what he could sell them for to some of the more unscrupulous people he knew in high society, he calculated he could add another £1,000 to his £2,000 share of coins and jewels. The £3,000 he received from this great plunder, plus another £6,000 he had in gold and silver coins buried in a safe spot in Tortuga would set him up quite nicely.

After letting their "newfound wealth" sink in for a few days, Avery gathered the pirates. "So, where do we go from here? Should we go find us another ship?" The crew always voted on where they would go next, plus how they'd divvy up their spoils.

Avery gave the crew time to think about it. Not wanting to tempt their good fortune, all voted to disband. Many decided to retire and go into hiding. For most of the crew, £1,000 was more than fifteen years' pay aboard any merchant ship. It was an enormous sum most would never see again. The rest of the fleet's captains and the remaining crew agreed to return to Madagascar and plan their next raids. For them, it was the only life they knew.

Avery decided he'd try to make his dreams come true in New York. He had been there before as a privateer for a British merchant and liked it.

He gathered his most trusted crew, twenty-five in all, and spoke with them away from the others. "Men, I have a plan and want you to come with me. But before I tell you, I need to know if you are with me. If not, no hard feelings, but I must ask you to leave while I inform the others of my plan."

"I'm with you," they all said one after another.

"Good. I want to sail to Tortuga. From there, we'll make another journey, but I'll tell you where after we arrive in Tortuga. You know the arrangement. I never tell anyone the plans in case someone gets caught by the authorities or other pirates. It's been our code this past year, and I see no reason to change it. Each of you will receive £40 when we reach Tortuga, and another £40 when we arrive at our final destination. Are you in agreement?"

"Aye, Captain," each pirate said.

"Excellent. We leave first thing tomorrow morning."

As the crew departed, Avery called over Seeds and Heisey. "Gentlemen, as always, you must keep this to yourselves. You are my most loyal men, and I trust you enough to let you know my entire plan. I'll need your help in making sure the others stay in line. There's going to be much to do, since there'll only be a few of us on the *Fancy*."

"Yes, Captain. You have our word."

"We will go to Tortuga first where I will gather my stash. We'll rest there for a day or two, and then sail through the rest of the Caribbean and up the coast to New York. Once there, I will tell those in port that the *Fancy* had been fitted out as a privateering ship but had no success in finding any pirates. I will show them my official papers I have from a privateering job I had with the East India Company back in England. The paperwork is only a year and a half old, which should still allow us access to the harbor in New York without any suspicion."

Heisey leaned over to Avery. "Tortuga can get violent. We'll have to be careful."

"You're right, but we won't be staying in there long. We must keep a tight rein on the crew to make sure they don't get into any trouble."

"And New York, Captain? That's going to take some time to get there, sir."

"That's true. But you'll like it there. It's a great city."

Avery gathered his thoughts. "In New York, I'll say I received orders from the ship's owners to sell the *Fancy* for the best price I could get. I will buy what the locals call a Hudson River sloop, and we'll sail up the Hudson River, where we will bury my loot in the nearby mountains. Everyone will get the agreed share of money owed, and then they can go on their way."

"Sounds good, Captain. Count us in to keep your plan secret."

"Thank you."

As Seeds and Heisey walked away, Avery went over his scheme in his head, counting off each part on his fingers. *One...bury the money in the mountains. Two...move the treasure to new hiding places a little at a time over the next few months, in case any of the crew has any ideas of sneaking back and robbing me. Three...buy property somewhere in the colonies and live the life of a wealthy gentleman. Should work. Sounds foolproof, or at least semi-foolproof.*

# 5

## BEAR MOUNTAIN
## NEW YORK

IT WAS A hot summer afternoon when Sam Barrett and his good friend and hunting partner, Micah Collins, heard someone screaming from the other side of the hill. As they ran toward the sound, they saw, about fifty yards away, a boy. He looked to be no older than fifteen years old and was running away from an enormous black bear. It was running full speed at the boy, roaring with its jaws gaping wide and fangs showing. It was on him in a few seconds. The bear knocked him off his feet with one swift swing of his gigantic paw. It was at least three hundred pounds and six feet tall when standing on its hind legs. The boy rolled to his side as the bear tried to bite him.

Sam saw the boy's arm dangling at his side, bent in an unnatural position. Crimson-colored blood was pouring onto the grass. The bear must have broken the boy's arm and gashed his bicep when it knocked him to the ground. The boy reached for his knife with his left hand, while he continued to scream in a language he didn't understand.

Sam's eyes grew wide as the bear threw the boy aside as if he were a stick. The boy tried to stand up but stumbled and his eyelids started to close.

He yelled again and then collapsed. The bear was standing on its hind legs, with his head swaying back and forth ready to pounce on the boy for the kill. Sam aimed his rifle and fired.

Waving away the smoke that rose from the gun, Sam saw he had shot the bear on its right shoulder, purposely aiming high to make sure he didn't accidentally shoot the boy. The bear staggered back, looking for what had hit him. It let out a loud, deep, death-curdling growl that froze the men in their tracks. Sam gasped and grabbed his pistol. The bear had forgotten about the boy and stumbled his way sluggishly toward the men.

Micah shot at the bear with his flintlock rifle, but it misfired as those guns often did. Sam, in a panic, dropped his gun, seeing the bear snarling and swiping at him as it moved closer. Sam reached down, grabbed his gun, fell back, and fired just as the bear loomed over him. The ground shook as the giant bear landed face down next to Sam, kicking up a cloud of dirt. Sam scurried to the side in case it was still alive. Micah came over and shot the bear in the head to make sure it was dead. Both men sat for a couple of seconds trying to catch their breath, and then ran over to the boy.

The boy's eyes grew wide, and he started shaking and vomiting. He passed out, and Sam gently tapped him on the face and lightly shook him. The young boy woke up startled, sweating, and shivering. His arm was bleeding badly and was bent to the side. He was getting pale. His head drooped slowly and then popped up again. This happened several times with the boy looking frightened as if he were being attacked again. He settled down long enough for Sam to ask who he was.

"What's your name?" Sam asked.

"Teme," the boy said, barely above a whisper. "I am Haverstraw—Turtle Clan." Then he passed out again.

Sam tore off part of his shirt and made a kind of tourniquet for Teme's arm to try to stop the bleeding. Teme screamed in pain when Sam pulled the tourniquet tight. It was beginning to get dark when Sam and Micah carried Teme down the other side of the mountain heading toward the Haverstraw's village. Teme groaned with each step they took. It would take them at least one hour to get there carrying the young man.

"Did you hear that?" Sam gasped as he turned to Micah, wide-eyed. "Sounds like wolves coming from the cursed part of the mountain. Nothing good is from there."

"I heard them," Micah said, looking over his shoulder. "They're not far away. We better get out of here. If they're that close, they're stalking us. They'll be circling soon."

"I was going to suggest one of us stay here with Teme, and the other go to his village for help, but now hearing those wolves, I think we better stick together."

"I agree," Micah said. "We should set him down and reload our guns just in case."

They gently leaned Teme against a tree and quickly loaded their guns while surveying the area for wolves. The howls seemed to get farther away.

"They must be going toward the bear we killed," Sam said. "Easy meal for them."

It felt like hours before making it to the outskirts of the village where they yelled for help.

Since it was summer, the Haverstraws were living in their temporary hunting camp—wigwams, made with wooden frames covered in animal skins and birchbark.

Men and women rushed out of their wigwams to see what all the yelling was about. A man exited his dwelling dressed in the normal men's Haverstraw clothing—breechclouts and leggings made from buckskin and red roach headdresses made of porcupine guard hair. A woman exited her wigwam wearing a wraparound tunic and cloak, while an elderly man came out wearing two feathers in his headdress. Everyone had tattoos. Those who had gathered around Teme parted as Sakima Maxkw came forward. The Sakima, or Chief of the Turtle Clan's, name was Maxkw, meaning Bear, because he was strong like a bear. His eyes grew big as he saw Teme's limp body being carried to him.

"We heard Teme screaming and ran to help him," Sam told the chief. "There was a large bear attacking him and we shot it dead. We brought Teme here as fast as we could."

Men and women gathered up the boy and took him to a wigwam to tend to his wounds. The Sakima and Teme's mother, Pschiki, meaning pretty, walked up to Sam and Micah with furrowed brows. "Thank you for saving our son," Maxkw said in perfect English as he shook their hands. "But I must ask your pardon so we can go tend to Teme. Thank you, again."

Maxkw looked at several of the men next to him. "Walk them back to their boats and see no harm comes to them."

"Thank you, but that won't be necessary," Sam said. "We can get back safely on our own."

"I insist," Maxkw said.

# 6

SAM AND MICAH arrived at Micah's house late at night. Sam's wife, Emma, was at the Collin's home keeping Sarah, Micah's wife, company while the men were hunting. The women rushed out of the house as their husbands opened the gate to the front yard.

Emma ran up to Sam. "Are you two all right? You've been gone so long. We were afraid something bad happened to you both."

"Sorry we worried you," Sam said. "But it was quite the day. We were up on the mountain hunting when we heard screams coming from the other side of a hill. We ran over to see a bear mauling a young Haverstraw boy. We shot it and took the young boy to his village."

Sarah's hands went over her mouth. "Oh, my goodness. Are you two hurt?"

"No, we're fine, honey," Micah said. "Just a little worn out."

"Is the boy…going to make it?" Emma asked.

"Not sure," Sam said. "His arm was badly damaged and he was bleeding a lot. He kept falling in and out of consciousness."

"I'm glad you two weren't hurt," said Emma. "I got nervous when you weren't home before nightfall."

"Sorry," Sam said. "It's late. Why don't we head on home and get some rest?"

Sam walked over and shook Micah's hand. "It's been a crazy day, hasn't it?"

"Sure has," Micah said. "You be safe going home. See you two soon."

Sam and Emma headed home in their wagon. It was a short journey to their house about two miles down the road. Sam squeezed Emma's hand and smiled. Emma inched closer to Sam and kissed him on the cheek and then punched him on the arm.

"Hey, what was that for?" Sam asked.

"For scaring me like that."

SAM AND EMMA relaxed the next day doing light chores around their farm and resting.

"I see you're reading the Bible again," Sam said.

"Well, one of us has to. You should read it more than you do, Samuel."

Sam grinned. "I know, but us Catholics don't read the Bible as much as you Protestants. It's a wonder you and I even got together in Derry, with us being from different religions."

"True. I'm glad we left and came to New York. Just too much tension between our two religions. Too much fighting."

Sam chuckled. "Our folks used to get mad at us for not going to Mass and services."

"I still feel bad about that. Our parents would have rested easier if we went to church with them more, especially before they got smallpox."

"You're probably right, but we do our best to treat others the way we want to be treated, and that's what they preach every Sunday, anyway."

"You look like something's on your mind. Are you worried about the boy from yesterday?"

"A little, but I'm concerned about our crops," Sam said. Things aren't growing like they used to. Seems to be slowing down some. We aren't quite making our fortune here like we thought. I guess we could buy more cows, pigs, and chickens."

"Oh, I don't know. You're doing a great job, Sam. One day we can hire someone to help."

"Perhaps. It's tough farming and having our store. But thank God for the store. We couldn't afford to live even here in our small house without it."

Emma smiled and then elbowed Sam. "You know…instead of hiring help, we can always have children."

"Someday, honey, but we got to get the store earning a better profit."

"I see more and more people and businessmen coming in every day."

"That's true. Even the governor and Mrs. Fletcher are regular customers now."

"We're doing better than you think. Customers are coming from up and down the Hudson River. No other store in the area sells as many different kinds of food, clothing, household and farm supplies like we do."

"You know what? You're right. Twice Governor Fletcher and his wife came to the store thanking us for our service to New Yorkers, and for charging fair and even below market prices to the store's patrons."

"Mrs. Fletcher mentioned to me in private how thankful she was we let customers put their bill on a tab when they don't have enough money and we don't charge any interest. I told her people go through hard times occasionally, and we know they'll pay us when they can."

❖ ❖ ❖

IT HAD BEEN one week since the bear attacked Teme when there was a knock on Sam and Emma's front door. Sakima Maxkw, Pschiki, Teme, with his arm in a sling, and several other Haverstraws stood out front with baskets full of deer meat, rabbit, turkey, fish, clams, and oysters, as well as beautifully carved knives and axes.

"These gifts are a small thank you for what you did for Teme," Sakima Maxkw said. "You risked your life to save my son. I will be forever in your debt."

Sam and Emma smiled at Sakima Maxkw. "Thank you," Emma said. "You are too generous."

"Yes," Sam said. "We were happy we could help."

Teme walked up to Sam and shook his hand and placed his hand on his shoulder. "Thank you for saving my life. You are a brave man. My name means wolf because I run fast, but not fast enough to outrun a bear!" Everyone laughed.

Sam smiled. "I'm glad you're feeling better. Everyone, please come inside our house and visit."

"Thank you," Sakima Maxkw said. "But we wish to go to Micah's house and thank him too." The Sakima walked up to Sam. "You and Micah no longer need to ask permission to go anywhere on Haverstraw land. It is now your land too. From now on, you call me Maxkw. We are friends. You do not need to call me Sakima."

"Thank you, Maxkw."

"If you ever need anything, just ask." They said their good-byes and Sam and Emma looked at each other, shaking their heads and admiring all the baskets of gifts they were given.

# 7

HABAÑA, CUBA

RATS RAN UP and down the alley sniffing for food. Water mixed with human waste splashed against the walls as the rain picked up. "That's far enough," a voice snarled at the man walking toward the red-painted door.

The man stopped and squinted in the darkness. He ran his hand across a scar running from his left ear to his chin. "You have a job for me to do?"

"Word is you can find a needle in a haystack. Is that true?"

"If the money's right."

"You'll get £50 now and £50 when the job's done."

"Who is it and where is he?"

"His name is Avery, and he has a galleon named the *Fancy*. Don't know where he is now. Find him and bring him to me."

"I don't think so," the man said and started to walk away.

"So, you're chicken."

The man stopped and slowly turned around. "The last person who called me that ended up with a knife in his belly. Took him a few days to die. It wasn't pretty."

A shot rang out, tearing off a piece of the man's shirt. "The next shot goes right between your eyes," the dark figure said, leaning against the red door as he pulled a second pistol from behind his back.

"I know who Avery is, and there's no way I can get anywhere near him. I can't go up against a pirate ship and simply knock him over the head and walk out with him. I'll have to hire another group of pirates just to get close to him. He'll probably end up dead in the process."

"I don't want him dead. I'll do that myself. I want you to bring him to me."

"Where do I bring him?"

"Knock twice on the red door I'm standing next to. Tell the person who answers you brought Avery to the Boss. Someone will answer, no matter what time day or night."

"It'll take more money. I may have to get him at sea."

The man in the shadows tossed a bag of coins at his feet and adjusted his hat. "I'll double the fee. Just get it done and bring him here."

"Consider it done."

"Failure is not an option, Mr. Cooper."

"How do you know my real name?"

"I know a great many things. Like you have a wife and a daughter here in Cuba. It'd be a shame if anything happened to them."

"If you touch them…"

"Do as I say and you'll get paid and your family will live. Fail and…"

# 8

## *TORTUGA, HISPAÑIOLA*

THE *FANCY* SAILED into Bucks Harbor, Tortuga a little after day-break on a hot and humid Tuesday morning. She flew England's co-lours, since many of the buccaneers and pirates on the island had a deep hatred of Spain and attacked any Spanish ship which sailed near the island. Avery kept at least ten men on the galleon at all times, due to the harbor being filled with men of questionable character who'd raid their craft if they had the slightest hint of the treasure onboard. They would stay a couple of days—long enough to rest and gather supplies for their journey to New York.

Carefully considering his options, Avery left Mountford and Burrow in charge of the *Fancy,* while he took Seeds and Heisey with him to dig up his stolen loot. Avery returned within two hours, pleased to find no one had been looking around the ship.

He gathered the crew and split up the men going into town. Merchants in Tortuga were accustomed to all sorts of sailors, pirates, and privateers coming to the port to buy supplies for their ships. Money and goods were exchanged. No one asked where the money came from.

Some of the *Fancy's* crew bought food, while others gathered more barrels of water for their next trip. Several purchased rope, linen, and hemp fabric in case they were needed to repair the sails and rigging.

The pirates met back at the galleon with their supplies and reported no one followed them.

Feeling somewhat relaxed that nobody was coming up to their ship and asking questions, except a few children running about the docks, Avery grouped his small crew together. "I have decided to let half the crew go into town tonight for a few hours to eat a decent meal. When they come back to the ship, the other half of you can go eat. No one is to get drunk or gamble. I do not want to attract any unnecessary attention, and I especially don't need any of you getting shot or ending up in prison. If anyone gets thrown in jail, you will be left to fend for yourself. Is that clear?"

"Aye, aye, Captain," the crew moaned.

Avery knew they'd been hoping for a night on the town drinking and gambling with the money they had stolen. He didn't blame them.

Avery pointed at his crew. "Keep an ear out and listen for anyone talking about our ship. If someone asks you what the *Fancy* is doing in port, tell them we're privateering for the king and will be on our way soon."

Later that evening, close to midnight, Avery stood before his crew again. "You will sleep in shifts watching the ship." Wanting to set an example, he said, "I will join the first set of men keeping an eye out while the other group sleeps."

Nothing happened during the first few hours. There was a heavy rain that kept many in town behind closed doors. Otherwise, there would have been more sailors out in the streets going to and from the local taverns.

Heisey walked up and stood next to Avery. "Captain, don't look around, but there's a man in the alley on the far street corner who's been there the past two hours watching our ship. Several men have been coming up to him every half hour. They talk and then the men walk away. Maybe I'm making something out of nothing, but I think he's up to no good. Want me to do something about it?"

Avery narrowed his eyes. "Take two men with you and bring him to the ship so we can properly ask him what he and his friends are up to. Make sure you're quiet about it and don't be seen by anyone. Knock him out if you have to."

"Aye, Captain."

Heisey and the two other crewmembers got off the ship and headed in the opposite direction of the alley where the man was standing. Once out of sight, they doubled back and grabbed the man before he could do anything. Heisey, six feet three inches tall, with fists like clubs, hit him over the head, knocking him out instantly.

One of the pirates looked wide-eyed at Heisey. "You didn't kill him, d'ye?"

Heisey laughed. "No. He's still breathing. He'll be out for a little bit."

Avery watched as Heisey and the others carried their captive back to the ship. He noticed three sailors stopped to talk to Heisey, but he couldn't make out what they were saying. The sailors were lifting their hands up in the air and shaking their heads. He saw Heisey act like he was drinking from a bottle and staggering. Avery saw the sailors laugh and then go on their way.

Once onboard, they brought the man belowdeck, tied his legs to a chair and his arms behind the back of the chair so he couldn't move. They put a rag in his mouth so no one could hear him if he yelled for help. They sat the man upright in the chair. Avery threw water in his face, waking him up, and then removed the rag from his mouth. Several pirates stood in front of the man, glaring and tossing their knives back and forth in their hands, looking like they wanted to use them.

The man moaned as he sheepishly shook his head and tried to gather his senses. "Hey…where am I?" His eyes widened, seeing the pirates surround him. He attempted to move, but the ropes didn't give.

"I'll be asking the questions," Avery bellowed. "Why are you spying on my ship, and who are you reporting to?"

"I'm not spying on your ship. I was waiting for some friends of mine that's all."

Avery looked over at Heisey and nodded in the man's direction. Heisey walked over to their captive and stood over him, cracked the knuckles of his enormous fingers, and pulled a large, sharp knife from around his back. Their prisoner looked up at the mountain of a man in front of him, swallowed hard, and decided it was in his best interest to answer Avery's questions.

"Calm down," the man said, his voice quivering. "No need to get testy. I'll answer your stupid questions, but you have to protect me. The men I work for won't take kindly to me telling you what's going on."

"Start talking," Heisey demanded.

"Captain Deering, the captain of the frigate in port, the *Scorpion*, got word a galleon was here. Some man Deering calls the *Boss* is paying us to find your galleon. Captain said he needs to find Avery and his galleon."

"*The Boss*?" Avery asked. "Who's the *Boss*?"

"I don't know. I was told to keep an eye on your ship. Some of our crew would come up to me every now and then asking what I saw."

"What d'ye tell them?"

"That you all were taking shifts keeping an eye out on things like we do."

Avery squinted and stared at the captured man. "What's so special about me and my galleon?"

"I don't know. He didn't tell me. He only tells everything to just a few of the men he trusts. But I saw our crew grouping together on our ship looking like they were planning something."

Avery shook his head and let out a deep breath. He thought for a minute, then tapped Heisey on the shoulder and pointed toward the hallway.

"We don't have enough crew to go head-to-head with another pirate ship. I was hoping we'd be able to stay in Tortuga longer, but it looks like we need to get out of here fast."

"You're right, Captain. But it's late now, and the weather's nasty."

"I know, but we've got no choice."

"Aye, Captain. Who do you think this Boss man is?"

"Not sure, but this is all I need. Someone coming after me. He's got to be either the emperor or one of his men."

"Do you think it's any of the other captains from our fleet? Maybe they had a change of mind and decided they wanted a bigger share."

"I thought of that, but I doubt it. They probably would have come after us sooner. Why wait until now."

Heisey punched his hand. "We'll be ready for whoever it is, Captain. You can count on your crew to have your back."

"Thanks, Heisey."

Avery walked into the room where their prisoner was being lifted up, while still tied to the chair, and being tossed back and forth among the pirates. They dropped the man when they saw Avery.

"Enough fun," Avery yelled. "It's time to leave, boys."

"What are you going to do with me?" the man being interrogated asked, his eyes darting from pirate to pirate.

"That is a good question. What's your job on your ship?" Avery asked.

"I'm the cook, and I help out as best I can."

"The cook and that's it?" Avery asked, shaking his head side to side.

Avery whispered to Heisey, "If we kill him, Deering would know something was up when they found his body. If we let him go, he'll run back to his ship and tell them what he saw…and we can't have that. We have quite a dilemma. Let's take him with us a ways and drop him off somewhere where he won't be a problem."

"Sounds good to me, Captain."

Avery called his men over. "Leave him tied up and gag him for the night. No need for anyone to hear him yelling for help. When we get within a league of Cuba, we'll let him go in the small rowboat, and he can row his way to the island. We'll be long gone before he reaches land."

Heisey shrugged. "What about Deering?"

"Hopefully, we'll be far away before Deering's men go looking for their cook. Once they do, they'll think he got tired of watching the *Fancy* and went to a local tavern and got drunk. It'll take his crew a few hours of searching before they realize he isn't in town anymore or is dead somewhere."

Avery walked back into the room and stood over his captive. "You can stay with us until we get to our destination, but if you give us any trouble, Heisey here will tear you to shreds and feed you to the sharks piece by piece. You hear me, cook? And…you better be a good cook, too."

The man mumbled. Avery removed the rag from his mouth.

"Yes, sir, Captain." The man gulped as he looked at Heisey, smiling. "Hey, how about cutting me out of these ropes?"

"We'll do that tomorrow…maybe. I don't trust you, and I won't have you roaming around my ship. And, if you don't behave, I'll let Heisey have at you. Gag him, men." Avery frowned and walked away.

❖ ❖ ❖

IT WAS TWO in the morning when the galleon sailed out of the harbor in rolling seas and pouring rain. Thunder was rumbling in the distance. The *Fancy* had all crew on deck as they left Tortuga and gradually made their way northeast of Cuba. By the time the sun rose, the rain had stopped. Under Finn's watchful eye from atop the lookout, it appeared no frigate or other ship had been following them.

The crew cut the ropes holding their captive and put him to work for three more days. Then they put him in the rowboat.

"Don't send me off to die," he screamed. "Let me stay on onboard as one of your crew."

His protests were met with Avery pointing a pistol at him. "Would you prefer I shoot you here and now, or take your chances rowing to Cuba? Don't be such a baby. It's not that far away." With that, the *Fancy* set a course of northwest. It was then Avery told the entire crew their destination was New York.

"I was wondering why we were sailing northwest," said Mountford. "I thought we'd end up in Port Royal and split up there. D'ye say New York? It's no longer New Netherland?"

"No, it's back with England now," Avery said. "It's best we don't go to Port Royal, anyway."

"Why?"

"They'll be expecting us to go there. Plus, there was a big earthquake and tsunami there a few years back. Destroyed almost everything and everyone. I heard they are rebuilding, but it's a slow process."

# 9

DEERING'S FIRST OFFICER, Smith, shook the captain, awakening him from his nap. "Captain, Captain,"

"What do you want?" Deering snapped.

"Pete was spying on the galleon in port like you ordered, and now he's disappeared."

"He's drunk in some tavern like he always is."

"I don't think so, Captain. We've looked in all of them and we can't find him."

Deering's face grew red and he clenched his fists. "D'ye check our ship?"

"Yes, sir. Up and down, and he's not here either."

Smith stared at the floor and whispered, "The galleon has left port too, sir. Rumor in town is it sailed several hours ago, and nobody knows where it was sailing."

Deering threw a dagger at the wall. "Why didn't you tell me that first? Who cares about Pete? He's useless. He probably got drunk, fell in the water, and drowned. Get the crew ready. I want to take off after that galleon when the weather lets up. I bet they're heading to Port Royal, Jamaica. They wouldn't leave Tortuga in pouring rain unless they had a good reason. Privateers my foot. They're pirates."

AN HOUR LATER, Deering was walking alone and stopped next to an alley.

"You're late," a voice snarled. "I told you never to be late."

"I'm a captain. I can't always drop everything and run when you want."

A knife landed between his feet. "You talk to me like that again and I'll cut off your nose and feed it to the pigs. You got me?"

"Aye. Tell the Boss I did as he ordered. I said the galleon would be here, and I was right. We should have raided it, but you told me not to."

"Don't question me, Deering. I've paid you handsomely to do what I say."

"Yes, but now the galleon's gone. I'm not sure where it's going, but I bet it's Port Royal."

"Then go to Port Royal. I want you to block his ship in port. Act as if your frigate broke down right next to it. Don't let him out. I'll meet you there. Remember…nobody harms Avery. The Boss wants him alive."

"Why all the mystery? Why don't you at least let me know who you are?"

A shot ricocheted off the wall next to Deering's face. "You'll know who I am when and if I want you to know. You're being paid to follow that galleon. Go do your job." The man rubbed the scar on his face and threw a bag of money at Deering's feet. "Now get out of my site, you worthless pirate."

# 10

IT WAS NOON when Deering's frigate sailed out of Tortuga on its way to Port Royal. Deering was usually grumpy, and now he was especially unhappy the *Fancy* slipped away in the middle of the night. It took five days to reach Port Royal, and Deering sailed past its rundown harbors looking for Avery's ship. He sent his crew searching through what was left of the town after the earthquake and tsunami, asking if anyone had seen the galleon. No one had. They hadn't seen any such ship in Port Royal for over a month.

"Where did it go?" Deering yelled as he stomped his foot and threw a knife at the deck. "It could be anywhere in the Caribbean." There were many islands where it could hide. It would be like looking for a black cat in a coal cellar. Then there was a big commotion among the crew, with everyone pointing at the dock.

"It's Pete, sir," Smith yelled as he waved the captain over. "He's here."

The crew helped Pete onboard, while Deering came over and grabbed him, lifting him off the deck. "Where have you been, and how come you're here? You better have a good answer, Petey boy."

Out of breath from all the excitement, and afraid of Deering, Pete looked everywhere but at Deering. "Umm…You see…"

"Spit it out, Pete, before I rip your tongue out."

"Aye…here's what happened. Some of the crew from that galleon in Tortuga saw I was spying on their ship. They snuck up on me where

I was hiding in the alley and knocked me out, tied me up belowdeck, and kept asking me what I was up to. I didn't tell them anything, I promise, but they sensed something was up. I mean, why else would someone be spying on them?"

"Go on," Deering said.

"They kept me tied up and set sail. It was terrible weather, but it let up at daybreak. As soon as we came within a league of Cuba, they let me off their ship in a rowboat and kept sailing north. A rowboat, Captain. I could have died out there. Anyway, I hitched a ride here to Port Royal yesterday, and I saw our ship so I came running over. That's the whole story, Captain."

Deering lowered Pete and surveyed him for any injuries. "Looks like you got a few bumps and bruises and a sunburn, but other than that, you look fine." Deering grumbled, "Where did they go?"

"I don't know where they were going. Just that they were heading north. When I was on their ship, they kept me tied up belowdeck. Their captain was mad someone was spying on them and told the crew it was time to sail out of there. They were nervous about something, sir, and didn't want anyone knowing their business."

"D'ye get what the captain's name was?"

"Not really sure, sir, but I think it's Avery. I overheard the crew talking about Avery wants us to do this, Avery wants us to do that. Maybe he was the captain. I don't know."

Deering smiled and caught himself. "That's probably his name." Deering paced back and forth trying to predict where the *Fancy* was going. Finally, he stopped and nodded. "They must be going somewhere in the colonies."

"Captain?" Pete asked. "Why are we going after the galleon? The man I think was Avery asked me that. I told him I didn't know."

"None of your business. Just do your job and cook us up something to eat."

"Yes, sir," Pete said and walked away with his head down.

Deering pointed to Smith. "Gather a few men and go into town and get whatever supplies you can for our trip. I know there isn't much here, but see what you can buy. Steal it if you have to. Be back in two hours. The rest of you, get us ready to sail. We're heading north."

THE BOSS WATCHED everyone coming in and out of the tavern. He smiled when he saw Mr. Cooper, from Cuba, walk up to the bar and sit next to Deering.

"So, I finally get to see who you are," Deering said to Cooper. "I got your message to meet you at this tavern. I came over as soon as I could."

There was a commotion at a nearby table. Two men started yelling over someone cheating at a card game. Cooper quickly poured a liquid substance into Deering's drink when he looked away. "I'm here because you said the *Fancy* would be sailing to Port Royal. You were wrong. I don't like mistakes. If you don't find Avery soon...well, let's just say you'll be at the bottom of the ocean."

"I have a lead," Deering said as he doubled over in pain. "The *Fancy* sailed north a few days ago. It must be going to Virginia or New York or somewhere up there."

"Feeling bad?" Cooper asked, smiling.

Deering put his head on the bar. "What'd you do?"

"Just a little warning shot across your bow so to speak. No more mistakes, pirate. You'll want to go outside now and throw up."

Deering stood and grabbed hold of his stomach. He ran towards the door, barely making it outside before vomiting.

A young boy ran up to Cooper. "The Boss wants to talk with you. Follow me."

The kid turned around and walked toward a man who was sitting alone at a table with his back against the wall.

The man flipped a silver coin toward the young man who caught it and tucked it in his shirt pocket. "That will be all, Tommy."

"Yes, sir," the boy said and walked out of the tavern.

The man nodded to the chair in front of him. Cooper sat down and studied the Boss.

"So, you're the Boss," Cooper said. "I didn't expect to see you... well, ever."

The Boss glared at Cooper. "You're trying my patience, Mr. Cooper. Where's Avery's ship?"

"It's sailing up to the colonies somewhere."

The Boss smiled and drank a shot of whiskey and nodded over to the other glass on the table. "I took the liberty of already pouring you one. I figured, depending on what you told me, it would either be your last or a congratulatory toast. Lucky for you, we're celebrating."

Cooper eyed the Boss as he downed his whiskey.

The Boss waved away Cooper. "Now leave me and go find that lousy pirate."

Cooper stood and walked a few feet toward the door. He stopped and turned around, facing the Boss. His eyes grew wide as he fell to his knees, grabbing his chest.

The Boss gave a tilt of his hat and watched as Cooper fell over on his back. People rushed over to help the collapsed man.

"Give him some air," the Boss said. "Looks like he's had a heart attack."

Cooper tried to raise his head, grabbed his chest again, and stopped breathing.

"He's dead," a man said after feeling for a pulse.

The Boss got up, adjusted his hat, and calmly walked out of the tavern.

# 11

ONE WEEK AFTER being looted, the *Ganj-i-Sawai* sailed into its home port in India, it was greeted with cheers as guards, servants, and bystanders came to greet the emperor's daughter from her overseas journey. The joyous reception was short-lived as word got back to the Grand Mughal about what had happened to them on their way to Mecca.

"Bring Ibrahim here immediately," the emperor ordered.

Ibrahim stared at the floor as he stood in front of the emperor.

The Grand Mughal's face turned red and he slapped Ibrahim. "Captain, and I use the term loosely, how could you let the *Ganj-i-Sawai*, with my daughter onboard, not to mention a large amount of my money and jewels, be robbed by a ragtag bunch of pirates?"

Ibrahim didn't dare look at the emperor. "Your Majesty, I feared if we fought the pirates any more than we did, your daughter might be harmed. They were ruthless men and would not think twice about killing everyone onboard. I know Mumtaz is more precious to you than all the jewels in your kingdom, and I could not risk her life."

"Some have told me you were a coward and only feared for your own life and not that of my daughter nor anyone else."

"Not true, Your Majesty. I was ready to fight to the death, but I thought it better to save your daughter's life than to be a hero."

"I see," the emperor thought out loud as he walked about the room, deciding what he'd do next. "I will give you another chance to save your reputation." He clapped his hands for his guards to come back into the room. "I am naming Kalam as the new captain of the *Ganj-i-Sawai*. You will be part of the crew assisting in the recovery of what was stolen from me, and to bring the pirates back to India. They will be made an example of what happens to those who steal from me. You will search every port until you find what is mine and bring it back to me."

"As you wish, Your Majesty," Ibrahim whispered as he bowed to the emperor.

"Kalam, come here," the emperor demanded. "Ibrahim, leave my sight."

"I chose you, Kalam, to be the captain because I am aware of your earlier days as a pirate."

"Your Majesty, I never—"

"Save it. I know everyone's background who is in my employ. That's why you're here. Sometimes you need a fox to catch a fox. And that's exactly what you will do. You will catch that pirate and bring him to me. Now I'm going to find out why none of the convoy was there to protect the *Ganj-i-Sawai*."

FIVE DAYS LATER, the massive ship sailed down the Arabian Sea to Madagascar looking for the pirates' galleon. The ship consisted of a large crew and as many weapons and supplies as it could hold. Madagascar was a haven for pirates, and Kalam hoped those who'd robbed the *Ganj-i-Sawai* might be there. Many of the crew aboard when it was plundered was onboard again. Most blamed Ibrahim for allowing the ship to be overtaken without putting up much of a fight. Kalam and the crew did their best to make the voyage miserable for Ibrahim. Kalam made him swab the decks, cook the meals, stand on lookout, and do any menial job he could dream up. He wanted Ibrahim and the rest of the crew to know he was now in charge.

People took notice as the ship sailed into port. Men stepped closer, shielding their eyes from the sun to admire the ship. Women "oohed" as the *Ganj-i-Sawai* glided across the water.

Kalam barked orders to his first mate, Khatri. "I don't see a galleon in port, but take twenty-five men into town. Ask around the taverns if one has been here and where it sailed off to. Take Ibrahim with you. Ibrahim, if you notice any of the pirates, bring them here to me."

AS CREW FROM the *Ganj-i-Sawai* entered a tavern called *Pieces of Eight*, they noticed two men duck out the back door. They ran after them. The two being chased split up when they came to an intersection. The crew chasing them did the same. They ran several blocks before catching up with one of them. They tackled him and held his hands behind his back.

"Why are you chasing me?" the man gasped.

"Why did you run when you saw us?"

"I was just leaving, and you all started running after me. Here take my £10. It's all I got on me."

"We're not here for your money, pirate."

"Then what do you want?"

"What do you know about a galleon that robbed our ship a while back?" an officer gruffly barked at him, while holding a knife to his throat.

"I don't know nothin' about no galleon. I work for Captain Sherman doing privateering for England. He's got a frigate not a galleon. You can ask him yourself," the pirate struggled to say. He was sweating and struggling to breathe as the knife was pushed against his throat. It was the only thing the pirate could think to say. He was hoping no one remembered what he looked like when he and the others in Avery's fleet robbed the *Ganj-i-Sawai*.

"Let's go find this Captain Sherman and see if he knows you," a crewmember barked at the wriggling pirate.

Still sweating, the pirate answered, "Oh, I just remembered he isn't here. He sailed back to England the other day."

Another *Ganj-i-Sawai's* sailor, with barely any teeth, stood inches from the pirate's face. "How convenient. You're coming with us." They hauled him down the street as the pirate kicked at the men.

❖ ❖ ❖

THEY BROUGHT THE pirate to a smiling Kalam. "So, what do we have here?" Kalam asked, chuckling. "You seem worried, pirate. Why do you keep looking around?"

One of the crew on the *Ganj-i-Sawai* came forward and yelled, "He's one of them scoundrels that robbed us. I'd remember his face anywhere. He made me carry some of the money onto his sloop. See if he has a scar on his right arm."

Kalam pulled back the pirate's sleeve to reveal a long scar. The pirate closed his eyes and hung his head.

"Well, pirate, you better start talking," Kalam yelled, drops of spit spattering the captive's face. "We can do this the easy way or we can do this the hard way. I mean the hard way for you. It's been a while since I used my knife to carve up a pirate."

"What do you want to know?"

"I want to know where our money and jewels are, and I want to know now."

"We split up the money, and we all went our different ways. My share is almost used up. The captain and a few men took their shares and the jewels and sailed away on his galleon, the *Fancy*. Rumor has it he was going to Tortuga, and then somewhere else. I don't know where he'll end up. He never tells us the final destination, in case any of us gets caught."

"What's the captain's name?"

"Avery."

Kalam's eyes grew big. "Black flag with skull and crossbones, Avery?"

"Yes. You know him?"

Kalam stroked his beard for a few seconds. "Are there any more of Avery's crew still here in Madagascar?"

"Just the one your men chased, but he used up all his money losing at cards and dice."

"How much money do you have?"

"£50 left, that's all. I lost a bunch at cards and…other things."

Kalam held out his hand.

"I'll give it to you if your men will let go of me."

Kalam punched the pirate in the stomach. "Tell me where it is."

The pirate tried to catch his breath. "In my left pocket inside my coat."

Kalam took the money and shoved the pirate into several of the crew. He scowled at the men gathered around him. "We're sailing to Tortuga first thing in the morning. Get this ship ready. We'll be at sea for a while."

"What are you…um…going to…to do with me?" the pirate stuttered, eyes darting from sailor to sailor.

"Oh, you're going with us, and you better not be lying. Put him belowdeck and tie him up. I don't want him getting any wild ideas."

# 12

THE BOSS ADJUSTED his hat as he walked down the alley with his hand on his pistol and looking for any movement. He put his key in the lock and opened the red door. A woman and a man stood on each side of the door with their pistols raised.

"Put your guns down. It's me."

"Sorry, Boss," the woman said. "You can never be too safe."

"No, Carmen. I want you to raise your pistols at whomever comes through the door. It may not be me."

"How'd it go in Port Royal, Boss?" the man asked.

"Mr. Cooper is no longer in our employ, Andrew. His services were no longer needed. Deering is sailing to Virginia to see if Avery is there. If he isn't, then he's going to New York. Deering feels Avery is going to one of those places."

Andrew glanced at the Boss and then stared at the floor. "Please be patient with me, sir, but I was wondering?"

"Wondering what, Andrew?"

"Well…Boss…um."

"Say it, Andrew."

"I was wondering why you were after Avery? Not that it matters. I will do whatever you order me to do. Never mind, Boss. I'm sorry. It's none of my business."

"You're right. It is none of your business."

Andrew backed up against the wall. "Forgive me, Boss."

The Boss' eye twitched and his hands shook. "Avery ruined everything in my life. That's all you need to know."

"I understand, Boss. Thank you for being patient with me."

The Boss walked over to Andrew and smiled. He turned away and then swung at Andrew, smacking him across the face. "Never question me again."

Andrew grabbed his face. "I'm sorry, Boss. Please don't hurt me."

"Be silent and do as I say. I want you to go to Virginia and New York and see if you can find Avery. I don't trust Deering. Who knows, he might end up joining Avery. Pirates either end up killing each other or joining together to plunder even more law-abiding people."

"Yes, sir. I will go immediately."

"Find out where Avery is, eliminate any of your informants, and come back here. Do not engage with Avery. You may find others looking for that dirty pirate. Misdirect them away from him. And don't attract attention. Then get back here and tell me where he is."

"Yes, sir."

THE CREW ON the *Ganj-i-Sawai* were not pleased about having to make the long journey to Tortuga, especially since they weren't even sure Avery and the treasure were there. It would take weeks to get there, but it was the only lead they had. They kept themselves busy cleaning the ship, mending the sails, cleaning, disassembling and assembling their weapons, and sharpening and practicing using their knives and swords.

After four weeks at sea, Ibrahim had some good news from atop the lookout. "Tortuga ahead at nine o'clock."

Kalam barked orders to his crew. "Get to your posts and keep watch for that galleon. I don't want any surprises or mistakes. Everyone be on your toes. Find me that ship and that pirate. I want our treasure back."

The *Ganj-i-Sawai* sailed into port at noon. Tortuga was packed with ships and men from what seemed every nation. Ibrahim screamed down from the lookout, "I see a galleon on the far side of town, sir."

Kalam smiled and gathered five of his best crew around him. "This is it, men. We can't just sail up to the galleon and take it over. We need to sneak up on them from town. Get seventy-five of the best soldiers and bring them here. We'll leave twenty-five men behind to guard our ship while the rest of us go take over that ship."

As the crew was leaving, Kalam stopped them. "If any of you find Avery, bring him to me. I don't want him dead if at all possible." The men looked at each other, furrowed their brows, and then went on their way.

Ten minutes later, about two blocks from the galleon, Kalam's crew gathered around him. He stood on a wooden box and pulled out his sword, waving it overhead. "Silence. We will break up into groups of ten men. Two groups will flank the galleon on the left and three groups on the right. The rest will go directly at the ship. Singh has informed me he's seen twenty men on the ship now with the rest of the crew in town. Singh's going back to town to see if he can find out for sure who owns the galleon and who and what might be onboard. We will wait for his return before we make our move."

SINGH STROLLED CASUALLY near the galleon and saw a man come off the ship and enter a tavern down the road. Singh entered the tavern and sat next to the man who was alone at the bar. Singh then ordered a bottle of rum. He knew he'd have to go against his religious

beliefs of not drinking alcohol if he was to fit in and gather information. The sailor from the ship was also drinking rum. They looked at
each other, held their bottles out, and clinked them together.

"Making our way back to India. How about you?" Singh asked the
man.

The sailor's face was flushed and his speech was slightly slurred.
"Sailing back to England after making the rounds about the islands.
Didn't find much to bring back. Privateering hasn't been good to us
lately. What brings you to Tortuga?"

"Trading spices for some much-needed supplies that are difficult to come by in my country. How long is your ship going to be in
Tortuga?"

"We're leaving tomorrow. Captain Peterson doesn't like us being
here long. Says there are too many ways we can get in trouble being in
town." The man laughed as he took a big swig.

"I thought your galleon was the *Fancy*?"

"No, that's Avery's ship. Ours is the *Wanderer*. An old friend of
mine in town told me the *Fancy* was here weeks ago, but took off out
of here real fast, in the middle of the night, heading northwest."

Singh sighed. "I should get back to my ship. My turn to stand
watch in a few minutes."

"Me too." Then the man walked out of the tavern.

Singh looked around and spoke to several other crewmembers of
the galleon and to the bartender. Each one said the same thing—it
wasn't the *Fancy*. Singh turned and headed back to his ship.

Kalam and the crew gathered around Singh as he returned to the
*Ganj-i-Sawai*. "Sorry, Captain, but that galleon isn't the one we're
looking for. I asked three of the galleon's crew and the bartender. It's
Captain Peterson's galleon."

Kalam punched the railing.

Singh looked down. "The one Avery is on headed northwest out of here weeks ago. That's the best I could get without drawing too much attention. Looks like our pirate belowdeck was telling us the truth. Avery was here."

Kalam grabbed the end of his sword and slammed it in the deck. "Bring our prisoner to me now." Several men dragged the pirate up the stairs and roughly shoved him in front of Kalam.

"Tell me everything you know about where Avery is going."

"I did. He said he was sailing here, like I told you."

"Where else did he say he was going?"

"He didn't say. He never does. He's real secret that way."

Furious, Kalam grabbed the pirate and lifted him high above his head. "Be thankful I don't kill you. If you run into Avery, tell him I'm coming after him. Tell him I will find him and he can't hide from me forever." Then Kalam threw him overboard into the water.

The pirate climbed onto the dock and ran away, bumping into people as he tried to get as far away from the *Ganj-i-Sawai* as possible.

The crew watched Kalam, waiting for his orders. He raised his sword. "We're sailing for the colonies at first light. We'll stop at each major port until we find him." Kalam walked down the stairs to his cabin and slammed the door. He lay on his bed whispering to himself, "Going back to where it all started." Then, he spoke as if he were savoring each word. "This time I will kill you, Henry."

# 13

AVERY AND HIS crew sailed the *Fancy* near port in New York and dropped anchor. Always wanting to make a good impression, Avery sauntered to his cabin below and put on his finest clothes.

Avery called over Seeds and Heisey. "Keep an eye on the men. I'm going into town to sell the *Fancy*, and I don't want anyone getting greedy and trying to take all the treasure for themselves. No need for a mutiny. I'm sure whoever wishes to buy the *Fancy* will want to inspect her first, so make sure the treasure is hidden from view."

"Aye, aye, Captain…will do," Seeds said as he saluted.

Avery called the crew over. "I want Seeds, Heisey, Mountford, Burrow, Wentworth, and five others—you decide—to stay with the ship while the rest of us go ashore. Those going with me can head into town for a bit. Just a drink or two, and some food at Fred's. I'm sure it's still there. That's all you're allowed to do, gentlemen. After I let it be known the *Fancy* is for sale, I will come get you and we'll return to the ship. Afterward, those left can leave the ship for a short break."

"Captain, when will we be getting our money?" Jamison, one of the older crewmembers, asked wide-eyed and smiling.

"You can have what shares you have coming to you for staying with me up to this point, or you'll get the full amount when I get a sloop and complete our journey. It will only be a few days trip and that's it. Think it over. Let me know your decision when I get back."

The men cheered, realizing they were even richer.

Avery held his hand up, signaling for his crew to stop. "From now on, I will be going by the name Thomas Sedgeport. I've never used that name before. He was my neighbor when I was growing up. Don't forget to call me that when we're in New York. Even better, address me as Captain. When whoever buys our ship comes aboard, I want all of you to stand aside in silence. Be dressed as properly as you can while they are onboard. Any questions?"

The pirates looked around and shook their heads. "We'll be on our best behavior, Captain," Seeds said.

A man came rowing up to the *Fancy* in a shallop, and the crew tied it up alongside the galleon. Avery and several of his men got on and helped row.

"Anything you need other than getting your men ashore, Captain?" asked the shallop's rowman.

"No. I will need you to stand by as my crew will be going ashore in shifts."

"Aye, aye, Captain."

"What's your name?" Avery asked.

"Speedy, sir. That's what they call me around here."

"Speedy, whom can I speak with about selling our lovely ship?"

"That would be Mr. Treadway, sir. He handles that sort of thing around here. Mr. Treadway knows who's in the market to buy and sell boats. He owns several ships himself. He might want to purchase your galleon, or know someone who might."

"Excellent. Take me to him once we get ashore."

"Yes, sir."

Once the shallop was tied to the dock, the crew went on to Fred's Tavern, while Avery followed Speedy to speak with Treadway. Speedy led Avery down the main street to a shop on a corner with a sign that read *Treadways*. Avery opened the door of the establishment and smiled. He liked what he saw. The chairs were covered in fine red linen, and tables made from mahogany shined to the point of seeing one's reflection. The entryway had lavish silk curtains at the windows.

A young lady was sitting behind a polished mahogany desk in a dress of the latest fashion. She had a British accent. "Good day. My name is Elizabeth. I am Mr. Treadway's secretary. How may I be of assistance, gentlemen?"

Avery cleared his throat and spoke in as proper a tone as he could muster. "I wish to speak with Mr. Treadway regarding the sale of my exquisite ship."

"I will see if he is available," she said, and pointed to the over-stuffed chairs next to the window. "Please have a seat." She knocked on the oak door behind her and waited until she heard "come in" from the other side.

Elizabeth reentered the room a minute later. "Mr. Treadway will see you now. Please follow me."

Avery and Speedy walked into Treadway's office to find a man with striking red hair sitting behind a large, ornately carved desk, chewing on tobacco and spitting in a spittoon.

Speedy pointed toward Sedgeport. "Mr. Treadway, this here is Captain Sedgeport of the galleon in port. He was wondering if you might be interested in buying it."

Standing up and holding out his hand, Treadway walked over to Avery. After greeting Avery, Treadway led him to another overstuffed chair. "Good day, Captain. Please have a seat. Speedy, thank you for bringing the captain to see me. That will be all."

Speedy gave a quick nod and walked out of the room.

Treadway smiled. "So, Captain, I noticed your ship as it sailed in earlier. How can I be of service?"

Sitting down with one leg crossed, Avery thought to himself, *This is what I want. This man has nothing but the best. I deserve to have this.* He sat up as straight as he could, held his head high and spoke using his best English. "The rather resplendent *Fancy* has been on several privateering missions for the East India Company. Unfortunately, we have been unafforded the opportunity to avail ourselves of any pirates. I have received instructions from the ship's owners to sell the majestic galleon for a price worthy of her. Here are the official papers indicating the East India Company's ownership of the galleon and them giving me authority to sell said vessel at my discretion. Of course, the Company would never allow me to sign as their representative, nor accept payment on their behalf, without their strict approval."

Stroking his red, trimmed beard, Treadway looked over the documents Avery handed him. "These are legitimate. I appreciate you bringing them with you. You'd be amazed at how many people try to sell me ships without proper documentation. That's one of the reasons I'm retiring later this year and moving up north. Now about your ship. It is a nice-looking ship, but I am not purchasing a galleon at this time. Perhaps in a month or two."

Avery could tell from Treadway's demeanor he had years of experience buying and selling ships. He was sure Treadway wanted to see what he was made of. Not wanting to be outdone in negotiating, Avery stood up, leisurely put on his three-pointed hat, and cleared his throat. "I understand, my fine man. I'm sorry we could not come to an agreement for the beautiful ship. Could you steer me in the direction of someone who may be interested in purchasing a galleon sooner than a month or two. If not, I am sure the gentleman in Virginia who saw the ship and wanted her then and there last year—and offered me a tremendously high price—would be willing to buy her. If you do not know of anyone else who may wish to purchase such a grand ship, then I wish you a good day, sir."

Treadway stood up. "Perhaps, Captain, if the price is right, I may be able to find room in my fleet for a galleon sooner rather than later. But it would have to be at a good price. I have several lovely ships already out on their own privateering duties, but I do remember a gentleman who asked if I could provide a ship for him to sail to the...I better not say any more due to confidentiality. You understand."

"Yes. Discretion in our line of business is most necessary. Now what were you thinking of offering for the majestic *Fancy*? The East India Company is judicious."

"I could not possibly go above £10,000."

"Sir, you insult me and my company. I thought I was dealing with a shrewd businessman, but your offer is ridiculously low, my good man. I have been ordered not to go below £15,000."

"£15,000? Now who is ridiculous? I'm a fair man. I will offer you £11,000 and not a pound more than that. After inspection of your galleon, and if all is deemed right with her, I see no reason why we cannot conclude our transaction very quickly."

Avery realized it was an honest offer, but not wanting to seem too eager said, "Sir, I'd be hanged if I returned with only £11,000. Make it £13,000, and we have a deal."

"I see this is not the first time you have been at the negotiating table, Captain. Let's split the difference at £12,000. I feel we can both live with that. Of course, I will need to inspect her first, and if there is no significant damage to her, then, sir...we have a deal."

Avery held out his hand. "Sounds fair." They both shook on it. "Now, I wish to discuss purchasing a Hudson River Sloop. Since the galleon was sold to you rather inexpensively, I expect to purchase a sloop at a reasonable cost. I noticed a single-masted sloop docked at port and was wondering if you owned it?"

"Yes, I do, and you're in luck. She is stunning looking, isn't she? I can sell her to you for a steal at £6,000. She sails like a charm."

"Mr. Treadway! Let's not play that game again. Of course, I wish to inspect her first. If she is worth all you say, I will pay you £3,000, and to quote you…I could not possibly go a pound more than that."

They both laughed. Treadway smiled and held out his hand. "I accept your offer, sir. The sloop is on the way to the galleon, so we can stop by there first."

Avery and Treadway made their way back to the dock, and Treadway showed Avery the sloop. It had only minor damage. The normal amount for any ship.

"Isn't she a beauty, Captain?" Treadway said as they surveyed the sloop.

"She is a fine sloop, Mr. Treadway. She seems all you have stated. I agree to pay £3,000 for her. She'll make a good sailing ship for our trip to Virginia."

"Very good, Captain. Let's go find Speedy and take a look at your galleon."

# 14

SPEEDY ROWED THE shallop up to the *Fancy*. Avery's crew tied her up and gave a hand to Avery and Treadway as they made their way onto the ship. Treadway walked throughout the galleon taking notes of items he saw needing repair.

"She is a fine ship, Captain," Treadway said to Avery. "I only see minor damage to her. The mast is weathered and needs to be painted, some of the deck boards are loose, and I noticed one of the decks has a large cut in it. Nothing out of the ordinary that would reduce my price for her."

"Outstanding, sir," Avery said, trying to hide the smile on his face. He was happy to get £12,000 for the galleon, especially since he paid nothing for her. "Shall we go to the bank, Mr. Treadway, and conclude our business transactions?"

"Good idea indeed, Captain."

"I will order my men to make way to the sloop with our supplies while we are at the bank. I hate to be a bother, but would you mind loaning us the shallop until morning while we transfer our goods aboard the sloop?"

"No bother at all, Captain. You may borrow the shallop for as long as you need."

"Thank you, Mr. Treadway."

Speedy took Avery and Treadway to the dock, and both men got out and walked to the bank. Since purchasing and selling boats was a normal business transaction for Treadway, he already had standard documents prepared for signatures at the bank. The men signed the contracts for purchase and sale of the *Fancy* and the Hudson River sloop.

The manager brought out £9,000 in two bags and placed them on the table. Avery counted it to ensure it was all there. He recounted the transactions. *£12,000 for the Fancy – £3,000 for purchasing the sloop.*

Avery stood up and shook hands with Treadway. "It has been a pleasure doing business with you, sir."

"Yes, Captain, it has indeed."

"I shall have my men and supplies off the *Fancy* by noon tomorrow if that meets with your approval."

"That will be acceptable. Due to the sizable sum of money in your possession, the bank has already summoned five officers, as is standard protocol, to escort you back to your ship. Pleasant sailing, Captain."

They both shook hands, and Avery left with the guards. Speedy was onboard the shallop waiting for Avery. The officers ensured the money got onboard the *Fancy* and then returned to the dock.

"Mr. Treadway told me you and your men wish to borrow the shallop," Seeds said. "He told me to pick it up at noon tomorrow. Do you need anything from me, sir, before I head out?"

"No, thank you, Speedy. We can handle it from here."

"Yes, sir. Have a good evening."

Avery gathered his crew around him. "I have sold the *Fancy* and have purchased a sloop. As I mentioned earlier, you may have your shares now, or you can get another £25 if you stay with me another few days to help me complete my trip. As usual, the details of the next stage of the trip will only be divulged to those who remain."

Twenty crew, including Finn, decided to stay, while four took their shares and left. They decided to see if any of the privateers in town might be looking for additional crew.

Avery took those who wanted their shares and gave them the money they were owed belowdeck. The men understood the code of not telling anyone what took place upon their ship, but Avery felt it wise to remind them. "We've been on a great adventure together. It has been my honor to be your captain. I wish you much wind at your back and good luck wherever the sea gods take you. Remember our journey must be a secret one known only to us. Until we meet again."

The men shook hands, and Avery motioned to Seeds. "Seeds, take the men to the dock." Avery saluted the crew leaving the *Fancy*.

When Seeds returned in the shallop, Avery gathered the remaining crew, including Finn, who remained, and told them the remaining plan. "I appreciate you staying the course until its completion. We need to gather all our supplies and treasure and place it on the sloop by noon tomorrow. We will move most of the supplies during daylight and wait until nightfall to move our most valuable items under the cover of darkness. My plan is to sail up the Hudson River tomorrow where we will bury the treasure on the mountain. After which I will give you your money. Now, let's move those supplies onto our new ship."

The crew hustled about the galleon moving barrels of salt pork, fish, beer, and water down to the shallop and then onto the sloop. They also carried a good amount of rope, linen, and hemp fabric for any future repairs to the sails and rigging their new ship might need.

As daylight turned to night, Avery called over his men. "Now that we have moved over all our supplies, I want us to be extra watchful as we transfer our loot. Make sure the money chests and containers carrying the bags of money are covered below before bringing them up. Heisey and Burrow, I want you two to stay with the sloop at all times. Let me know if anyone comes nosing around."

"Aye, aye, Captain," the men said in unison.

Avery called Finn over and walked with him to the poop deck where they could talk in private. "Finn, you have been with me these past two years and have been a great help not only to me but to the crew. You have certainly earned your keep."

Finn smiled. "Thank you, Captain."

"You are free to go whenever you wish, but if you want to stay on with me when we finish burying the treasure, you may do so. Not as a servant or anything like that, but as my assistant. I can always use a trusted hand, and you have more than proved yourself. You are more than welcome to join me wherever I end up."

Finn lost his breath for a second. "Captain, that is very generous of you. I'd be honored to be your assistant. Thank you, sir."

Avery held out his hand, and Finn shook it appreciatively.

It took the crew two hours to move all the loot over to the sloop and to make sure everything they wanted was taken off the *Fancy*. Avery took one last look throughout the galleon to ensure all the valuables were removed.

Once aboard the sloop, Avery walked over to Heisey and Burrow. "Anybody come around?"

"No, sir. It's been quiet."

"Good. Let's get ready for tomorrow."

# 15

IT WAS A brisk day when Avery and his crew of nine sailed out of port under a British flag sailing up the Hudson River. Avery stood at the helm of his newly acquired sloop and was thinking about what to name her.

Avery called over his crew as he puffed out his chest. "I have decided to name our sloop the *Pharaoh*, after the great Egyptian pharaohs in the Bible. So, does it fit her?"

"The *Pharaoh?*" Seeds asked. "I don't think many people would know what the name means, but you're the captain, so whatever you say goes. I remember you telling me Pharaohs were big leaders back in those days."

"They certainly were," Avery said.

Avery kept his pirate flag hidden belowdeck. They sailed at a moderate pace. Not too fast as to arouse suspicion but not too slowly, since he was anxious to bury his treasure.

Yet, Avery was used to moving through the seas as quickly as possible and started to grow impatient at their current pace. "Tighten up that line, men. Let's see what she's got."

With Avery's command, the crew pulled on the lines and the sail caught full wind. The sloop moved swiftly through the Hudson River waters, and the men came to life. They saw several other boats on the river, and each one waved to the sloop as it sailed by. It was a different experience for all of them. They weren't used to such friendly interactions with other ships. They were used to robbing them.

Avery walked about the sloop going to each crewmember. "Be nice and friendly. Don't give anyone anything to be concerned about. Give them a wave."

It was mid-afternoon when Avery called out. "I want to make it to Salisbury Island before nightfall. We should be there in the next couple of hours, and go up the mountain tomorrow morning. Even though everyone on the river so far looks friendly, keep a sharp eye out for pirates. They've been known to hide out near the island and come around the back end and attack ships as they're sailing by."

DEERING WAS BELOWDECK in his cabin when his frigate was less than one league away from the New York port. It was three o'clock in the afternoon. He was throwing maps around the room and cursing, until he came upon a map of New York and the surrounding area. *I hope I haven't wasted my time trying to find that galleon,* Deering thought to himself. *I would have bet £100 it was going to be in Virginia.*

Deering jumped when one of his deckhands came below and knocked on his cabin door.

"What do you want?" Deering snarled.

The deckhand cautiously opened the door. "Umm, Captain, sir…"

"What is it?"

"Sir, we spotted a galleon in port."

Deering smiled, stood up, and ran up the steps to the deck. "I bet it's her, boys. I want everyone alert. When we get to port, I'll do all the talking."

Looking up to see what flag they were flying, he noticed the British flag he'd ordered to be flying wasn't hoisted yet. "Where's that British flag?" Deering yelled, spit flying everywhere. "Why aren't we flying British colours? Hoist it immediately and make sure our red hourglass flag is belowdeck."

"Aye, Captain," a crewmember cried out while hoisting a British flag.

The frigate dropped anchor near the docks as Speedy came out in the shallop to bring the crew into port.

Deering gathered his crew. "The rest of you stay on the ship, while I go to see about that galleon. Be ready to move out when I return."

"Captain, how many of your crew are coming into port?" Speedy shouted in the direction of the frigate.

"Just me for now," Deering said.

"They call me Speedy. What brings you to New York, sir?"

"On privateering duty for the East India Company. We're stopping off in New York for a bit before heading back out to sea." Deering pointed to the large ship in port. "Who owns the galleon over there?"

"It belonged to Captain Thomas Sedgeport. Have you met him? He was privateering for the East India Company too, but they didn't find any pirates. The Company told him to sell it. He sold her just the other day to Mr. Treadway. Have you had any luck finding any pirates?"

"It appears we've had somewhat better fortune protecting the Company from those scoundrels than Captain Sedgeport. Where's he now?"

"After selling the galleon, he bought a sloop and he and his men went for a short spell up the Hudson River. I'm not sure where they're going after that."

"I see. So, when did Captain Sedgeport leave?"

"He and his crew left yesterday sailing upriver."

"Would you be able to provide me with a map of the river? I'm going to try to meet up with Captain Sedgeport. I have information that may be useful to the East India Company, which he can relay for me when he returns to England."

"Aye, Captain," Speedy said as he tied the shallop to the dock. "Please follow me and I'll get you some maps. It's real nice sailing up the Hudson this time of year. I'm sure you'll find Captain Sedgeport either upriver or on his way back."

"My crew and I will be going into town tonight to stretch our legs and get a decent meal, Deering told Speedy. "Any recommendations?"

"I'd say the men would probably like Fred's Tavern. The food isn't bad, and the beer and whiskey aren't too watered down."

"Sounds good. How about I throw £5 your way and you let me borrow the shallop for the night so the crew and I can come and go into town? I'll make sure it's tied up nice and neat for you to use in the morning."

"I'm not supposed to, sir, but I don't see any harm in you using it this evening. It has been pretty quiet around the dock today, and it doesn't look like things will be getting any busier this evening."

"Very good. Sounds like we have a deal. Here's the £5. Have a fine evening, Speedy."

"Thank you, Captain."

Deering rowed the shallop back to his frigate, while his men readied the ropes for him to climb aboard. Once on the ship, Deering called his crew over. "All right, bilge rats…"

"Bilge rats?" a crewmember yelled out.

"Oh, be quiet and listen."

"It looks like we just missed Avery. He's going by the name Captain Sedgeport here in New York to keep a low profile. That's got to be his galleon. It has all the markings the Boss said it would have. Avery sold it the other day and bought himself a sloop."

"What now, Captain?" one of the crew asked.

"You can go to town tonight for some decent food and beer. Stay away from the strumpets. We're leaving at first light. I promise we'll leave without any of you, if you aren't back in time. Avery's going up the Hudson River, and I plan on meeting him there."

Deering stomped to his cabin and slammed the door shut. He plopped down on the wobbly chair behind his tattered desk, grabbed a half-empty bottle of rum, and took a big gulp. He wiped his brow and looked up at the ceiling. *The Boss is probably going to try to kill me, whether I find Avery or not. I might as well take what I can from Avery and kill him. If the Boss catches up with me, I'll tell him Avery must have been killed by other pirates.*

# 16

THE *PHARAOH* SAILED up the Hudson River with Salisbury Island on their port side. They sailed to the back of the island hidden from anyone passing by.

"Get ready…now set anchor on the starboard side," Avery commanded. "We'll stay here overnight and head up the mountain at dawn. Get something to eat and make it an early night."

"What's the plan, sir?" Seeds asked.

"We're going high in the mountain. I don't want anyone on a day hike to find my treasure."

"Where are you going to bury your loot?" asked Heisey.

"In one of the caves on the mountain."

"Why not bury it in the ground like we usually do?" Seeds asked.

"The bears and other animals living in a cave will be a natural deterrent for anyone. A little history lesson for all of you—the mountain is called by several names. The Haverstraw call it Wanakawaghkin, or 'good land,' and the New Yorkers call it 'Bear Mountain.' Bears like to live in caves. Get my meaning now?"

"Not a bad idea, I guess," Heisey said. "You're in charge. It's your money."

Avery spotted a light from a distant ship and pointed to Finn. "Climb up one of those trees over there and keep a lookout for any boats on the river. I want to make sure no one sees us over here. Tell me if a boat comes within close range of us."

"Aye, Captain," Finn said as he got off the sloop and headed for a tall oak tree he spotted.

After two minutes, Avery walked over and stood under the tree Finn climbed. "See anything?"

"Nothing, Captain. That light you saw from a ship earlier hasn't moved. It's stopped at a dock for the night. Looks like it's a barge moving lumber."

"Good. Come on down and help us get ready for our hike up the mountain tomorrow. There's still food left over. Better eat since I want you to go with us."

"Yes, sir. Be right there."

It was a quiet night, and Avery and the other pirates slept on the sloop uninterrupted. The crew kept watch every few hours in shifts like they normally did. When morning came, there was a heavy fog surrounding the island, and hardly any ships sailing or rowing on the river.

Avery was the first man to awaken. He walked around and jostled each crewmember. "Time to get a move on. Grab a quick bite to eat. I want all of us to go up the mountain. We'll careen the *Pharaoh* in case anybody has any ideas of taking her while we're gone. It'll be high tide in about an hour, so that'll make it easier for us."

"Aye, Captain," the pirates said in unison.

"Make sure we keep the treasure covered in tarps the entire way. I don't want anyone seeing what we have. You never know who we might come across. Let me do the talking if we run into anyone. I'll tell them we purchased some land on the mountain from the local Haverstraws and are looking for a good place to build a cabin. That should hold their curiosity at least until we bury the treasure and be on our way. Any questions?"

"No need to eat now, Captain," Heisey said for the crew. "We'll grab food to take with us. We're ready to go."

Avery's eyes gleamed, anticipating being able to use the loot soon. "Excellent. Let's careen the sloop and get that treasure up the mountain."

As high tide was coming in, the pirates offloaded all the treasure from the sloop. They moved Avery's loot to the foot of the mountain, to be moved later, and, not wanting to risk someone stealing their shares while they were gone, they buried it in the woods close to the beach. They tied a halyard to the mast and pulled on it until the sloop was on its side. The pirates secured the halyard to a large chestnut tree on the island, ensuring the boat would stay careened until they returned.

Wanting to double check all was clear before they left, Avery pointed to the tree Finn had climbed the previous day. "Climb up there and tell me if you see any ships nearby."

"The fog is heavy, Captain, but I don't see any boats at all," Finn called down to Avery.

"Good. Let's go!" Avery cried out.

An eerie haze covered Bear Mountain making the worn foot paths barely visible. No one said much as they were getting used to their land legs. Plus, carrying the heavy money chests and other loot left the pirates winded.

Occasionally, Avery stopped so everyone could catch their breath, and he could draw where they had walked on his makeshift map. He wanted to make sure he'd be able to find exactly where his treasure was buried when he came for it later. Avery noticed the men were getting tired and looking at him impatiently.

"Captain, when are we going to stop and bury the treasure?" one of the men asked Avery.

"Soon."

"Do you know where the caves are?"

"Not exactly, but rumor has it they are close to the top, and it looks like we're almost there. I bet in another half hour."

"Quit your belly aching," Seeds scolded the crew. "We'll get there when we get there, so hush up."

A rock flew from the woods hitting one of the pirates in the leg and causing him to fall. "Hey, who threw that at me?"

The pirates all looked at each other and shook their heads. "I didn't throw it."

"Well, one of you lousy bilge rats threw it at me. If I find out who, your face is going to meet up with my fist."

"I'll hit each of you in the head with a rock if you don't knock it off," Avery yelled.

Just then a boulder came flying, landing in front of the pirates, and two more landed on each side of the trail.

❖ ❖ ❖

THE ENORMOUS CREATURE lifted its head and sniffed the air. It narrowed its eyes and grunted. Humans. It hated people and detested them coming into its territory. The male beast was nine feet tall and weighed seven hundred pounds. Its head sat on shoulders that measured five feet across. It was the largest and meanest of all the creatures on the mountain.

Its hair was mostly brown with patches of black scattered throughout his body. The deep scar on its neck and the missing left eye were due to a fight with a bear years ago. It had only two fingers on its right hand. The other three were shot off two years ago by hunters who'd accidentally stumbled upon it. It killed them and threw their bodies down the side of the mountain.

This was his territory.

It sniffed the air again and looked at its right hand. It rubbed the stumps and rocked its body left and right. No other humans had gotten this near to him since he was shot. No person would ever hurt him again. The beast motioned with its head toward the men it smelled. The other beasts moved in the direction it gestured. They did whatever he commanded. He was their leader. None of them dared question him. Those that had met with swift and painful deaths.

There were seventeen in all. Its leader made a chattering noise, and several of the beasts climbed up trees. The rest darted silently through the forest, running on their knuckles. They looked at their leader for a sign as to their next move. It scaled a tree and looked for the men. Seeing them nearby, it whistled and pointed. It jumped down and landed heavily on the ground. Dirt flew everywhere from its massive weight. The other animals lowered their eyes and slowly walked in the direction their leader pointed. It picked up a large rock and whistled again. The creatures stopped and copied their leader by picking up rocks. The leader narrowed its eyes. It violently shook its head and roared. The others raised their rocks, growled, and ran toward the humans.

# 17

"GET DOWN," AVERY whispered. The pirates hit the ground while pulling out their guns and rifles, pointing them in every direction. "Someone doesn't want us up here. Could be homesteaders or Haverstraws. I never heard of anyone ever living up here, and the Haverstraws are friendly."

"What was that noise, Captain?" Finn asked, his eyes darting around.

"I don't know."

"I can't see anything. It's too foggy. And what's that smell. It smells like something's rotted. Captain, let's get out of here."

"Quiet, Finn," Avery whispered.

"I can't help it, Captain," Finn murmured. "I can't catch my breath."

"Stand next to me. Don't let them see you're afraid."

It started raining and the wind blew harder. The large oak trees swayed and limbs cracked all around them. The terrible smell wafted through their nostrils as they heard the pounding of something running in front of and behind them. Whatever was surrounding them would crash through the trees, throw rocks at them, and retreat. Afterward there was silence. This happened several times, and then it finally stopped for a few minutes.

Avery stood up slowly, holding his hands in the air. "We aren't here to cause any problems. We're just walking to the top of the mountain.

Show yourselves. We won't shoot." He looked at his men and nodded. "Point your guns down."

The area surrounding the pirates was quiet for a minute, and then came a thunderous roar from ten yards in front of them. Avery saw the men's eyes grow big, and then everyone dropped to the ground.

The hair on the back of Avery's neck stood up. It was as if the sound shot straight through his body. The pirates stared at each other.

"What was that?" Seeds asked.

"Who knows," Heisey said. "It didn't sound like a person yelling or screaming, and it wasn't a bear."

"I was in Africa and saw an ape caught in a cage," Donegan said. "It kinda sounded like that, but I don't think there are any apes here. Had to have been a bear."

"Let's get going," Avery commanded. "Keep an eye out and have your guns at the ready."

Avery and his crew continued walking up Bear Mountain on the still barely visible path for another half hour. They felt like someone or something was watching and following them. They didn't hear any more roars, but Avery occasionally heard what sounded like someone hitting a tree trunk with a club on one side of them, and then the same sound a few seconds later on their other side. Sporadically, he thought he heard chattering sounds coming from the thick woods around them. He couldn't make out any words. It almost sounded like children talking in some made-up language or animals making noises trying to communicate with each other. It was all strange and had the pirates on edge. To make matters worse, it started raining even heavier.

Next to the path, they noticed several trees were unnaturally bent over and looked like they were connected to other bent trees. It didn't appear to have been altered from the wind or snow or even from other trees falling over on them. They weren't tied together with anything but seemed to be interconnected. It looked similar to what someone would do when initially building a temporary structure in the woods for sleeping. But these trees were too broad and tall to be possibly bent over by a person or even several people with ropes. Plus, there were no ropes on the trees. The path also had large limbs across it every few feet. They appeared to have either fallen due to heavy rain or, perhaps, they were even pushed across the path on purpose. It took three pirates each to move them before they could walk forward on the path.

Avery stopped. "Do you hear that?"

"Hear what?" Seeds asked.

"Exactly," Avery said. "I don't hear anything. No birds, no animals. Nothing. It's too quiet. I don't like it."

They walked another one hundred yards when they came upon an entrance to a cave in the side of a hill.

# 18

"WE'RE HERE," AVERY said while holding his nose. "I knew there were caves on the mountain, and it looks like we found us one. Hope it doesn't smell as badly inside as it does out here."

Seeds covered his nose with his hand and inched backward. "Captain, I thought that smell was from a skunk, but it kind of smells more like wet, rotting flesh. I wonder if something died in there."

"It is pretty bad," Avery noted. "Who wants to be the first to go in to make sure a bear isn't in there?"

"Not me," each pirate said.

Avery shook his head and frowned. "You all are a bunch of chickens. I'll go in first. You have no problem brawling with sailors and pillaging ships on the high seas, but a little stink in a dark cave makes you all cowards."

Avery turned away from the cave's smelly entrance and lit a torch. He took a deep breath and held it, turned back toward the cave, and went in. He stooped as he entered the low opening. After a few feet, the cave opened to where he could stand up straight. Avery looked around, noticing the cave to be about half the size of a ship's deck with several tunnels near the back end.

Avery saw deer bones and carcasses littering the earthen floor. He even saw several fish bones scattered around the cave. There was a half-eaten bear leaning against one of the walls. There weren't any fire marks that indicated people lived there. *Must be a bear cave, but do bears eat other bears?*

Avery choked back vomit as the smell was horrendous. He looked around but didn't see any live animals, or any signs that humans had been there. He drew a picture of a cave with an *X* inside it on his map to mark the location of his treasure.

He walked back to the entrance of the cave. "It's all clear. It smells bad, but that just means no one will be coming around and the treasure will be safe. I walked back one hundred feet or so. That'll be a good place to start digging. It may help if you put a rag over your noses. There's a bunch of animal bones and carcasses on the ground."

The pirates lit their torches and walked inside the cave with the two money chests of gold and jewelry, and ten bags of money. They stopped where Avery had gone earlier and started digging when he pointed to a spot on the floor of the cavern. It took them only a few minutes to dig a hole big enough to put in one of the chests and a few bags of treasure. They began digging another hole nearby when a large rock flew at them from deep within the cave.

The pirates stopped and looked at each other. "Not this again," Seeds said.

"I've had enough of this," Avery barked, walking in the direction from where the rock was thrown. "Who threw that rock?" A hairy figure crouching on all four legs peeked out from behind a rock formation.

"A bear," yelled Avery as he fired a shot. The animal fell back and screamed in pain from the round ball that slammed into its shoulder. A larger animal grabbed the injured one and dragged it farther back in the cave.

"Oh my God, what was that?" Avery cried out as he backed up. He was starting to hyperventilate. "I thought it was a bear, but when I saw it fall back and the other one drag it away…it…it…didn't look like a bear."

The pirates backed up as deafening roars came from where the injured animal was taken. Then, an enormous creature came charging at them.

"Fire," Avery yelled at the pirates.

Shots rang out as massive beasts came rushing at them. Ricocheting bullets echoed throughout the cave. Loud roars, like the ones the pirates heard before, came from farther inside the cavern. The sounds were deafening. Shadows of massive creatures flashed around the sides of the cave reflecting off the lit torches. The roars became louder as the shadows of the hulking beasts came closer. Twelve enormous ones ran at the men at full stride, swinging their huge hairy arms and hands and pummeling the pirates.

Many of them were at least seven feet tall with shoulders almost as wide. Their bodies were covered with hair, and they had pug noses. Most had brown or black hair, but a couple, what appeared like older ones, had white hair. Their faces looked like a combination of a man and an ape, and their eyes glowed red in the reflection of the torches. Some were bleeding from where bullets hit them, but it didn't slow them down.

Several more massive creatures roared and rushed at the pirates with their gigantic feet pounding into the ground of the cave. The horrible smelling brutes grabbed the men and threw them about like soggy bags of flour.

Avery saw "Paddy" O'Reilly being lifted in the air and thrown to the ground, his leg bent backward. Paddy screamed as he was dragged farther into the cave.

One massive creature stomped on Donegan's back, breaking it instantly, and then turned its attention to Avery. It swiped at him, tearing his shirt and leaving deep claw marks across his chest. Avery regained his composure and aimed a shot from his gun directly at the animal's face. The kickback from the blast threw his arm back and spun him around. Avery turned back quickly to see the creature slam dead on the ground.

Avery's adrenaline kept him from feeling the pain in his chest, but he knew he was hurt badly. The cuts were deep. He steadied himself against the wall of the cave as his head started spinning and his legs wobbled. Then everything turned dark and he hit the ground.

# 19

FINN HAD HIDDEN as best as he could in a crevice in the cave once the shooting started, but now he could see a creature creeping near him, sniffing the air, trying to locate him. It had locked onto Finn's scent. With the beast inches away, Finn darted out and ran as fast as he could toward the cave's opening. The creature took a swing at him with one of its massive arms. Finn screamed as its claws tore at his back. Four large streaks of blood ran down his shirt as he made a mad dash out of the cave.

By now there were several pirates and creatures dead from the battle taking place. Those men who were still alive were screaming and waving their torches at the animals. The fire was the only thing that held the creatures back. The beasts roared and snorted as they retreated slowly to the far end of the cave. Two of the pirates grabbed Avery by his shirt and dragged him toward the cave's opening. The others gathered firearms, the unburied money chest, and several bags of money. They slowly walked backwards, making their way outside the cavern. The brutes continued throwing rocks at the men but didn't come any closer.

Finn saw Avery was still unconscious as the men dragged him farther and farther away from the cave. Once they retreated about one hundred feet, ensuring none of the creatures followed them, the remaining pirates yelled at each other, trying to figure out what had just happened.

Finn shook his head. "What were those creatures?"

"I don't know," Seeds said. "I've never seen anything like them. They looked half-man and half-ape. Only bigger than any man or beast I've ever seen."

SEEDS, TOOK CONTROL of the situation. He counted the number of pirates grouped around him. "Looks like twelve of us made it out alive. Avery's in bad shape. Finn, it looks like they clawed you too."

"I'm all right. It just really stings."

"Here, put my shirt across your back and tie it in front," Seeds said. "It'll help slow down the bleeding until we can get to the ship."

Seeds pointed to two of the pirates. "Suggs and Perry, you two carry Avery. The rest of us will haul the remaining money chest and what bags of money are left down the mountain. Hopefully, Avery will be fine, and we can figure out what we're going to do once we're on the sloop. I'm done with this mountain."

The pirates were on edge as they started their long journey back to Salisbury Island and their sloop, in what was now a torrential downpour. The mountain was covered in a fog, making the trip all the more treacherous. The crew was still on the lookout for the enormous creatures. Any snapped twig had their heads on a swivel trying to see where it came from.

It was about dusk, and the weather grew colder. Wisps of clouds covered their path. The shadows from the trees and rocks lying across the path looked like gigantic human stick figures. The men were soaking wet and worn out when they spotted their sloop.

Seeds looked at Finn and scrunched his brow. "How you feeling? You took a pretty good swipe from one of them creatures back there."

"Aye. It still stings but not too badly."

"Once we get back to the sloop, we'll see what the doc left us and try to fix up you and the captain."

"Thanks."

Seeds pointed at Suggs. "Stay here with the captain under the trees until we get the sloop upright. He doesn't need to be out in this weather any more than he has been. We'll do our best to help him until we sail back to town and get him to a doctor. I wish we had the doc with us. He'd know what to do."

"I'll tell you if the captain gets worse."

"Good." Seeds pointed to the ship. "Let's get to that sloop."

The sloop gradually came upright as the pirates cut the halyard tied to the large chestnut tree and attached to the sloop's mast.

Seeds pointed at Sully and Jones. "Go get the captain." The two ran off to where they had left Avery and Suggs.

"How's he doing?" Jones asked Suggs.

"Not good. He's breathing really slowly and he looks pretty pale to me. Plus, he's got the shivers. Let's get him onboard and under a bunch of clothes and sheets. Hopefully, that will warm him up."

Several of the pirates lifted Avery onto the sloop and carried him belowdeck to his cabin.

"Give him some air," Seeds told the other pirates. "I'll let you know how he's doing in a few minutes."

Seeds found the doc's bag of medicine and tried to figure out what to give Avery to help him. He shrugged as he looked through the satchel. He closed it and placed it on the table next to Avery's bed. *"I don't have a clue what's in these bottles. I'll keep him warm as best I can."*

Seeds opened Avery's shirt to see the claw marks on his chest already looking like they were getting infected. He grabbed a bottle of rum and poured some on the cleanest sheet he could find and dabbed at the wounds. Avery moaned. Seeds stopped and tapped Avery's face. "Captain, Captain, you awake?"

Avery sat straight up, staring wide-eyed at the walls. Then he screamed. "Shoot them. They're everywhere. Red eyes…huge…don't let 'em get me. SHOOT!"

"Captain, it's me, Seeds."

Avery blinked several times. "Seeds? Where are we?"

"We're on the sloop."

"Get us out of here!" Avery yelled. "They're everywhere!" Then he went unconscious.

Seeds climbed back on deck.

"He all right?" several of the crew asked. "We heard the captain screaming."

"He's pretty out of it," Seeds said. "He thought he was back in the cave trying to fight off those creatures."

"Should we try to make it to town tonight?"

"Weather's terrible. Probably best to wait until mornin'. Hopefully, it'll clear up by then. If not, we may have to go anyway. Looks like the captain's wounds are infected. Finn, how are your cuts?"

"Not bad. Suggs poured some rum on them and cleaned them up. Burned like crazy, but I'll be fine."

The pirates kept watch in shifts throughout the night. It was quiet on the river. Avery woke up every few hours in a rant about creatures attacking him. Other than that, the only thing heard were the sheets of rain hitting the sloop.

# 20

DEERING'S FRIGATE, THE *Scorpion,* and his crew of pirates sailed up the Hudson River at a good pace while keeping a sharp lookout for a sloop. They flew a British flag, ensuring not to draw any unnecessary attention. They had sailed quite a way when a sloop had passed them coming down the river. Deering yelled at his crew to ready themselves for a fight, but its passengers were families with children.

It started raining harder and the pirates saw fewer and fewer boats of any kind on the river. Deering decided to pull up next to shore, drop anchor for the night, and pursue Avery in the morning. He went belowdeck for the evening and told his crew to take their normal shifts and to inform him immediately if they saw any sloop sailing up or down the river. The night passed by without the pirates spying any ship.

Early the next day, Deering awoke to find it had stopped raining and the sun was beginning to show itself. He gave his crew the command to pull up anchor and to start sailing.

The *Scorpion* had sailed two hours up the Hudson and came upon Salisbury Island. It was still fairly early in the morning, and Deering and his men had not seen any boats on the river. The *Scorpion* was sailing past the island when a pirate in the lookout turned to look toward the back of the island. Cupping his hand around his mouth, he yelled down to the deck. "There's a sloop, Captain. She has British colours. Doesn't look like she's moving."

"Swing us around," Deering commanded. "I want to get a better look. Go straight at her. Men, get to your stations and get ready for a fight. Prime your guns and get your weapons ready. If it's Avery and his crew, I don't want them to get away."

"Give me the spyglass so I can take a closer look at her," Deering demanded. He saw several men on deck who didn't look like passengers on a boat or sailors from the British navy. "Pete, get over here and tell me if you recognize any of them," Deering said, while handing Pete the spyglass.

"Let me see, let me see," Pete whispered as he strained to look through the spyglass. "Are any of you those scoundrels?" Pete's eyes narrowed. "Yes, Captain, that's them," he yelled. "I'd remember them anywhere. They're the ones."

"Come on, you rapscallions," yelled Deering. "Get ready for a fight."

Deering stood tall, adjusted his cutlass and pistol on his waist, and readied himself for battle.

❖ ❖ ❖

SAM AND EMMA Barrett sat on the east side of Salisbury Island having their usual Sunday date. They were eating chicken, corn, and bread, and sipping hard cider from mugs.

The island was nearly five hundred fifty acres in size with a large marsh adjacent to it. It was a wonderful place for fishing and for exploring the various wildlife in the area. Many varieties of birds resided on the island including osprey, wood duck, geese, swans, hawks, eagles, and a multitude of others.

Sam smiled at Emma as he looked out at the river. "I love watching the different kinds of ships sail by on the Hudson."

"I do too," Emma replied. "Especially the sloops zigging and zagging around the larger ships. I wonder what adventures they had on the ocean getting here, and where they're going upriver. I wonder if some of them dropped off items for our store."

"Hope so," Sam said. "We need more supplies to sell."

The Haverstraws, Mahicans, Mohawks, and Minsis also rowed past the island in their dugout canoes made from several types of trees. These boats were sturdy for difficult waters, yet light enough to be carried by one man if need be.

Sam and Emma were holding hands watching a flock of geese fly by. Their peaceful outing was suddenly disrupted when they heard men shouting on the other side of the island.

SEEDS WAS CHECKING on Avery when Suggs yelled down to him, "Frigate coming straight toward us."

"What colours is she flying?" Seeds cried out as he ran up from belowdeck.

"She's flying a British flag, but I don't like that she's coming straight at us and sailing fast. Not real friendly like."

"Get ready for a fight, boys," Seeds yelled.

Suggs snuck downstairs during all the commotion. He saw Avery lying there unconscious. He reached into Avery's coat pocket and pulled out the map showing where the treasure was hidden on the mountain and stuffed it in his pant pocket. He dug in another pocket and found the two keys to unlock the money chests' padlocks. "I think I should hold on to these for safe keeping, Captain, especially if you don't make it." He saluted and returned on deck.

Seeds shook his head. "Doesn't look good. There aren't many of us to skirmish a gang on a frigate. Who knows if that flag is legit?" Seeds called over Jack and Finn. "Better get the captain off the sloop and take him up there on the mountain. It'll be safer for him up there. Jack you come back once you get him to safety. Finn, you stay with the captain."

Jack picked up Avery under his arms, and Finn grabbed his legs as they carried him up top. "Help us with the captain," Jack yelled to several of the nearby pirates. They lowered Avery into the arms of three crew below, and Finn and Jack climbed onto the beach. Jack and Finn carried Avery a short way up the mountain and laid him beside a tree.

"See you later, Finn," Jack said. Then he ran back to the sloop.

# 21

"GET READY TO fire a cannon shot at her," Seeds commanded, fully in charge now.

"Aye, aye," Smith cried out, standing next to the big gun.

Seeds raised his rifle. "Prime your guns and rifles. Get your cutlasses and—" Before Seeds could finish, there was a loud *boom*. A cannonball hit the top of the sloop's mast, breaking it in two, and rocking the sloop.

"Fire," Seeds yelled. The cannonball flew through the air and slammed into the side of the frigate, killing five men instantly.

Two more *booms* rang out from the frigate as a cannonball landed squarely in the middle of the *Pharaoh's* hull while another tore a hole in its deck.

"We're not protected while anchored," Seeds yelled, shaking his head. *I knew we should have gotten out of here sooner.* "Gather your weapons. Grab the money chest and bags of money and let's fight that frigate from land. I don't want the treasure ending up in the river. Smith, give her one more shot before we leave the *Pharaoh*. Steve, Rick, Charlie, and George, go bury the chest and our money by those trees where we buried our money before going up the mountain. Hurry and then get back here."

"Take that," Smith shouted as the roar from the cannon shot slammed onto the deck of the frigate, killing several more pirates. "We got 'em good on that one," Smith shouted. "I see smoke, and I can hear their crew yelling for help."

"Good job," Seeds cried out. "Now come on down and let's get 'em from the beach."

Several of Avery's crew grabbed all their bags of money, threw them down to the four pirates below, and jumped off the sloop into the shallow water below. Two of the pirates carried the money chest and lowered it below as best they could as gunshots ricocheted around them.

Four pirates ran with the chest and bags of coins straight to the tree line on the beach. Two men carried the money chest and several bags of coins on top of it, while the other two carried the rest of the coins. Shots rang out around them as they ran.

Seeds saw one of the crew shot, while another ran to help him.

"Charlie's hit. Charlie's hit," Simpson yelled as he threw his bags of coins to the others and ran to help him. He kept patting him on the face. "Where'd you get hit? Come on, Charlie. Tell me where'd you get hit?" Simpson's face turned red, realizing his friend was dead. He balled up his fists and stood facing the frigate, firing pistol shot after pistol shot at the pirates on the ship.

The others threw the bags of money in a hole already dug from before and covered it over with leaves and dirt as fast as they could. They ran and grabbed Simpson, pulling him back under cover of the trees. "Come on. Get over here. You're going to get yourself killed."

"The money. Charlie's bags of money," Simpson protested as he ran back and grabbed the bags Charlie dropped when he was shot. A shot rang out from the frigate and exploded one of the bags of coins Simpson carried. The other pirates were yelling at him. "Let it go, Simpson. Leave it."

Seeds looked upriver to see how close the frigate was to the island. He was trying to determine quickly how much time they had before the crew on the frigate got to the beach. "We only have a minute or two before they're here."

There was a momentary lull in the fighting when Jack came running down the hill from where he'd left Finn with the captain.

"How's he doing?" Seeds asked Jack with a furrowed brow.

"About the same. Finn's watching after him."

"Looks like they tore the *Pharaoh* apart, but we got them good too."

Sweat and dirt covered Seeds' face. "Aye, the sloop is pretty much done for. I figured we had a better chance fighting them on the beach."

# 22

THE *PHARAOH* SHUDDERED from another cannon blast. The sloop rocked violently but remained afloat. Sand exploded when a cannonball hit the beach twenty yards away from the nearest pirate.

The crewmembers on the *Scorpion* ran the frigate onto the beach and scrambled down the ladders on its sides amid gunfire from Avery's crew.

"Give it to them," shouted Seeds as the pirates from Avery's crew ran at the attackers.

Pistol shots rang out from both ends of the beach as each side lost men to bullets hitting their targets. The pirates ran at each other screaming and swinging their weapons. Metal cutlasses and scabbards clanged as the pirates swung at each other ruthlessly.

After noticing, who he guessed was the captain shouting orders to his men, Seeds charged him. He wanted to kill the man in charge of the enemy. Deering shot at Seeds with a pistol in one hand while swinging a cutlass high above his head.

A round lead ball from Deering's pistol hit Seeds in the shoulder, knocking him to the ground. He got up to one knee, steadying himself. Deering raised his cutlass and glared at Seeds. A shot rang out from behind Seeds, hitting Deering in the chest, knocking him off his feet and slamming him backwards onto the sand. Deering got up on one elbow, shook his head trying to gather his senses, but fell back onto the sand, dropping his cutlass.

Jack ran over to Seeds, after he made sure Deering was dead. "You all right?" he asked.

"Never better, Jack. Thanks for shooting him. I'd be a dead man if you hadn't."

"No problem. You going to be good here?" Jack asked as he looked at Deering's lifeless body.

"I'll be fine," Seeds said as he lay there, knowing his life would end soon. "I saw that sailor we let go near Cuba. They must have followed us here. Go get 'em, Jack."

THE BARRETTS STARED wide-eyed at each other, holding their breaths. It was as if a small war was going on, but they couldn't see anything from where they were standing.

"We should leave," Emma said.

Sam's heart was racing. He wiped the beads of sweat from his forehead. "You're right. Let's pack up our picnic and head home."

The gunfire continued for what seemed like ages to Sam and Emma, and then it abruptly stopped.

Emma took hold of Sam's hand. "Do you think it's over? What if they're coming over here?"

Sam checked to make sure his dagger was still attached to its sheath, and his pistol was primed and ready.

"I don't see anyone coming our way," Sam said.

"Don't care," Emma said while putting the picnic basket in their boat. "Let's get out of here."

"I know we should, but it's quiet now," Sam said. "Don't you want to see what happened?"

Emma put her hands on her hips. "Samuel Barrett, you have that look on your face. Don't let curiosity get the better of you. We need to go now."

"Let's give it a few minutes," Sam said.

They stood silently, listening for any more fighting. But after fifteen minutes, it was still quiet.

"I realize we shouldn't…" Sam said, shaking his head. "But since the shooting seems to have stopped, let's go see what happened."

"No, Sam," Emma pleaded. "Let's go home."

"Just a quick look," Sam said. "Then I promise we'll go home."

Emma held on to Sam's arm. "Very well, but only for a second."

The couple slowly made their way to the other side of the island. As they came around the corner on the island's east side, they peeked around a tree. They saw two ships badly damaged. As they got closer, they noticed dead men lying about the beach.

Emma gasped and turned her head away from the gruesome scene, but held Sam's hand as he moved forward. They walked closer to the men and the smoldering ships.

"Emma, look at all the weapons."

Weapons of every kind lay around the men. Most looked like the type one would use for hand-to-hand combat. Blunderbusses, musketoons, bucklers for protection, cutlasses, boarding axes, boarding pikes, and numerous kinds of knives were strewn across the sand. As they glanced around, they heard the groans of two wounded men lying about fifty feet away. Sam and Emma ran over to them to help.

"Find any pieces of cloth or clothing you can and apply pressure to that man's wound while I work on this one," Sam hollered to Emma.

Emma grabbed a piece of a torn-off jacket she found next to the man and pressed it hard against the large cut on his head. Tears rolled down her cheek as she applied pressure to the wound. She noticed another cut on the man's neck and looked around trying to find anything else she could use to help stop the bleeding. She grabbed a hat laying there and held it against his neck with her left hand while continuing to keep pressure against his head with her right. "Please don't die," she said. "I've never seen anyone die before."

Emma kept repeating, "Please don't die, please don't die," while she continued to apply pressure to the man's cuts. She constantly wiped the tears from her eyes and prayed God would save him. Several minutes later, the man's chest stopped rising and falling. Emma checked for a pulse. She felt none. Bowing her head, she crossed herself. She tearfully walked up to Sam and held him tightly. "He's gone."

"I'm sorry. Mine's barely alive, but he's trying to tell me something."

After coughing and wheezing for a good minute, the injured man Sam was trying to save placed keys and a map in his hand. The man gathered strength and whispered, "Can't spend any of it where I'm going. Captain's probably dead. Beware of creatures in a cave up on the mountain. Bigger than bears. Shoot them if you see them."

Sam leaned next to the man's ear. "What cave, and what creatures? I don't understand."

The pirate's eyes grew big and he pointed to claw marks on his chest. He tried to say something but collapsed and died in Sam's arms. Sam placed the man's head on the ground and closed his eyes.

"What did he say, Sam? I couldn't hear him."

"He was talking about creatures bigger than bears in a cave up on the mountain. I never heard of animals like that on the mountain or anywhere. He gave me a map with an X on it. It must show where they buried treasure and ran into those creatures he was talking about."

"You can ask Maxkw when you see him next," Emma whispered.

Sam put his hand on his face and shook his head. "Did you see those claw marks on his chest? They don't look like bear marks. They're fresh cuts too."

FINN WIPED AWAY tears as he saw all his friends lying there. He prayed they weren't dead. He wanted to go down there and help his mates, but he couldn't move. It was as if he were frozen, and it seemed like time had frozen too. The trees stopped swaying, and even the birds flying by appeared as if they were caught in a stiff breeze.

Then Finn's fear turned to anger. He clenched his teeth and punched the ground. *Who's that man and woman? I can't believe Suggs took the captain's map and keys and gave it to them.*

AFTER TRYING TO help the two wounded men, the Barretts checked to see if anyone else was alive. They split up but came back together a few minutes later.

"Any luck?" Sam asked.

"No," was all Emma could muster. Then she gasped and pointed toward the tree line. "Look over there near the woods. Coins are scattered all over the ground. Looks like they were tossed toward those trees."

Sam walked over and stared at a large amount of gold and silver coins. There were silver Pieces of Eight and gold doubloons. He looked around and had to hold on to a tree. He couldn't believe what he saw—a mound of leaves half covering what looked like an ornate treasure chest.

# 23

SAM AND EMMA inched closer to the money chest and noticed the lid was slightly open. She almost stepped on a dead pirate lying next to it holding a boarding axe. There were numerous jewels on the chest's lid.

"My goodness, Emma," Sam said, pointing to the dead pirate. "He broke off the padlock with his axe."

"Look at all the jewels on the cover!" Then she peeked inside. "I can't believe it. There are carved pieces of ivory, rings, necklaces, and pendants with rubies, garnet, emeralds, and gold. They're beautiful. I've never seen so much jewelry."

Looking around, Sam thought these men looked like pirates, but he didn't want to alarm Emma. "We need to be careful, but we should see if anyone's alive on the ships."

They climbed onboard the sloop as best they could due to all the damage. They didn't see anyone. Several half-ripped bags of coins lay on the deck.

Sam noticed that while the sloop was flying British colours, there was another flag lying in a corner. It was a black flag with white skull and crossbones on it. "Let's go check on the frigate."

They didn't find anyone aboard the frigate but found more bags of coins and another strange flag lying next to the mainmast. It was a red flag with a white hourglass pictured on it. This confirmed to Sam both vessels were pirate ships, based on what he was told from sailors he had run across at the local tavern. They told of seeing ships with these kinds of flags on them, but Sam thought they were just stories told by drunken men trying to impress each other.

"What kind of flags were those?" Emma asked.

"I didn't want to frighten you when I first saw them, but…they're pirate flags."

"What? Pirates that close to us on the island?"

"Unfortunately, yes. Skull and crossbones flags are flown to instill fear in the ships they're attacking. I'm trying to remember what the flag with the hourglass means. Oh yes, there's a certain pirate, whose name escapes me, who uses that flag to warn his victims that 'their time is up.'"

"Sam, what are we going to do?"

"I don't know. There may be more pirates coming. What do we do with all the coins, jewelry, ivory and the map?"

They sat there, overwhelmed.

"Let's get out of here," Emma pleaded.

"We've got to think this through for a second," Sam said.

It was getting late, and they had a decision to make. Sam went over their options. "We can gather up the treasure we found and leave within the next few hours so we can be home before nightfall. We can try to bury the dead as best we can, stay the night, and sail back home tomorrow. But there are too many for us to give them all a proper burial. I saw only a couple of small shovels."

Sam scratched his head and looked around at the deadly scene in front of him. "This loot was probably stolen from many ships, and I'm sure some country or countries want it back. But this treasure ended up on Haverstraw land and Maxkw should decide what to do with it. Let's quickly go to him and see what he decides."

# 24

FINN STARTED TO walk down to the beach when someone grabbed his shoulder.

"Better not go down there," an old man said, smiling.

Finn leapt back, startled. "Who are you?" He couldn't help but stare at the man's long, straggly grey beard, his deer skin pants and shirt, and hat made of leaves.

"I'm Thaddeus Figglebottom. At yer service," he said, bowing. "An' who might yeh be?"

"You're joking? Thaddeus Figglebottom?"

"That's me name. I admit it's a little fussy. Most folk call me Fig."

"Um, I'm Finn. Where d'ye you come from? You scared me half to death."

"Sorry about that. I live here in these hills. I saw yeh an' yer friends yesterday goin' up the mountain an' comin' back down. I see yeh all had a bit of trouble on the beach. Looks like yer friend here is hurt."

"Yes, but I better get down there and see if I can help any of my other...friends."

"I hate to tell yeh, but they're all most likely dead or will be shortly. There's nothin' yeh can do for 'em now. Do yeh know the man an' woman walkin' around the beach?"

"No, I need to get down there."

"I wouldn't if I were yeh. Who knows what in the ding-dong-did-dly-dew they're up to? Yeh could end up like yer friends. Been in a few fights myself over the years, an' it's the unexpected that always gets yeh hurt or killed. It's up to yeh." The man pointed at Avery. "We ought to get yer friend here to me place so I can look after his injuries. Seems like he's in bad shape. What happened to him?"

"We all got attacked by huge creatures in a cave at the top of the mountain, and they clawed him up pretty good. I think it's infected. I need to get him to a doctor in town."

"Wait a minute. Yeh said yeh was in a cave up at the top of the mountain an' ran into some huge creatures?"

"Aye."

"Were they bears?"

"No, they looked like they were half-man, and half—"

"Half-ape?" Figglebottom interrupted.

"What they are?"

"Yer all lucky to be alive. The Haverstraws up here call 'em *Mhuwe*. They usually leave folk be an' hide amon' the trees. Sometimes they throw rocks an' sticks at yeh if yeh get too close to their territory, but they just want to be left alone. They keep to 'emselves most of the time, an' yeh hardly ever see 'em. Yeh smell 'em when they're close-by. They stink somethin' awful. Yeh also hear knockin' on trees an' hollers at night, an' sometimes whistlin' sounds in the woods. That's when they're talkin' to each other. They leave me alone 'cause I give 'em some deer when I go hunting about once a month, an' I don't go into their territory. Since I do that, they tolerate me bein' up here. Sorry. Listen to me carry on. I haven't talked to anyone in a while."

"How do you know so much about them?"

"I've lived up here now goin' on twenty years. Just me since my wife an' kids died from the pox. Couldn't stan' to be amon' people after that. A stray dog came around a few years ago an' we keep each other company. The Haverstraws don't go as far up the mountain where I live because of the *Mhuwe*. Not too many townsfolk come up here 'cept to hunt, an' when they do, they don't go that fer up the mountain."

"How can you tell when you're in their territory?"

"Yeh all see trees bent over an' either stuck in the ground or tucked under other trees. That an' when yeh start gettin' rocks an' things thrown at yeh an' hear tree knocks an' the whistlin' I told yeh about. It's best to stay away when that starts happenin'."

"That's what happened to us. Guess we ended up in their territory, and possibly where they live in that cave."

"Sounds like it. Let's get yer friend to my place an' take a look at him. I have herbs that should help him. With both of those ships wrecked, yeh can't go into town anyway. We'll make somethin' to put him on so we can carry him. Too hard to lift him by ourselves. My place is a good hour from here. Grab some thick tree branches. We can use 'em for poles. Sorry, but we're going to need yer shirt too."

Finn cut down two long tree limbs and brought them over to Figglebottom.

"Take off yer shirt so we can run the tree limbs through the sleeves," Figglebottom said. "We can tie 'em together with rope I have."

Finn took off his shirt and handed it to Figglebottom.

Figglebottom scrunched his nose. "Looks like yeh got clawed by the *Mhuwe*."

"It's not too bad. Just stings every now and then."

"We can take care of that back at my place too. I still can't imagine why they would attack yeh an' not only throw rocks at yeh."

"Well, Captain thought one of them was a bear coming from the back of the cave and shot it. He wounded it because it screamed something awful. Another one of those, what you call them, *Mhuwe*, dragged it back in the cave. Captain said the one he shot was on all fours but was probably six feet tall if it had been standing up."

"Now I know why they attacked yeh. That makes sense. Only six feet tall—it must have been a youngin'. Yer captain hurt one of their babies, an' their protective instincts kicked in. Yeh all are lucky any of yeh survived."

"I still don't feel right leaving my friends there," Finn said.

"It's up to yeh, but like I said, it's best to go. Sorry, but I don't see anyone movin' but that man an' woman. Hate to say it, but I think yer friends are dead."

Finn looked down, shook his head left and right, and wiped away a tear. "You're right. I can't believe they're all...gone."

"Sorry," Figglebottom said, putting his hand on Finn's shoulder. "It's tough on anyone, especially someone at yer age."

Finn nodded. "Let's go. Hopefully we can save my...uh..."

"Yer friend?" Figglebottom interrupted.

"Yes, my friend."

They put Avery on their crude stretcher and dragged him up the mountain. Avery sporadically woke up moaning, and then would fall back in a stupor. At one time, Avery yelled out, "Run, they're coming at us. Shoot them." Another time he screamed, "Get out of the cave. Creatures...too many of them."

Finn didn't say much. He kept one eye on Avery, making sure he was as comfortable as possible, and another on Figglebottom. Figglebottom was a strange man, but Finn felt he didn't have much choice other than to go with him. He hoped this mountain man could help his captain. Finn's mind was racing. *What if the captain dies? Where do I go? What do I do? What if all our loot is gone? What if this mountain man really is crazy? How will I protect the captain and myself?*

# 25

"YEH BEEN PRETTY quiet, boy," Figglebottom said. "Yeh all right?"

"I'm good. We almost there?"

"Not much more ter go. Yer friend will be fine. Don' worry."

An hour later, Finn looked up to see a small hut with the roof covered in moss and leaves. The opening to the hut was low to the ground. A scraggly dog came running up to them, barking.

"This here is Cucumber, Pickle, Sweetie Pie," Figglebottom said, petting the dog that jumped into his arms. "My place isn't much, but it works fer me. Don' get any guests up here, an' that's the way I like it. Sweetie Pie is a love bug. She'll just lick yeh ter death, but she's a good watchdog. Anybody or anythin' comes close-by, she'll bark like crazy."

Finn didn't say a word but looked around not knowing what to make of the shack and his host.

"How yeh like my place?" Figglebottom asked.

"It's all right, I guess."

"Where's yer friend hurt?"

"He got clawed in the chest," Finn said as he carefully removed Avery's shirt, trying not to awaken him.

"They tore him up pretty good, didn' they? They're tough creatures, them *Mhuwe*. I got herbs over here that I'll boil up an' put on them cuts. It should take the 'fection away. Yeh could use some of this fer yer back. Once we get rid of the 'fection, he should wake up. 'Fections wipe yeh out."

Finn sat next to Avery as he watched Figglebottom grab a bag of herbs from the top of a rickety shelf made from twigs and a few cut tree limbs. Figglebottom put water in a pot and set it over a small fire pit outside his hut. Once the water started boiling, he added the bag of herbs and several strips of cloth.

"We need ter let them boil fer a good fifteen minutes. The cloth will soak up most of the medicine from the herbs, but I'll put them directly on his cuts ter so he gets as much of it as he can. Same fer yeh, ter, Finn. No sense in yeh gettin' a 'fection ter."

"Thanks. I just want to make sure Sedgeport gets better."

"Sedgeport's his name. Is he yer father?"

"No, he's the captain of our ship."

"Oh, so yeh all are sailors. Ever hear of this one?

All by the dark an' lonely sea

Flowin' wherever it may please

Nowhere ter go

Nowhere ter flow

Flows by so calm

So calm ter see

The calmness of the sea

Ferever it will be."

Finn rolled his eyes. "No...can't say I've ever heard that one. At times the sea can get pretty violent."

"Oh, I can change it some," said Figglebottom clearing his throat. "Ever hear this one?

All by the dark an' tumultuous sea

Flowin' wherever it may please

Nowhere ter go

Nowhere ter flow

Flows by so violent

So violent ter see

The violence of the sea

Ferever it will be."

"Can't say I've ever heard of that one either," Finn said, raising his eyebrows and looking away.

"Reckoned yeh hadn't," Figglebottom said, laughing loudly as if he had made the best joke in the world. "I made it up myself. Right here on the spot. Kind of fancy myself as a poet. So, what yeh doin' on land, goin' up the mountain? I saw yeh carryin' stuff. Yeh wouldn't want ter be settlers since yeh all are sailors. That's mighty strange."

Finn looked at Figglebottom, not saying anything.

Figglebottom winked at Finn, and stroked Cucumber, Pickle, Sweetie Pie's head. "I know what yer doin'. Yer pirates buryin' treasure up high in the mountain where nobody can get ter it. Very clever. Very clever indeed, until yeh ran into the *Mhuwe*."

"No, we were looking at land up here to build and settle. We aren't pirates. We were on a privateering mission for the East India Company."

"Have it yer way. Yeh don' need ter tell me the truth. Yeh don' live as long as I have an' not learn a thin' or two about people. I figured it out when yeh all came down the mountain all careful about what yeh were carryin'. Nobody is that careful about supplies, especially carryin' someone who's hurt. Plus, a lot of dead people on a beach an' two ships? Not ter hard ter figure out. But I won't bother yeh. It isn't any of my business anyway. I don' want any of yer treasure anyhow. What would I do with it up here?"

"I don't know what you're talking about," Finn said.

Figglebottom snickered and shook his head. "No, even if I had money, I wouldn't go back ter town no matter what. I'm livin' my life real quiet like up here, an' I like it that way. No…no money fer me. Don' need ter worry about me takin' any of yer money."

"Um, that's good," Finn said, staring at the ground. *What have I gotten the captain and me into? Come on, Captain. Wake up.*

# 26

SAM AND EMMA got into their small boat and sailed to the Haverstraw's village to speak with Maxkw. Emma looked back at the beach. "That's strange."

"What?" Sam asked.

"I just saw a beautiful parrot fly and land on the shoulder of one of the dead pirates."

When they arrived at the Haverstraw's village, Sam quickly recounted to Maxkw what had occurred on the beach. "After the gunshots and cannon fire stopped, we waited a while to go over and see what happened. We tried to help the two pirates who were wounded, but they died. Then we saw all this money and jewelry in a money chest. Before one of the pirates died, he gave me a map with an X on it. He told me the treasure was in a cave on the mountain but to be aware of huge creatures that lived there. He looked really scared and had large claw marks on his chest. He said they were bigger than bears."

Maxkw took a step back. "Hmm. The man said huge creatures?"

"Yes, do you know what he could have been talking about?" Sam asked with a knotted brow.

Maxkw nodded. "He must have meant the *Mhuwe* that live in that part of the mountain."

"*Mhuwe*? I've never heard of them."

"We do not talk of them much outside our people. They are big, hairy creatures who live mostly inside the caves that cross through the mountain. We Haverstraw don't go where the *Mhuwe* live."

"Why?"

"Legend says they are people who have eaten human flesh and turned into these beasts. Some Haverstraw who went to that part of the mountain years ago never came back. The few who returned told of terrible tales of creatures much bigger than a bear. Some were eight feet tall and weighed many hundreds of pounds. At times you can smell them coming, but usually they appear out of nowhere. They let out a deafening roar that goes straight through your body. At times we can hear them from our village at night. You don' want to go anywhere near them, Sam."

"What would you like to do with the treasure on the beach?" Sam asked Maxkw. "It's on your land. You should be the one who decides what should be done with it."

Maxkw smiled and put his hand on Sam's shoulder. "It is a good thing you have come to tell me what happened. We do not need the money nor jewelry. We see men, from time to time, bury their money on our land. We saw these men going up and down the mountain with their treasure. We could have gotten it at any time if we had wanted. Do with it as you wish."

"Are you sure? There's a lot of money there."

"Yes, I am sure."

"Thank you, Maxkw. Emma and I will try to do what's best with the money."

THE BARRETTS SAT quietly while they sailed back to the Island. They looked at the river flowing by and lifted their faces to feel the warm wind kick off the Hudson.

After a while Emma looked at Sam. "What do you think we should do?"

"It'll be getting dark soon," replied Sam. "We can't just let all the treasure sit there on the beach and in the ships! And it's too late in the day to give all the dead a proper burial tonight."

"Sam, I don't want to stay on the beach all night, especially with all those dead pirates. What if more pirates come to the island?"

"You're right, Emma. Why don't we take the chest, as many of the bags of loot we can carry, and the map home. Then we'll meet with Governor Fletcher and give him the treasure we found. It wouldn't be right for us to keep it. It belongs to some country."

"I'm sure he will be fair and honest with us."

Sam shrugged. "I hope so. No, you're right. I'm sure he'll do right by us."

"We'll simply tell the Governor what happened and rely on his sense of fairness to give us any reward he sees fit," Emma said, holding her head high.

They carried the beautifully ordained money chest and all the treasure inside it, plus twenty-five bags filled with coins from the beach and ships, and loaded it onto their boat and set sail for home. They left the household goods, tobacco, sugar, cloths, spices and weapons on the beach, assuming the governor would send his men to the island to recover these items along with any other coins and jewelry they could find.

The Barretts returned home an hour after nightfall. They hid the money chest in their bedroom under blankets and put the bags of coins under their bed, feeling it was the best place to keep the treasure for now.

# 27

FIGGLEBOTTOM PROUDLY STOOD next to his concoction boiling in the pot. "I think the herbs have cooked long enough. We'll let them cool off fer a minute or two. Don' want ter burn him. He's hurting plenty as it is. Yeh get some ter, Finn. Them *Mhuwe* don' stink fer no reason. They got all sorts of dead an' decaying things on their hair an' claws."

Finn closed his eyes and scrunched his nose. "Will it hurt much?"

"Shouldn't," Figglebottom replied. "Yeh aren't scared, are yeh?"

"No. It's just…You sure you know what you're doing?"

"I use these herbs when I get a cut, an' it don' hurt me none. It's cool enough now. Let's put 'em on yer friend's chest."

"All right."

Avery moaned as Figglebottom put the herbs directly on his cuts and covered them with the strips of cloth that were in the boiling pot. Figglebottom looked at Finn and smiled. "Yer next. See it didn't hurt yer friend none."

Finn pulled off his shirt, and Figglebottom put the herbs on Finn's cuts. "It doesn't hurt at all," Finn said, sticking out his chest. "But boy does it stink."

"Told yeh. Most medicine that's good fer yeh stinks an' tastes bad. Need ter put the herbs on yer captain every few hours ter get the full effect. I'll brew us up some more. Yeh eaten anythin' today?"

"No. I was getting kind of hungry."

"Say no more. I'll fix us up somethin' in no time. Yeh like deer?"

"Never had it, but it can't be any worse than the grub I've eaten on the ship."

"That's true. I'll throw in potatoes an' carrots ter. In an hour we'll have us some stew. Yeh will love it. It's Cucumber, Pickle, Sweetie Pie's favorite."

"Thanks."

"I'll put more herbs on yer captain's wounds an' then make us that stew."

Finn, Figglebottom, and Cucumber, Pickle, Sweetie Pie all sat together eating the stew while Avery, still unconscious, lay on Figglebottom's makeshift bed in the hut.

"There's the cracking sound again," Finn said, jerking his head toward the trees.

"That's the *Mhuwe* lettin' each other know where they are. Yeh will hear another smackin' sound against a tree in a little bit."

"There it is again," Finn said, his breathing growing shallow.

"No need ter worry, none," Figglebottom said. *Mhuwe* don' bother me. They probably saw yeh an' yer friend come up here with me an' are checkin' on us. *Mhuwe* get curious whenever somethin' or someone new is up on the mountain."

"Shouldn't you give them some of the stew so they'll leave us alone?"

"I gave them a bunch last week. They'll be fine. Yeh two are a different smell ter them up here. They'll look yeh over from a distance an' then they'll go on their way. Eat some more stew. Yeh need ter keep up yer strength on account of yer cuts."

"What if they're the ones from the cave?" Finn asked as his eyes bounced from tree to tree.

"If they were those *Mhuwe*…well…we'd all be dead by now. They would have killed us as soon as they saw yeh an' yer captain comin' up the mountain. The trail yeh went up is a ways over ter our right. These must be a different group that live closer ter me. There are a bunch of them *Mhuwe* up here."

Cucumber, Pickle, Sweetie Pie tilted her head, looked at Figglebottom, and walked into the hut.

"Baby girl must have heard yer captain makin' some sounds. Let's go see how he's doin'."

Avery was blinking his eyes and moving his head around trying to gather his senses. "Where am I? Finn, is that you?"

"Yes, Captain Sedgeport," Finn said, nodding over at Figglebottom to remind Avery of the name he went by while they were in New York. "You've been out for a day. How you feeling?"

Avery nodded a couple of times, letting Finn know he understood his reminder about his name. "Not sure, really. The room's spinning around. Where am I? How're the crew doing?"

"We got ambushed by a pirate ship on the island when we returned to the sloop after those creatures came at us in the cave. Sorry, sir, but everyone got killed by those pirates. You and me are the only ones who lived."

"Nobody else is alive?" Avery asked, slamming his hand on the cot.

"No, sir," Finn said, stepping back. "Seeds had me and Jack take you up on the mountain once we realized we were going to be at-tacked. He wanted us away from the fighting. Jack ran back to help with the fight. He told me to stay with you."

Avery closed his eyes, let out a big sigh, and shook his head. "Glad you made it, Finn." He opened his eyes to see Figglebottom stand-ing next to him. Avery tried to get up but collapsed on the bed. Avery scrunched his forehead. "Who are you?"

"Thaddeus Figglebottom—at yer service."

"You're joking, right?"

"Yeh both said the exact same thin' when I introduced myself. Yes, that's my real name, but like I told him, people call me Fig. We better put more herbs on those cuts of yers if yeh are goin' ter heal up."

"Thanks for helping us."

"My pleasure. I suspected yeh were hurt bad when I saw them carryin' yeh down the mountain."

"You saw us?"

"I was watchin' yeh all goin' up the mountain an' comin' back down."

"We didn't see you."

"Yeh don' live up here as long as I have without knowin' how ter keep an eye on thin's without bein' noticed."

"I was wondering if you mind giving me and Finn a few minutes alone? I kind of want to get my bearings straight and go over things with him. Lots happened while I was out of it."

"No problem. Me and Cucumber, Pickle, Sweetie Pie will go fer a little walk an' give yeh two some time alone."

"Who?"

"My dog."

"Oh…Thanks. Much appreciated."

"See yeh two in a little while."

# 28

AVERY PULLED FINN close to him. "Tell me what happened, and how I got here."

"Yes, sir, Captain, but no need to whisper or hold anything back. Fig figured out why we're here on Bear Mountain."

Avery's eyes widened. "He did?"

"He thinks your name is Sedgeport. He doesn't know your real name."

Finn told the entire incident to Avery, about carrying him down the mountain from the cave, taking him off the sloop and hiding, the pirate attack, burying the remaining treasure on the beach, Suggs giving the man on the beach the map, and meeting Fig and bringing him up to Fig's hut.

"I can't believe I was unconscious through all of that. That creature almost did me in. And Suggs taking the map…He better have a good reason, but he is, after all, a pirate, so…"

Avery thought out loud, trying to figure out what to do next. "So, Fig figured out we're pirates and got into it with other pirates after we buried some of our treasure on the mountain and ran into those creatures in the cave?

"Aye. Fig calls them *Mhuwe*. That's what the local Haverstraws call them."

"He saw the treasure on the beach?"

"Yes."

"He probably thinks that's ours too."

"Captain…he told me he doesn't want any money."

Avery snickered. "Of course, he wants it."

"His wife and kids died of smallpox a while ago. After that, he just wanted to be up here by himself, left alone."

"I see. Probably why he is a little different, huh? But still, watch your back with him. I don't trust him."

"I will, but I'm pretty sure he's harmless. He even saved your life. I didn't think you'd make it. None of us on the ship thought you'd live. You were bad off. But Fig made this brew of herbs and you came to really quick."

"That must be what stinks."

"Aye. I have herbs on my cuts too."

"You good?"

"I'm all right. I didn't get clawed as bad as you."

"Guess I owe him. He would have already killed you and me near the beach if he was going to do us in."

"I guess so."

"But I've learned never to trust anyone where money is concerned. Everyone but you, Finn."

"Thanks, Captain. You should rest some, sir."

"Not now. I've got to think of a way to get to the treasure on the beach and in that cave. I didn't tell you earlier, but my plan was to move the loot a little at a time to different spots on the mountain over the next few months. Some of the crew may get a notion to come back and take it all for themselves."

"I figured you'd do that."

"You did?"

"No one would leave it in a spot where a bunch of pirates knew it was buried. At least one of them would come looking for it after a while."

"Guess you've learned a thing or two since being with our unruly crew."

"Aye," Finn said, smiling.

Avery tried to get up but fell back on the makeshift bed. "I need to get to that beach and see if any of my loot's still there. This can't be happening. Everything I've ever wanted…everything I've ever dreamed of is tied up in that loot. I can't lose it all."

Finn puffed out his chest. "Captain, I'll go and bring back what's left. I can go with Fig. I think you're too weak to go. There's no real path from here to the beach. Fig knows the way."

"I can make it. Help me get up. I don't want Fig to get any of the treasure."

"Aye, Captain. 1…2…3…up," Finn said as he strained to lift Avery. Finn and Avery fell on the floor of the hut. "Fig, help!"

"What yeh two tryin' ter do?" Fig asked, shaking his head.

"Finn was trying to help me get up. I need to get to that beach and check on my boat and things."

"If yeh can't stand up, yeh can't make it ter the beach. It's about an hour from here, an' in yer condition, it may take a day."

"I know, I know," Avery snorted. Changing his mind, Avery shrugged. "Can you take Finn and bring back my stuff from the boat, and anything else of value that may be lying around?"

"Sure, an' if by 'anythin' of value' yeh mean treasure, I'll brin' that back ter. Like I told Finn, I don' want any of yer money."

"Thanks," Avery said with a nod. "By the way, you don't fool me. You put on this act as a crazy hermit, but you're a lot smarter than you let on."

"Well, I wouldn't go sayin' I'm smart. Guess I can stop using my old mountain man accent, since you figured out I'm not that nutty."

Finn nodded. "You are pretty hard to understand sometimes."

Fig laughed. "True. But I meant what I said about not wanting any of your money. I had all I needed before, and I wasn't happy. I'm better off up here alone. Nobody bothers me, and I want to keep it like that."

"Sounds good to me."

"And…I bet Sedgeport isn't your real name, but I don't want to know it. It's better that way. Now how about Finn and I go see what's left of your loot on that beach first thing in the morning? It's too late now. Don' want to end up *Mhuwe* food if we get lost an' stray into their territory."

"Thanks," Avery said, holding out a hand.

Fig nodded and shook Avery's hand. "I'll leave you food and water. Cucumber, Pickle, Sweetie Pie will stand guard and bark if anyone comes around. We'll be gone and back before you even wake up tomorrow."

"Thanks, Fig. If anybody is down there at the beach, just wait until they're gone. Better if people think we're all dead," Avery told Fig with a wink.

"Aye, aye, Captain," Fig said with a salute, and walked out.

Finn walked over to Avery. "You should sleep, Captain. I'll let you know what we find tomorrow."

"Thanks, Finn."

Finn walked out, and Avery stared at the roof of the makeshift hut. His face turned red, and he grabbed the cup of water next to him and threw it on the ground. *My fortune and my future are in the hands of a boy and a hermit.*

# 29

THE NEXT MORNING, while Emma opened the store, Sam went to see if they could have an audience with Governor Fletcher at his earliest convenience.

The governor's assistant, Kenneth Herndon, asked why they wanted to meet with the governor. Sam did not want to state the real purpose for the meeting, for fear word of finding a vast treasure would leak out to the public. Sam said they intended to purchase property on Haverstraw land and sought the governor's assistance.

Herndon arranged for the Barretts to see the governor at ten o'clock the next morning.

That night, Sam and Emma talked about what might happen when they met with the governor.

"Hopefully, the governor will give us a reward," Sam said. "I understand privateers usually get about fifteen percent of what they recover from pirate ships. With any luck, Governor Fletcher will give us the same."

Emma smiled. "We could buy a big plot of land and build a beautiful home with fifteen percent of what we found on the island. Who knows how much more they'll find when they discover what's hidden at the map's location!"

"But what if he doesn't give us a reward?" Sam asked. "Would that be the end of it?"

"We should get something. I mean...we could have kept it all for ourselves, sell the store, leave town, and build a mansion somewhere. We could even build it here. People would wonder how we got all that money though."

They had a fitful night's sleep wondering what might happen the following day.

The next morning, Sam and Emma put on their best clothes, and traveling by horse and wagon, first stopped off at their store and placed a sign on the door that read "Closed." They arrived at Governor Benjamin Fletcher's office at nine forty-five AM with a handful of Pieces of Eight, doubloons, the map, and some jewelry tucked inside Sam's jacket.

After letting the Barretts into the governor's office, Herndon bid farewell, leaving the Barretts and Governor Fletcher alone to conduct their business.

"Please be seated," the governor said as he gestured toward the seats in front of his desk. The governor wore a curly powdered wig and dressed in fine apparel imported from England.

"Governor, I must first ask your forgiveness," Sam said, eyes cast down.

"What do you mean?" Fletcher asked, furrowing his brow.

"We are not here to ask for assistance to purchase land."

"Herndon, come in here," Fletcher yelled.

"Sir, sir, please hear us out," Sam said. Our request for this meeting will be of great benefit to you, but we needed to meet with you without anyone knowing the true purpose."

The door opened and Herndon stood at the entrance. "Yes, Governor? Is everything all right, sir?"

"Mr. and Mrs. Barrett, you have one minute to tell me the true purpose of this meeting. Mr. Herndon, please stay."

"Thank you, sir," Sam said. "I will explain why we said what we said." Sam looked at Emma and back at Fletcher.

"Continue," Fletcher said, staring at Sam.

"Two days ago, my wife and I were picnicking on Salisbury Island when we heard gun and cannon shots on the other side of the island. We went to investigate and stumbled across many dead pirates. Two were barely alive, but we couldn't save them." Sam further recounted what had happened, including the massive creatures on the mountain that Maxkw called *Mhuwe*.

Fletcher paced behind his desk. "This is unbelievable. I'm astonished all of this could have taken place so close to town."

"We didn't want to state the true intentions for our meeting, in case you wished to handle this event discretely. Also, and not to disparage anyone, but both ships were flying British flags."

Sam took out the coins, jewelry, keys, and map he had in his coat and handed them to the governor. "Here is some of what we found, sir."

He told the governor Maxkw did not want any of the treasure.

"He doesn't?" the governor said wide-eyed.

"No, sir," Emma said. "And we didn't believe it fair for us to keep all the treasure for ourselves."

Fletcher put his hands behind his back and nodded. "I see. That is most generous of you."

Sam noticed the governor's demeanor change immediately as a big smile came upon his face. "You Barretts are truly remarkable and honorable people. Not only did you try to save those you could, at great personal risk, but you also decided not to keep all the treasure for yourselves. Yes, you are truly remarkable. I only wish I would do the same in similar circumstances."

"Thank you, Governor," Emma said.

"Yes, thank you, sir, for your kind words," Sam replied as he glanced at Emma, keenly aware Fletcher was trying to charm them.

"Come to think of it…" Fletcher said, looking up at the ceiling, "I recall several British ships were taken over by pirates last year."

"They were?" Sam asked.

"Yes, we assumed the ships' captains were killed. We haven't received word from them in quite some time. I wonder if these two ships were commandeered by those pirates lying dead on the beach. I shudder to think those captains turned to piracy themselves and are among those dead on Salisbury Island. I'm sure that didn't happen. I'm certain those captains were honorable to the end, if indeed they are now with the Lord."

Sam and Emma watched the governor scratch his chin and walk about his office.

Emma leaned in close to Sam. "What's he going to do?" Emma whispered.

"I'm not sure," Sam whispered back. "It looks like he's trying to decide."

Governor Fletcher stopped walking and stood in front of the Barretts. He smiled and put his hand on Sam's shoulder. "Mr. and Mrs. Barrett, you must receive a reward for your actions, but we cannot tell anyone about the treasure until my men have had a chance to retrieve all of it. If word got out, I can only imagine how many people would sail to that island and climb the mountain trying to get what they could."

"Yes, sir. That was why we were less than forthright with you and Mr. Herndon about our purpose for wanting to meet with you," Sam said.

Fletcher nodded. "That was smart of you both. You said the pirate who gave you the map said there were large creatures in the cave where they hid their loot?"

"Yes, sir," Emma said. "Maxkw said they were what the Haverstraws call *Mhuwe*, and to stay away from their territory. The Haverstraws do not go to that part of the mountain in fear of them."

"I never heard of *Mhuwe*. Probably just big bears."

"Neither had we, sir," Sam said.

Sam and Emma watched Governor Fletcher glance at Herndon and then look back at them.

"Now, what to reward you both for such a heroic act?" Fletcher stood in front of Sam and Emma, twirling the curls in his wig. After a few seconds, Fletcher held his finger in the air. "I know what I'll do. I'll give you the same commission I would privateers. I have leeway to pay privateers under my command up to twenty-five percent of the pirate's booty, with twenty-five percent of the recovered items staying under my authority here in New York. The rest going to the king of England."

Sam and Emma quickly glanced at each another. They held their breath, waiting on the governor.

The governor puffed out his chest. "That's what I will do. I will pay you, Mr. and Mrs. Barrett, a combined twenty-five percent of the recovered booty and whatever is found on that map you were given. You may have your percentage however you wish. Coins, or coins and jewelry and other items recovered. Take as long you wish to decide."

Sam and Emma stared at each other with big smiles on their faces.

The governor straightened his jacket and held out his hand to the Barretts, indicating their meeting had come to an end.

Sam and Emma shook the governor's hand. "Thank you, Governor, for giving us such a generous reward," Sam said.

"Yes, thank you very, very much," Emma said, grinning.

Sam held Emma's hand. "We will tell you our decision quickly.

Sir, how do you wish to retrieve the treasure we have hidden at our home?"

"I will have ten men go to your house later today with a wagon to retrieve the items and bring them back to my office. I will assemble a group of soldiers to go to the island tomorrow."

Sam and Emma shook the governor's hand again and again. "Thank you so much," Emma said.

The governor puffed out his chest and smiled. "No, thank you for recovering what looks like stolen British money and goods. I will have my men meet you both at your home later this afternoon."

Sam and Emma said farewell and walked back to their horse and wagon and headed home. They had planned on opening the store when they finished their meeting with the governor but decided to keep it closed for the rest of the day. The news they received was too life changing to go back to work that day.

They were quite pleased at the governor's reward and understood immediately their lives would never be the same. While they weren't sure how much twenty-five percent of the booty might add up to, they knew it was more money than they had ever dreamed of having or making.

# 30

IT TOOK FINN and Fig an hour to arrive at the hill above the beach. Finn was nervous about seeing his deceased friends.

"There it is," Finn said, pointing down toward the beach, one hundred yards in front of him, down a steep side of the mountain.

"Let's move real slow like," Fig said. "Listen fer any sounds of people."

They inched toward the sloop and hid behind it for a good two minutes, looking and listening for any signs of life. Hearing nothing but buzzards and other birds flying above, they cautiously walked out from behind the boat.

Finn saw all his fellow pirates from the *Fancy* lying on the beach, dried-up blood pooled around them. *I've got to see if any of my mates have survived. I won't forgive myself if I don't.*

Finn rushed to check their pulses. It was such a gruesome site, even a pirate boy, and his eyes teared up. No one had a pulse. Only then did Finn allow himself time to search the beach and on the boats for the treasure. There was none to be found. He checked where they tried to bury the bags of money and money chest among the trees. It was all gone. He climbed onto the *Pharaoh* and the frigate and looked around the ships—no treasure on either. It had all been taken. Dead pirates and a half-sunken sloop and frigate were all Finn saw on Salisbury Island.

Finn paused as he thought he recognized a dead man on the beach who wasn't one of the crew on the *Pharaoh*. "Who is he?" Finn asked himself.

"Sorry," Fig said as he put a sympathetic hand on Finn's shoulder. "Do you have any clothes or anything you want to take off your boat for you and your captain?"

"I'll grab a few things," Finn said, his head lowered. "Should we try to bury them?"

"I know you want to, but it'll be better if we leave things alone as much as possible. Don't want anyone figuring out anybody from one of the boats is still alive. Better folk think everyone is dead, and you all killed each other."

Finn looked away from Fig. He wiped a tear and shook his head. "I'll go get my clothes and Captain's belongings."

"Do you want any help, or do ya want to do that alone."

"Thanks, I'll go by myself."

"Don't be too long."

Finn climbed aboard the *Pharaoh* and carried out a few bags containing his clothes and Avery's garments. He picked up several rifles and put two pistols in his waist and multiple shot in his pockets.

Fig grabbed some weapons and shot too.

Finn surveyed the beach for a full minute and sighed. He looked at Fig and nodded. They left and went back up the mountain, walking in silence the entire way to the hut.

Cucumber, Pickle, Sweetie Pie barked as Finn and Fig walked up to the makeshift home.

"We're here," Finn yelled out to Avery so he didn't think a stranger was coming into the campsite.

"You're not carrying much," Avery said, frowning.

Finn stared at the ground. "Sorry, Captain. It's…gone. I brought back some of our clothes. Got a few rifles, pistols, and shot too."

Avery slammed his fist into the bed. "That's it?" After a few seconds of grumbling, Avery gathered himself. "Well, I guess there's still a good amount in that cave. I need to figure out a way to get rid of those creatures first."

"Doubt you're going to be able to kill off the *Mhuwe*," Fig said. "Have to come up with a way to get them out of the cave. They're too big and there are too many to kill them all. Plus, they have your scent and you killed some of them. You go back there and they'll be coming for you. You think there are only of a few of them 'cause that's all you see. Trust me, there's a lot more hiding in these mountains. They'll smell you the moment you step foot in their territory. And they haven't forgotten what you did in that cave."

"Great, now I have monsters that want me dead, and that man and woman on the beach probably have a bunch of my money and jewelry. It was easier dealing with pirates."

Finn stood and pulled his shoulders back. "I was thinking, I can go into town and spy around. Listen for anybody talking about treasure and dead people on the island. People in town won't think a kid was involved. I'll also be on the lookout for that man and woman I saw and see what I can find out about them."

"I don't know," Avery said. "You've already been through a lot with those *Mhuwe* clawing at you and seeing what you saw on the beach. I'm the one who needs to go to town and find out what happened."

"But people saw you in town buy a sloop."

"True," Avery said.

"I appreciate you kept me out of all the…difficult stuff when we were on our, um, privateering missions, but I can do this," Finn pleaded with Avery.

Avery shrugged. "What do you think, Fig?"

"Guess it would be all right, "Fig said, pursing his lips. "I can take Finn to the closest dock. I have some money so he can ride a ferry to town. He could stay a day or two, and head back here on the ferry and tell you what folks are sayin'. By then you should have gained your strength and be better able to decide what to do next."

Avery shook his head. "I don't like it. I don't like it one bit. But I have a feeling each day we sit here is a day closer to losing all my money. You sure you want to do this, Finn?"

"I've got this, Captain. I can stay in the background and sleep out in the woods. No one will suspect a thing. I'll look around and keep my ears and eyes open. Be back in two days. Maybe even several of our crew are still in town and can tell me what's going on and if they heard anything."

"Fine, let's do it, but be back here in two days…tops."

"Aye, aye, Captain," Finn said. He turned to walk away then spun around. "That's who he is!"

"Who are you talking about?" Avery asked.

"I saw a dead man on the beach who wasn't part of our crew who looked familiar. Couldn't stop thinking I had seen him before somewhere. Turns out, he was that sailor we, uh, left off near Cuba. His crew must have found him and followed us here."

"That would explain why a ship all of a sudden attacked us out of nowhere. Wonder how they learned we were sailing up the Hudson River?"

"I'll try to find out when I'm in town, Captain."

# 31

"GOOD MORNING, MR. and Mrs. Barrett. Lovely to see the two of you again," Herndon said as he led them to the sitting area. "I'll tell the governor you are here."

Fletcher shook each of the Barretts' hands with both of his as he led them through his office door.

Sam gave Emma a quick wink, held his shoulders back, and smiled at Fletcher. "We do not wish to take up much of your time, Governor. We realize you are a busy man."

"No bother at all. Please have a seat. May I get you anything to drink?"

"No thank you, Governor," Emma said. "That is very kind of you."

"Have the two of you come to a decision regarding your reward?"

Sam glanced at Emma and nodded. "Yes, Governor. We wish to have the reward in coins to be deposited in the bank."

"Very wise. Very wise indeed."

"Thank you, sir."

"I have done an accounting of the money and money chest of jewelry my men brought back from your house. It comes to a total of £270,000, making your reward £67,500 so far."

"My goodness," Emma gasped.

Fletcher smiled. "Remember, that's only a portion of the money you'll receive. We need to see what we find on that map. I will have my men deposit the money to your bank account. You do have one, don't you?"

"Yes, sir, we do. But it's a modest amount."

"Well, it won't be after today," Fletcher said, chuckling. "This afternoon, I will draw up a contract documenting our agreement. It will state you will receive twenty-five percent of the accumulated money and jewelry we collect from this discovery. Your share is to be provided to you in coins and deposited into your account. The contract will be in effect until we complete gathering all the treasure from Salisbury Island and the location on the map."

"Thank you very much, Governor," Sam and Emma said in unison as they shook the governor's hand.

"I'll be in touch and inform you regarding what we find on that map. I have sent a ship to Salisbury Island this morning to examine what took place there, and to see if they can find any clues as to what parties were involved. Enjoy the day, Mr. and Mrs. Barrett, and thank you again for bringing this matter to my attention."

"Thank you, Governor," they said, unable to contain a large smile.

Sam and Emma looked at each other in amazement as they stood outside the governor's mansion.

"I knew it would be a lot, but I had no idea we'd get that much!" Sam said wide-eyed.

"And that's only part of the money. Once they recover what's hidden on that map, we'll be getting even more! We're rich! We never have to work another day the rest of our lives!"

"Can you imagine? Just a couple of regular folk from Ireland trying to make their way in New York, and now we're rich."

# 32

THE GOVERNOR'S SHIP dropped anchor on Salisbury Island as vultures flew away making rasping, hissing sounds. The sailors disembarked covering their mouths and noses with neck scarves to help mask the stench of decomposing men. They stood in silence looking at the dead men on the beach, and the badly damaged sloop and frigate nearby.

"We'll search the island and inspect the boats before we bury the dead," Captain Martin commanded. "But first let us all bow our heads in silence as we ask God to have mercy on their souls." Martin counted to ten to himself.

"Gentlemen, we will split up into two groups." He pointed to a cluster of officers standing nearby. "You group of fifteen sailors will inspect the sloop. You twenty over there will inspect the frigate. Simmons, you are the team leader of the sloop's inspection, and Tenley will be team leader of the frigate's inspection. Everyone be careful. Those ships are in bad shape. I don't want anyone getting hurt. Search high and low and bring out anything of value. After that, we'll scuttle them. Simmons and Tenley, come here first before you gather your men. The rest of you, at ease."

Pulling the team leaders off to the side so no one else could hear, Martin spoke quietly. "Gentleman, what I am about to tell you must stay between the three of us. We don't know who sailed those ships. They're flying British colours, but I have been informed we may find pirate flags on them. I'm not saying any of our fellow British sailors or privateers may have crossed over to piracy, but if you find anything hinting of that, you will inform me immediately."

"Yes, sir," they both said, saluting.

"Any questions? None heard. Get to it."

The sailors walked gingerly on the decks of the ships amid the creaking and groaning sounds underneath their feet made by the damaged boards. Five minutes later, Simmons walked over to the captain with a folded flag in his arms. A few seconds after that, Tenley was carrying something similar.

"Captain, we found this on the deck of the sloop," Simmons said as he unfolded a skull and crossbones flag.

Tenley held up the flag he brought. "Captain, we found this red hourglass flag on the deck of the frigate."

Martin sighed. "Not a great sign of meritorious activities with those flags aboard. I doubt they were souvenirs from overtaking pirate ships. Good job. Any indication of who these ships belonged to?"

"No, Captain, not at this time," Tenley said.

"No, sir," Simmons replied.

"Inform me if you find anything else of, shall we say, a sensitive nature."

"Yes, sir."

Tenley walked up a few minutes later. "Captain, we found these three bags containing Pieces of Eight hidden in a cabinet in, what we assume, was the captain of the frigate's cabin."

"I see. Tear that cabin apart, and rip off the deck boards before leaving the frigate. Tell Simmons I said to do the same thing with the sloop. They may have hidden valuables there, too."

"Aye, Captain."

It was late afternoon when the governor's sailors had finished going through the ships and burying the dead. They discovered three bags of coins from the frigate, plus numerous weapons from both ships and those found on the beach. No additional money was found on the sloop. The sailors scuttled the ships by making good-sized holes in their hulls, allowing water from the river to sink them to the bottom of the Hudson. The team leaders and captain took one last look around the island, ensuring those who were dead had been buried, and no weapons or anything else of value was left on the beach.

"Our job here is done," Martin shouted. "Raise the anchors and hoist the sails. Let's sail back."

# 33

A SIZABLE CROWD of men and women, boys and girls stood watching as the magnificent *Ganj-i-Sawai* sailed into port. Speedy rowed the shallop out to the ship to transport anyone wanting to come ashore.

Kalam grabbed Ibrahim's arm and pulled him aside. "Is that the galleon that robbed you?"

"It could be. I'm not sure."

"Come with me," Kalam demanded. "We're going ashore to speak with the governor. Then we'll see if it's Avery's ship, and if he's still in town." Kalam looked at Asrav. "You are in charge while I'm gone. Make sure no one leaves the *Ganj-i-Sawai*. I will give the crew their orders upon my return."

"Very well, sir," Asrav said then bowed.

Ibrahim sat quietly as Kalam stood and crossed his arms, waiting for Speedy to finish tying up the shallop on the dock. "I wish to have an audience with your governor," Kalam said.

"I will take you to Mr. Herndon. He is Governor Fletcher's assistant. He will be able to arrange a meeting with the governor." Speedy pointed in the direction of a large mansion at the top of the street. "Please follow me this way."

Herndon walked up to meet Kalam as he entered the doors of the mansion. Shaking Herndon's hand, Kalam handed him a formal declaration of his mission from the Grand Mughal. Kalam announced, "I am the captain of the *Ganj-i-Sawai*. The Grand Mughal, the Emperor of India, sent me to find and retrieve the money and jewels that were stolen from the *Ganj-i-Sawai* in the Arabian Sea not long ago by pirates. They are led by a scoundrel named Avery, and he sailed a galleon much like the one over there in your harbor. I wish to have an audience with the governor to speak with him regarding this matter."

"I see," Herndon said, as he pointed to a room with overstuffed chairs. "Please have a seat while I speak with the governor. I will be back momentarily,"

Herndon knocked on the governor's office door, waiting for a reply.

The governor clenched his fist and hit the desk. "Come in," he yelled.

"Governor, I am sorry to disturb you."

"What do you need, Herndon?"

"There are two men from India wishing to speak with you regarding the matter of the famous robbery on the *Ganj-i-Sawai*. Herndon repeated what Kalam had said. Here's the document he gave me from the emperor himself. Do you think it could be the ship they're looking for?"

Fletcher stood up and straightened his jacket. "Well, there's only one way to find out. Send them in."

Kalam and Ibrahim bowed as they stood in front of the governor. "Thank you, sir, for seeing us on such short notice."

"Of course, of course." Fletcher waved his hand toward the chairs in front of his desk, gesturing for the men to sit. "Please stay, Mr. Herndon." Herndon stood to the side of the office. Fletcher smiled at his guests. "Am I to understand you believe the galleon docked in our port may be the one used to rob your ship?"

"To be honest, sir, we are not absolutely sure. Ibrahim, here to my left, was the captain of the *Ganj-i-Sawai* when it was looted by the pirate some say is Avery. We won't be sure until we see the man who owns the ship. The emperor's ship was robbed of a vast sum of money and two money chests containing many jewels. These were meant to be gifted by Princess Mumtaz, the daughter of the Grand Mughal, while on pilgrimage to Mecca."

"We must get to the bottom of this, especially if the galleon in my port was used in pirating. My understanding, based on a report given to me, is the ship was owned by the East India Company, which commanded its captain, Captain Sedgeport, to sell her after its privateering mission proved unfruitful, and they wished to cut their losses."

Kalam narrowed his eyes. "What did this man look like? He could be going by an alias."

"I have not seen him. Mr. Treadway purchased the galleon. If you wish, you may leave me with a list of the items robbed. I will contact you, if you are still in town, or get word to the emperor if the items should show up at a later date."

"I see. Perhaps your assistant can take us to Mr. Treadway. Ibrahim, please hand the governor the list of items stolen. Thank you for your time, Governor."

Fletcher glanced at the list Ibrahim gave him. "I'm sorry I could not be of better service to you and your country. I will notify you immediately if I hear of any news regarding the items taken from you."

Kalam and Ibrahim bowed.

"Thank you, Governor," Kalam said. "Good day."

Fletcher nodded. "Mr. Herndon, take these gentlemen to Mr. Treadway.

"Yes, sir," Herndon replied and gestured toward the door. "Please follow me, gentlemen."

# 34

THE MEN WALKED down the street in silence until they came to Treadway's place of business. Herndon opened the door and allowed his guests to walk in first. "We wish to speak with Mr. Treadway regarding a very important matter," Herndon said to a young woman sitting at an ornate desk.

"I see. Please wait one moment while I get Mr. Treadway. Please have a seat."

Herndon looked at Kalam and Ibrahim. "She's Mr. Treadway's secretary."

Ten seconds later, Treadway's office door opened and he came out to greet his guests. "Gentlemen, please come into my office," he said, shaking his guests' hands.

"Mr. Treadway," Herndon said, "these gentlemen are from the ship, the *Ganj-i-Sawai,* and just had a meeting with the governor regarding the galleon in port. The governor suggested they talk with you regarding your purchase of the ship and its captain."

"I see. Is there an issue with my purchase from Captain Sedgeport?" asked Treadway. "I also sold him a Hudson River sloop."

"Mr. Treadway, I am Captain Kalam, and this is Ibrahim. I am the captain of the *Ganj-i-Sawai*, and Mr. Ibrahim was her former captain. The Emperor of India has commanded me to find the pirates who robbed our ship of valuable money and jewels several months ago in the Arabian Sea and sailed away in a galleon. We in no way suspect you of any wrongdoing. We were wondering if you might be able to tell us something about the man who sold you the ship?"

"Good gracious. Yes, of course. Captain Sedgeport sold me the galleon. He is a privateer for the East India Company. He showed me his papers and they were legitimate. It was suggested by those in town that he meet with me to see if I might be interested in purchasing the ship. I was."

"Hmm. Please tell us what the man looked like," Kalam asked, inching forward in his chair.

"Yes. He was a large, muscular man. You could tell he had been at sea for quite a number of years due to his leathery skin. I guess all us sailors get that way over the years."

Ibrahim began to speak, but Kalam put his hand on his arm to stop him. Kalam laughed. "Yes, especially after being at sea for so long. You said he bought a Hudson River sloop from you?"

"That's correct. It is a useful ship in these parts."

Kalam stroked his beard and shook his head. "I'm sure he wasn't involved. He doesn't match the description of the pirate who stole from us. Did Captain Sedgeport say where he was going? Perhaps he might be able to tell us if he's seen any other galleons during his journey here."

"I always make it a point not to ask too many questions."

"Yes, of course," Kalam said, frowning.

"Have you ever been in the colonies before?"

"Only in and around New York," Kalam said.

Treadway smiled and looked directly at Kalam. "I hear Virginia is quite lovely this time of year. You must try to get down there if you have the chance."

Kalam cocked his head to the side, his eyes widened, and he nodded to Treadway. "Thank you. We will try to go there if time permits."

"It's been a pleasure meeting both of you," Treadway said, standing up.

"Thank you," Kalam said, bowing slightly. "Mr. Herndon, would you please direct us back to the dock?"

"No need. Please follow me."

As they arrived at the shallop, Kalam shook Herndon's hand. "Thank you, Mr. Herndon, for taking the time to help us. We are most grateful."

"My pleasure, Captain. Please contact me if I can be of any further assistance. Good day."

The men sat in silence as the shallop made its way back to the *Ganj-i-Sawai*. Kalam looked at Speedy. "Thank you. We may call on you again this evening as the crew may want to go into town for a while."

"Yes, sir. Wave a flag at the dock, and I'll see you and come on over."

"Excellent," Kalam said as he handed Speedy a gold coin for his service.

Once on the *Ganj-i-Sawai*, Kalam told Ibrahim, "Go to my cabin. I will be there in a few minutes after I address the crew."

Kalam stood on a barrel and waved the men over. "Gentlemen, we are making progress in finding the scoundrels who stole from the emperor. We may be in New York for a few days. I am allowing half of you to go into town this evening. The other half can go tomorrow. Listen for any rumors about anyone robbing our ship a few months ago, plus anything about where the pirates may now be hiding. Remember my rules whenever we are in port. There is to be no gambling, no drinking, no carousing with women, and no fighting. Anyone breaking any of these rules will be severely punished. Be back on our ship no later than midnight. Mr. Asrav, divide the men into two groups, and make sure they behave while in town."

# 35

KALAM CONCLUDED IT was probably Avery's galleon, by the way Ibrahim reacted in Treadway's office. But he couldn't have Ibrahim giving away the upper hand, especially if Treadway or the governor were working with Avery. Kalam certainly wouldn't tell Ibrahim he and Avery used to work together years ago as privateers. Or that Avery had a debt to pay and Kalam was going to collect on it one way or another. Kalam kept things close to the vest when dealing with Ibrahim. He'd give Ibrahim tidbits of information only when it proved helpful to finding Avery.

Kalam walked into his cabin and shut the door. He put his feet on his desk and glared at Ibrahim. "What was it you wanted to say when we were in Treadway's office?"

"His description of Sedgeport sounded just like that pirate Avery who robbed us."

"Just as I suspected, but I didn't want you to give that away to Treadway. They could be working together. If Avery knows we are on to him, he'll pack up and leave town and take the treasure with him."

"I see. Good thinking. What is your plan?"

"I will have another meeting with Governor Fletcher tomorrow to inform him I believe Sedgeport and Avery are one and the same person. I wish to see his reaction. Hopefully, Avery hasn't paid the governor to hide him from us. We don't have much choice but to tell Fletcher what we think. Tonight, I am going to go into town and listen for any rumors involving Sedgeport and his men. I want you to go see if that ship was the same one that robbed you."

Ibrahim nodded.

"Later this evening, come to my cabin and report what you find."

"Yes, sir," Ibrahim said with a slight bow.

IBRAHIM WALKED TO the galleon and saw a beehive of activity. Sailors were carrying barrels of supplies, food, and water onto the ship.

Treadway was standing on the dock when he noticed Ibrahim. "Mr. Ibrahim, I thought I might find you here this evening."

"Yes, I just had to come see the galleon up close."

"Still think she might be the ship that robbed you?"

Ibrahim leaned left and right looking at the ship. "Difficult to say. She has the same number of masts and decks. It also has an elongated hull and a low forecastle. The same as the galleon that robbed us, but I cannot be sure. Is she being taken out to sea again? I see the crew bringing on supplies."

"Yes, she's going out tomorrow on a privateering mission for the homeland. I am being compensated handsomely for the use of my newly purchased ship. Seems like pirates have been looting England's ships on a more regular basis lately, and the king has had enough. The galleon is heading to the Caribbean to retrieve the valuables the pirates have stolen. There's the captain over there. Would you like to speak with him?"

"Yes, I would. Thank you, Mr. Treadway."

"My pleasure, and by the way, he looks nothing like Captain Sedgeport. I noticed you wanted to say something earlier when I described him, but Mr. Kalam gestured to you not to say anything."

"You noticed?" Ibrahim said, his mouth dropping open slightly. "You are most observant."

Treadway smiled as he walked Ibrahim over to meet the captain. "I have been in business a good number of years and have lived a good number too. Better to be observant and notice what's going on than to be surprised."

Treadway waved at a burly man giving instructions to the sailors. "Captain Drinkwater, if you have a moment."

The captain held up a finger. "One second." He handed a handful of papers to one of the sailors and walked over to Treadway.

"Captain Drinkwater, I wish to introduce you to Mr. Ibrahim. He was the captain of the *Ganj-i-Sawai* when it was raided by pirates in the Arabian Sea some months ago. They had a galleon similar to—"

"Pleased to meet you," Drinkwater said, interrupting Treadway. "I heard about that robbery. It's a wonder anyone lived."

Ibrahim looked down. "Yes, we were most fortunate."

"I hope this galleon that was purchased by Mr. Treadway isn't the same ship that looted you. No offense, Mr. Treadway. Not that you had anything to do with it."

Treadway frowned. "No offense taken."

Ibrahim shook his head. "I can't be sure, but she looks very, very similar if she isn't the same ship."

"Well, as you can see, I am not a pirate. My wife does call me one though when she's unhappy with me," he said, laughing. "I am on a job now to find pirates who robbed our English ships. Bring them to justice for what they've done. It seems they're getting more and more daring. Feels like there are more pirates than privateers on the waters, but I hope to put a dent in their activities."

Ibrahim noticed a sailor out of the corner of his eye lower his head and turn away when he came near. "Thank you for your time, Captain.

I can appreciate how busy you are, and I do not want to take up any more of your time. I wish you much luck on your voyage."

Drinkwater shook Ibrahim and Treadway's hand. "Thank you, Mr. Ibrahim. It's been a pleasure meeting you. Evening to you, Mr. Treadway."

Ibrahim and Treadway walked a few feet away. Ibrahim bowed and shook Treadway's hand. "Mr. Treadway, you have been most gracious and understanding. I appreciate it. I think I am going to walk around your lovely town. Do you have any suggestion where I may have a bite to eat, and would you like to join me?"

"Thank you. I would join you, but I must return home for the evening to be with my family. Most people end up at Fred's Tavern. You will likely find many of your crew there. I hope you find what you're looking for."

"Best wishes to you, sir," Ibrahim said.

Ibrahim walked down the street past the galleon and ducked into an alley. He watched the crew load supplies onto the ship from the dock. *Was that man avoiding eye contact with me?* Ibrahim wondered. *Could he be one of the pirates and is now one of Captain Drinkwater's crew?*

A few minutes had passed when Ibrahim noticed the same man he saw earlier speaking with another sailor. Ibrahim's eyes grew big when the two men walked out into the street and he got a better look at them.

# 36

FRED'S TAVERN WAS bustling and noisy, filled with sailors from the *Ganj-i-Sawai* and the usual locals. Kalam sat at the bar eating and drinking rum. He didn't follow his religious norms of not drinking alcohol. He listened for any rumors about treasure or pirates. He hadn't heard anything noteworthy when Ibrahim came rushing in.

"Sir, I saw two of the pirates who robbed us loading supplies onto the galleon," Ibrahim whispered. He looked at the rum but didn't say anything.

"You did?"

Ibrahim rambled on, barely stopping to take a breath. "Yes, I was standing by the galleon when Mr. Treadway saw me and came over. He even introduced me to its new captain—a Captain Drinkwater, who, if you're wondering, is not Avery. He is privateering for England, and they are going to the Caribbean in the morning."

"Slow down, man. Slow down."

"Sorry. I remembered seeing both of them. They were two of the pirates who looted the *Ganj-i-Sawai*. I didn't say anything to them, and they didn't see me watching them. I came over as quickly as I could to inform you of my finding. I didn't confront them because, like you say, I wanted to get the upper hand on them. I didn't want them to realize we are on to them."

Kalam smirked. "Perhaps you may redeem yourself after all. Let's

145

go see if we can speak with the governor. Hopefully, he hasn't retired for the evening."

Kalam and Ibrahim walked the short distance to the governor's mansion and found the candle lights still on in the offices. Their knock on the main door was met with an immediate response from the governor's assistant.

"Mr. Herndon, we apologize for our arrival at such a late hour. We have some important information we've only now uncovered. It is most urgent we meet with the governor tonight if possible. It cannot wait until morning."

"Please be seated and let me see if the governor is available," Herndon said. Five minutes later, Herndon walked back into the room. "The governor will meet with you, but I do ask you make it as brief as possible due to the hour."

"Of course, and thank you."

"Good evening," Governor Fletcher said, frowning.

"We apologize for coming to meet with you at this late hour," Kalam said. "And we are extremely grateful you granted our request for an audience."

"You're welcome. I understand you have an urgent matter about which you wish to speak with me?"

"Yes, sir. We will be brief. Mr. Ibrahim noticed two sailors loading supplies onto the galleon who were pirates that robbed the *Ganj-i-Sawai*."

Fletcher furrowed his brow. "You are certain, Mr. Ibrahim?"

"Yes, sir. I am most certain. One of the men saw me as I was having a conversation with Mr. Treadway and Captain Drinkwater. He turned away quickly as to avoid eye contact. I later saw him speaking, in hushed tones, with another sailor who too was a pirate who looted our ship."

Fletcher sighed. "This is quite a situation we have here, gentlemen. That ship is scheduled to leave tomorrow morning, upon my order, on a privateering mission for King George, III. It is the reason why I am still in my office tonight. That, plus there is a matter regarding your stolen treasure I wanted to speak with you about tomorrow. But first things first. You are absolutely sure these two men were pirates who looted your ship, Mr. Ibrahim?"

"Yes, Governor. I am."

"Very well." Fletcher stood up and opened his door. "Mr. Herndon," Fletcher called out.

"How may I be of assistance, sir?" Herndon asked.

"It appears we have at least two pirates masquerading as sailors who are set to go on our privateering mission. I'm certain their background is unknown to Captain Drinkwater. Gather several officers. Let us go at once to have a word with the captain and to bring those pirates to justice."

"Yes, sir," Herndon said, standing at attention. "I can meet you outside with the men in two minutes, sir."

Fletcher nodded and walked over to Kalam and Ibrahim. "Let's go outside, gentlemen, and wait for Mr. Herndon."

Less than one minute later, four large officers, in full uniform, armed with rifles and pistols, stood at attention in front of the governor. "Gentlemen, we have pirates aboard the galleon. The captain will line up his men so Mr. Ibrahim here can point out the two who are pirates, plus see if there are any others. Do you have any questions?"

"No, sir," they said in unison.

Fletcher adjusted his hat and jacket, took a deep breath and let it out. "Let's go."

A few minutes later, the governor, Herndon, four officers, Kalam, and Ibrahim stood at the bottom of the walkway to the galleon.

Captain Drinkwater came rushing over. He saluted and stood at attention. "Governor, it is an honor. I see there are officers with you and Mr. Ibrahim, who I met earlier this evening. Is everything all right?"

"No, Captain. It isn't. Mr. Ibrahim has brought to my attention that there are two men on your ship who were pirates who robbed the *Ganj-i-Sawai.*"

"Pirates? I will not stand for pirates being on my ship. Please tell me who they are and I will bring them to you immediately, sir."

"I have a better idea," Fletcher said. "Mr. Ibrahim only saw these two, but there may be more. He has not had a chance to see all the sailors onboard. Please arrange for all the sailors to line up on the dock immediately. Mr. Ibrahim will look at each one and point out those pirates who looted his ship. My officers will remove those men and bring them to jail."

"Yes, sir," Drinkwater said. "At once, sir." He saluted and walked quickly up the walkway with the guards.

Close to one hundred men marched down the walkway and lined up single file along the dock. Suddenly, five "sailors" bolted and ran in different directions down the town's streets and alleys. The four officers chased after them and caught two of the men. They brought them in front of the governor, guns pointed at their heads.

"Are these two of the pirates who robbed you?" Fletcher asked Ibrahim.

"Yes, they are, but these aren't the two I saw earlier. There are two others."

"Please look at the men lined up on the dock and see if there are any more. It's obvious the ones who fled are."

"I apologize," Drinkwater said to the governor, Ibrahim, and Kalam. "I had no idea some of the men were pirates. We interviewed each crewmember and they all seemed legitimate sailors. Again, my apologies."

"Not necessary," Fletcher said. "It is expected there will be a few bad men among a privateering crew of over one hundred men. Those caught and those who escaped will be brought to justice. Let's see if there are any other men Mr. Ibrahim recognizes."

Ibrahim walked up and down the line of sailors, looking each man in the eye. He walked over to Fletcher shaking his head. "I see no others, Governor."

"Captain, we will let you get back to your duties," Fletcher said. "You have a long night ahead of you if you are to leave on time in the morning."

"Thank you, Captain. Again, my sincerest apologies. I am glad those pirates will pay the price for what they did."

Fletcher stood in front of his officers and puffed out his chest and narrowed his eyes at the captors. "Gentlemen, escort these villains to jail. Mr. Kalam and Mr. Ibrahim, please follow me back to my office." Fletcher shook his head as he walked.

# 37

CAPTAIN MARTIN WAS waiting for Governor Fletcher when he arrived at the governor's mansion.

Fletcher smiled at Kalam and Ibrahim and motioned them over to the state room. "Gentlemen, if you'd be so kind as to wait a few minutes while I speak with Captain Martin. His report may be of importance regarding what I wish to discuss with you."

"Of course, Governor," Kalam said.

"Please have a seat, Captain," Fletcher told Martin as he sat behind his desk rubbing his hands, awaiting Martin's report.

Martin cleared his throat. "Thank you, Governor. Upon arriving at Salisbury Island, we found forty-three men dead on the beach from various gunshot and knife wounds. We buried them on the beach as they were decomposing rather rapidly."

"Could you tell if any of the dead men was a muscular, tall man?"

"Sorry, sir. The bodies were pretty decomposed when we got there. Not to be too graphic, but animals and birds had already gotten to the bodies."

"I see…continue."

"There were two badly damaged ships near the beach—a sloop and a frigate. Neither of the ships had any men on them. It appeared there was a battle between two pirate ships, even though both ships were flying British colours. We found a skull and crossbones flag on the sloop. The frigate had a red flag with an hourglass."

Fletcher shook his head and rubbed his forehead. "I wonder… never mind. Continue your report."

"We found three bags of coins hidden in what we assume was the captain's cabin on the frigate. We discovered no other money or jewels on either ship or on the beach. I gave the bags of coins and the pirate flags to Mr. Herndon. We found and brought back with us numerous weapons lying about the beach and what remained on the ships. We have stored those in our garrison. We then scuttled both ships and returned, sir."

Fletcher stood up, put his hands behind his back, and paced around the room. After a minute, he stopped and leaned on his desk in front of Martin. "Fine report, Captain. From what the Barretts and you have told me, we've had pirates in our midst. Thank you, Captain. That will be all. I will call for you if any further action is needed. Tell Mr. Herndon I wish to speak with him."

"Thank you, sir," Martin said, saluted, and left the room.

"Yes, Governor?" Herndon said as he closed the door behind him.

"What I am about to say must stay between the two of us."

"As always, sir."

"I cannot afford to have another incident where the Crown believes I am in partnership with a pirate. The king still isn't convinced my arrangement with Thomas Tew was a legitimate privateering commission to attack the French."

"I understand, sir. I believe we can keep the event at Salisbury Island quiet."

"We mustn't have anyone think New York is a place that harbors and protects such villains."

"Of course not, sir."

"Regardless, either the pirates who had the sloop or the pirates who had the frigate probably looted the *Ganj-i-Sawai*."

"I agree, sir. My understanding, from my conversation with Mr. Treadway, is the captain of the galleon was a Captain Sedgeport and the frigate's captain was a Captain Deering."

"I cannot have an international incident between England and India on my hands."

"That *would* be most unfortunate, sir."

"I have already given the Barretts their share of the treasure they found, plus a promise of more when we find what is on that map. I'm sure some of what was found on the island is from the pirates on the frigate, but part of it is most likely from that sloop too."

"Most certainly, sir."

"The Grand Mughal will want all the treasure looted from the *Ganj-i-Sawai* returned to India, or a large portion of it."

"I'm sure Mr. Kalam will be quite insistent, sir."

"Yes, he will. I want those men we captured tonight to be interrogated immediately. Hopefully, they will give us useful information."

Herndon held his shoulders back and stood up straight. "Consider it done, Governor."

"I'm not going to tell Mr. Kalam all we've learned. He seems like an astute man and will figure it out if he hasn't already."

"Yes, sir."

"Perhaps if our sides can work together, we can avoid an embarrassing international incident. Please call them in. And thank you for listening to me. You are a trusted friend."

# 38

FLETCHER WALKED TO the state room and nodded at Kalam and Ibrahim. "Please come and meet with me in my office."

Kalam and Ibrahim followed Fletcher and stood in front of his desk.

Fletcher rubbed his eyes as if he were trying to remove the events of the past few days. "It's getting late, and I am having the pirates we caught interrogated as we speak. Perhaps it is best if we meet again in the morning when I have more information to share with you."

"Governor, you said earlier there is a matter regarding our stolen treasure you wanted to speak with us about tomorrow," Kalam said. Before Fletcher could respond, Kalam continued. "Could we discuss that now?"

"Very well. I wish to be as forthcoming as possible." Fletcher stood up and walked back and forth behind his desk. "Two pirate ships attacked each other the other day, not far from here, on Salisbury Island. A fair amount of money and jewels were found. I am not saying any of it was the treasure taken from the *Ganj-i-Sawai*. I am telling you as much as I have learned as a goodwill gesture between our two countries. Hopefully, by laying my cards on the table, as the saying goes, you will do the same."

"Thank you, Governor, for your honesty," Kalam said with a slight bow. "The news you have provided gives us hope we may recover what was stolen from the emperor. To be open with you also, we suspect

Captain Sedgeport is really Captain Avery. We think he sold the galleon to Mr. Treadway and bought a sloop from him."

"I see," Fletcher said, sitting back down, his hands folded in front of him.

Kalam looked at Ibrahim and then back at Fletcher. "I am glad our two countries can work together in a spirit of cooperation. Perhaps it is best for us to meet tomorrow morning when you have received more information. We will go back to our ship now and await word from you. Again, Governor, we appreciate your openness with us."

"By the way, one of the pirate ships involved in the battle the other day was a sloop. Again, it may be a coincidence. We just don't know yet. I'll have Mr. Herndon inform you, in the morning, as to when we will meet tomorrow. Have a pleasant rest of your evening, gentlemen."

❖ ❖ ❖

A FEW BLOCKS away in the local jail, Officer James Oakley nodded and grinned when Herndon told him the Governor wanted the captors interrogated immediately.

"Make them sing," Herndon said. "This is quite a stain on the governor and our community. Governor Fletcher wants to know everything about the *Ganj-i-Sawai* robbery. I'll leave you now so you may go about your business."

Oakley cracked his knuckles. "It'll be my pleasure, sir."

Oakley slowly locked the main door to the jail, smiled, and opened the cell containing the two chained-up men who had run. He wanted them to wonder what he was up to. He took one of the jailed men and moved him to a cell at the end of the hall as far away from the other inmate as possible. There were no other jailees that night.

"So, pirate, looks like it's just you, me, and Gertrude here," Oakley said, tapping a large knife fastened to his belt. "I've always been told pirates are tough, and they can withstand a lot of pain. Is that true or is it only an old sea tale?"

The man glared at Oakley.

Oakley held up his right hand with the index finger missing. " I used to be a sailor myself. Lost this finger in a fight with a pirate. I barely flinched when it happened. Hurt a good bit, but I didn't show it none. Are you as tough as me, pirate?"

"What do you want?" he asked Oakley.

"Just what I said. I want to know how tough you are."

"How about we make a deal? I tell you what you want, and you leave me alone."

Oakley pulled out the gleaming knife and glared at the pirate. "Now what fun is that? I'm working the night shift. I've got to have something interesting to do to make the time go by faster."

Sweat dripped off the pirate's forehead. "Stop! You've had your fun. I'll answer your stupid questions."

"Just as I thought—an old sea tale. I'll go easy on you if you tell me everything. It will end up, how shall I put this, badly for you if I have to drag it out of you. Understand?"

"Yes. What do you want to know?"

"For starters, why did you five run?"

"I don't have a clue why the other men ran. I didn't pay my bill at Fred's and reckoned I'd end up here if I didn't take off."

"How about your friend down the hall? Why'd he run?"

"Like I said. Don't know and don't care. I have no idea who he is."

"I'll ask again. Why did the other men run?"

The prisoner shrugged. "I dunno. Look, I signed up to hunt pirates, and I wanted to have some fun the night before we sailed. I didn't pay for my drinks. What's the big deal?"

Oakley threw his knife an inch from the prisoner's head. It stuck into the wall with a clang. "Gertrude and I don't believe you. I told you not to make me drag it out of you. I was nice and gave you a chance. Looks like we're going to have to do this the hard way."

"Give me a break. I told you the truth."

"The hard way then," Oakley said, grinning. He picked up a chair and broke it over the prisoner's head, knocking him unconscious. "Let's see what your friend has to say."

# 39

"LET ME OUT of here," the prisoner down the hall yelled as he saw Oakley walk toward him.

"Now why would I do that," Oakley laughed. "Your friend told me everything. He said you took part in the robbery of that ship from India. That's why you ran."

"He's lying. I wasn't part of any of that. I was just looking for work."

"Then why'd you run?"

"Those officers looked right at me like they were going to come and get me for something. I was scared and ran."

"I believe you," Oakley said. "But your friend said you were a part of that robbery, so you're going to end up here for a long time like him."

"I wasn't. I didn't rob that ship." He slumped his shoulders and lowered his head. "I stole a horse a few weeks back to go see my wife. That's the truth. I thought those officers were going to arrest me…so I ran."

Oakley pulled out his knife and waved it in front of the prisoner's face. "You better not be lying to me, pirate."

"I'm not a pirate. I swear."

"What do you know about the *Ganj-i-Sawai* robbery?"

"If I tell you, will you let me go?"

"Maybe." Oakley peppered him with questions, trying to trip him up. "What's your wife's name?"

"Marjorie Wilson."

"Where do you live?"

"We've got a small farm a few miles up the road."

"I've never seen you before."

"We moved in a few weeks ago. She goes shopping at Barretts' store. We got twenty acres, and a few cows. Come on. I'm telling you the truth."

"Why'd you steal a horse to go back home?"

"I'd been in town a week trying to make some extra money before going to sea. We're going to have a baby."

Oakley ran his hands through his hair and moved his head from side to side. His neck made a cracking sound. "You getting out of here depends on what you give me. If it's something I can use, then maybe, just maybe I'll let you go."

"I heard the galleon was the one the pirates used to rob the *Ganj-i-Sawai*," the prisoner said.

Oakley tossed his knife from hand to hand. "Go on."

"The man down the hall's one of them, but he's trying to live a regular life."

"How many more of them are in town?"

"Not sure. I think a few. They're pretty tight-lipped. I overheard them talking. That's how I learned about it."

Oakley held his knife to the prisoner's throat. "You wouldn't be lying to me, would you?"

"No. I'm telling you the truth. Let me go."

"Maybe," Oakley said. "Got to make another visit to your friend."

Oakley walked to the other jail cell and slammed the door shut behind him.

The prisoner rubbed the back of his head and sat up. "You're crazy. Why'd you hit me over the head?"

"Two reasons. One, I don't believe you. And two, I don't like your face."

"Give me a break. I told you the truth."

"Your friend told me the whole story—about you being one of those pirates. Tell me the truth and I'll see to it you don't spend the rest of your life here or hanging from the end of a noose."

"He's lying. I came up here from Virginia looking for work. That's how I got on with this privateering group."

Oakley grabbed the shillelagh he had tied to his waist and held it over his head. "Looks like your head needs another visit. This time from Arthur." Oakley swung the shillelagh and hit the prisoner over the head.

Oakley left the cell and got a bucket of water. He walked back to the cell and threw the water on the prisoner.

The detainee shook his head and rubbed the back of it. "Come on. How many times do I have to tell you? I'm not a pirate."

Oakley held the shillelagh over his head. "Very well…Arthur…do your thing."

"No…no," the prisoner said, holding up is hands. "I'll tell you what you want to know."

"Now we're getting somewhere. Start talking."

The prisoner shut his eyes and lowered his head. "The man from India with the governor was the captain of the *Ganj-i-Sawai*, and we were afraid he noticed a couple of us earlier."

"So?"

"Come on. Do I have to spell it out for you?"

Oakley waved the knife in front of the pirate's face.

"Stop. We were part of the group that looted the ship from India. Reckoned if he saw us, we'd be caught and end up in jail like I am now. You will cut me a deal? Right?"

"Depends. Was the galleon the one you used to rob the *Ganj-i-Sawai*?"

"Aye. A bunch of us ended up here in New York. I reckoned I'd get some honest work for a while and see how that went."

"How many of you are in town?"

"There are four of us on the galleon. Don't know how many others are still in town. The other crewman you got locked up isn't one of us. Can't tell you why he ran. There were more of us here a week or so ago."

"Where's the rest of them?"

"Like I said, I'm not sure where the others are. The captain's very secretive. He didn't tell me his plans. That's the truth."

"What was your captain's name?"

"You know I can't tell you that."

Oakley grabbed the prisoner by his shirt and slammed him into the wall, knocking out his breath.

The man coughed. "His name is—" He stopped in mid-sentence and shook his head left and right. I can't. It's against the code."

Oakley shoved the prisoner into the wall again.

"All right. His name is…Avery."

# 40

OAKLEY SMIRKED AND rubbed his chin. "Did your ship fly a pirate flag?"

"Aye. We usually flew a British flag, but then a skull and crossbones flag when we attacked a ship."

"Where was your hideout?"

"We had a place in Tortuga. We got everything we had buried and came here. We were breaking up as a group, since we made so much money from robbing that ship."

"How much did you take from her?"

"Around £600,000 in money and jewels."

"£600,000?" Oakley asked, wide-eyed.

"That's why we decided to break up and go our separate ways. Some of us wanted to make a fresh start, like me. Some stayed in Madagascar, some remained in Tortuga to carry on with another captain, and a handful of us came here to New York with Avery."

"You said jewels. What kind of jewels?"

"I get less jail time, right?"

"It's looking a little better for you. Go on."

"You promise?"

"Keep talking."

"We took two large money chests off the *Ganj-i-Sawai*. They were really fancy. They had jewels on the chest itself, and there were lots of diamonds and rubies inside. Real heavy, too. Took two men each to carry them. Most of us didn't want the jewels. Too tough to sell those things without raising suspicion. Captain kept most of those and gave us a greater than usual share of the money. He could sell the gems and get more for them than we could. We all got our shares. Some stayed with the captain and some took the money and left."

"Why did you come to New York?"

"Captain had a plan but wouldn't tell us unless we decided to go the rest of the way with him. Those of us who didn't want to go no farther—well, he paid us our shares. No hard feelings, and off he went to sell the galleon. Around twenty crew decided to stay with him.

"Why's a frigate in town, and why do they want to speak with Avery?"

"A frigate? I saw one in town the other day, but I don't know anything about it. Wonder why they want to speak with Captain? Avery told people we were here privateering for the East India Company. Guess he wanted to speak with him about that."

"You sure you don't know anything about that frigate?" Oakley said, raising his shillelagh.

"I'm sure. Uh…what's the frigate's captain's name?"

"I think it's Deering."

"Deering? Deering? That name rings a bell. Wait a minute. I remember now. There was a captain in Tortuga whose name was Deering who was nosing around asking questions about us. We got one of their men and questioned him, but he didn't say much. Gave us his captain's name though. Said it was Deering."

# 41

HERNDON KNOCKED ON the governor's door an hour after Kalam and Ibrahim left. "Officer Oakley has finished interrogating the prisoners and would like to speak with you, sir."

"Bring him in. Stay with us while he gives his report."

"Yes, sir."

Herndon escorted Oakley into the governor's office. Oakley stood at attention.

Fletcher sat at the end of his chair, eyes wide. "So, what did you find out from those scoundrels?"

Oakley sighed. "Sorry, sir. I don't think they have anything to do with the galleon or pirates, sir."

Fletcher stood up and raised his hands. "Didn't you, um, encourage them to tell you what they know?"

"Yes, sir. I even hit one of them over the head twice, knocking him out. He ran because he didn't pay for his drinks at Fred's. The other one ran because he stole a horse the other day."

Fletcher slammed his fist on the desk. "We're back at square one. You got nothing useful from them?"

"I'm afraid not, sir. Like I said, I don't think they had anything to do with the robbery. Perhaps if we can catch the others who ran they may have information we can use."

Fletcher shook his head. "I guess it's not your fault. Keep them locked up. We'll end up putting them on trial later. Inform me immediately if they tell you anything else."

"Yes, sir," Oakley said, saluting.

OAKLEY WALKED BACK to the jail, on the lookout for anything suspicious. He saw a man standing on the edge of an alley. Oakley put a hand on his knife as the man walked toward him.

The man stopped in front of Oakley. "You got the information the Boss wanted?"

"Yes."

"Meet me behind the jailhouse at midnight," the man said.

Oakley walked back to the jail and stared at the lantern clock on the wall. When it struck twelve, he jumped to his feet, grabbed his gun, and hurried to the door. He looked out the window to make sure no one was walking around late at night. Seeing no one, he quietly opened the door and locked it behind him.

Oakley walked around the back. He saw the man hiding in the shadows.

"What'd you learn," the man said.

Oakley relayed everything he'd discovered from the prisoners about the galleon, the robbery, and Avery.

"Outstanding," the man said. "The Boss will be pleased. Here's the money promised."

Oakley walked over and smiled as he counted the money. "Looks like I won't have to work any longer."

"Not anymore," the man said as he thrust a dagger into Oakley's stomach. "Not anymore." The man grabbed the money he gave Oakley and shoved it in his coat pocket. "Time to head back to Cuba."

# 42

NO ONE PAID attention to Finn as he gave his money to the attendant and walked onto the ferry. He stood by the rail and watched ships sail past. It had been a pleasant three-hour journey down the Hudson River.

"We'll be docking shortly," the attendant shouted. "Prepare to disembark."

Finn stepped off the ferry and stuck with the large crowd hustling onto the busy streets. He decided to make his way toward Fred's Tavern, hoping to gather some useful information there. He was too young to go inside, but he could hang around outside it and not attract too much attention.

It was eleven forty-five in the morning and people were making their way to Fred's. As Finn had guessed, no one noticed him as he leaned on a wall next to the alley. People walked by and continued their conversations as if he wasn't there. Finn hadn't seen any of his former crewmates nor overheard anything newsworthy.

Then he saw someone who looked like the captain of the *Ganj-i-Sawai* and another man from India walking up the road. *What's he doing here? I don't think he saw me on the Fancy, but I'm not sure.* Finn stayed belowdeck when the fighting took place but went above helping the crew load the treasure from the *Ganj-i-Sawai* onto the *Fancy*.

Finn decided to follow them at a distance. After a few blocks, he saw the ship. "Ohhh nooo. The *Ganj-i-Sawai*—Why's it here?" Finn caught himself and put his hand over his mouth. He realized it had to be the ship's captain he saw in town. Finn watched him and the other man walk into a large mansion.

Finn stopped a woman walking nearby and smiled. "Excuse me, ma'am, what is that building over there?"

"Why, it's the governor's mansion, son," she replied. "It's a real beauty, isn't it?"

"Yes, ma'am, it is," Finn said. "Thank you."

Finn was heading back to Fred's Tavern when he heard someone calling him. He stopped and looked around. He saw a man in an alley with a hat covering most of his face, waving him over.

Finn slowly walked over. "Who is it?"

"It's me—Isaac."

Finn grinned. "It's great to see you. What are you still doing here?"

"I was going to ask you the same thing. Better we take this somewhere quieter. The authorities are looking for me. Come on. Let's go a little outside of town where no one can see us."

Finn's eyes watered as he recounted what had happened. "Our whole crew is dead."

"Wow. Sorry to hear that. What can I do to help?"

"Have you heard anything about the treasure or our fight on the island?"

"No, nothin' at all. Not sure how much good I can be to you and the captain with the law looking everywhere for me. They caught Mike. He's in jail. Not saying anything bad about any of the crew, but sooner or later, it's all going to come out about us robbing the *Ganj-i-Sawai*. I'm sure they probably have most of it figured out by now. I mean, why else would that captain be here. It's crazy he's here in New York. Oh, and there's been a man asking if anyone knows Avery."

"What's he want with the captain?"

"Don't know."

"D'ye talk to him?"

"No. I heard him asking around at Fred's and I took off. Can't be a good thing though."

"I'll tell the captain when I get back."

"We should split up," Isaac said. "You don't want to be seen with me, especially if I get caught. No sense both of us going to jail. Let's come back here at six tonight and see if either of us have heard anything."

"Sounds good. See you later."

Finn and Isaac looked around to make sure no one could see them. Finn walked toward Fred's Tavern, and Isaac walked in the opposite direction. Finn was almost at Fred's when there was a big commotion behind him down the road. He turned around and noticed two officers holding Isaac by the arms.

Isaac was screaming. "You have the wrong man. I'm here on business. Let me go." The officers dragged him toward the jail not far from where Finn stood watching. Isaac looked in Finn's direction, gave a slight shrug, and started protesting again. "Why are you doing this to me? I'm a businessman. Let me go. You'll hang for embarrassing me in front of all these people. My wife…my wife. Please, someone tell her what's happened."

# 43

THE DINING ROOM table was prepared for the formal event. The governor's best china, silverware, and crystal glasses were set. Waiters stood next to the walls with their gloved hands folded behind their backs. Kalam and Ibrahim were escorted into the dining room as the waiters pulled back their chairs from the table, waiting for them to sit.

Fletcher smiled at his guests from India and motioned to their chairs. "Gentlemen, please be seated. Welcome back. I am honored you will be having dinner with me tonight. I can understand how anxious you are to learn what I have uncovered regarding your stolen treasure, but let us enjoy the meal first. My chef has prepared our banquet. I hope you will find it satisfactory. We shall start with turtle soup; several dishes of stew consisting of turkey and duck, followed with jellies and pies."

"That sounds wonderful," Kalam said.

"Exquisite, sir," Ibrahim agreed.

The men dined for two hours discussing current events in India and New York.

Fletcher leaned back in his chair and wiped his mouth with his napkin. "It has been quite a busy and eventful couple of days. I hope you enjoyed your dinner."

"It was excellent," said Kalam.

"Excellent indeed, sir," Ibrahim replied with a slight bow.

"I wish we were meeting under better circumstances. Let us go to my state room where we may enjoy a more comfortable setting in which to discuss business."

"That sounds outstanding," Kalam replied.

Fletcher, Kalam, and Ibrahim each lit a cigar and sat in fine leather upholstered chairs. Fletcher took a long puff from his cigar. "Now that we're all comfortable, I will tell you what has transpired the past few days. It is a remarkable series of events. I have decided not to withhold any information from you, so that you may know the full extent of what has happened."

"We appreciate your honesty and integrity," Kalam said.

"Thank you. Feel free to stop me at any time, if you have any questions." The governor spent the next fifteen minutes explaining in great detail all that had occurred with the pirates and the treasure.

Kalam and Ibrahim glanced at each other. "You said your officers came upon only one ornate money chest?" Kalam asked.

"That's correct, and several bags of silver and gold coins."

"Do you still have the money and chest here at your mansion?" asked Kalam.

"Yes, I do.

"May we see it to determine if it is one that was aboard the *Ganj-i-Sawai?*"

"Yes, of course. Please follow me."

Fletcher took Kalam and Ibrahim to a secure room. "Please do not take what I am going to ask you as a sign I do not believe in your integrity."

"Ask us what?" Kalam asked.

"Before I lift the tarp covering the money chest, please tell me what it looks like and what's inside."

"I completely understand," Kalam said without showing any sign of being insulted. He waved to Ibrahim and nodded for him to describe the money chests.

Ibrahim raised his chin. "The outside of the two money chests are adorned with rubies and emeralds. Diamonds, more rubies and emeralds, and sapphires are inside."

Ibrahim looked at Kalam. "May I tell the governor the special adornment on each chest?"

"Yes. That will leave no doubt that it was on the *Ganj-i-Sawai*."

"Rubies forming the shape of the letter '*M*' are on the corner of each chest. This is in honor of the emperor's daughter, Mumtaz."

Fletcher removed the tarp covering the money chest. "Here is what was found on Solomon's Island. It is just as you described."

Ibrahim ran his hands over the money chest as if he found a long-lost friend. "Yes, and there in the upper right-hand corner you can see the '*M*' in rubies. I thought I would never see it again."

"You also mentioned there were several bags of gold and silver coins found," Kalam said.

"Yes. We have done an accounting of what was found, including the money chest, and have concluded the total value is £270,000. I have already given the couple I mentioned who found the treasure their share. Of course, we are unsure what is at the map's location."

"You've given away some of the emperor's money?" Kalam said loudly, his eyes widening.

"Now you must understand," Fletcher said, holding up his hands. "We are not even sure all of it is from India. I made the agreement with the Barretts prior to your arrival. Again, the money chest may be the only thing left of the robbery that is here in New York."

"I see," Kalam said, shaking his head. "I am trying to be as honorable as I possibly can, but this is an outrage. This is the emperor's money and precious stones. You cannot simply divide it up amongst yourselves because it is now here in New York."

"I understand you are upset, but let me remind you the property in discussion is in New York and is legally ours now. I am being as fair as humanly possible."

Kalam stared at Fletcher and then looked up at the ceiling. He took a long puff from his cigar and smiled at Fletcher. "We were hoping you found much more. We estimate that approximately £600,000 in Pieces of Eight, gold, silver, diamonds, and jewelry was onboard the *Ganj-i-Sawai* when it was robbed."

"My goodness," Fletcher said. "That is a vast amount. I can see why the emperor wants it back. I hate to say it, but if I were a betting man, I'd wager that most of it has already been divided among the pirates." Fletcher handed the map to Kalam. "Perhaps more can be found on this map,"

"Do you know where this is?"

"I'm aware of the general location. But first let's discuss how we are going to handle the disbursement of what has been found. Plus, whatever else we find when we follow the trail of the map. Hopefully, we can come to a consensus both sides will find acceptable."

Kalam folded his arms across his chest and frowned. "I see. You wish to have leverage over us,"

"It's not so much leverage I seek, as I wish for us to come to an agreement reasonable to both sides. It is unclear how much of the treasure found on Salisbury Island is from the *Ganj-i-Sawai*. What is clear, however, is that the money chest we found was on your ship. An unknown percentage also came from the frigate. We aren't even sure the map is Avery's. It could be from someone on the frigate. Also, and not to be too legalistic here, the money and money chest were found in New York, so technically it is the property of England."

Kalam slammed his hand on the table. "You are correct regarding the law, but I thought you wished to come to a mutually beneficial agreement."

"Calm down, sir, or this discussion is over," Fletcher said, standing up from his chair.

"I will not apologize for letting my love for India get the best of my emotions."

"Let's all take a breath," Fletcher said. "We need to decide how we can come to a consensus regarding this matter. There is no need for a winner or loser here."

"Agreed," Kalam said with a nod.

"Here's my proposal," Fletcher said, standing behind his chair. "India will keep any money chest found with the rubies spelling out the letter 'M' on it, and all contents inside said money chest. Any coins found will be split with seventy percent going to England and thirty percent going to India. However, my men found three bags of coins in the cabin of the frigate. Those coins should remain the sole property of England, since the frigate did not rob the *Ganj-i-Sawai*."

"You cannot be serious, sir," Kalam said, throwing his hands up in the air. "A seventy-thirty split is ridiculous. That is way too much for England. I propose a fifty-fifty split."

"I could not do that. Does a sixty-forty split with sixty percent going to England sound fairer to you?"

Kalam looked up in the air and let out a long breath. Then he glared at Fletcher. "Unbelievable. I don't like it one bit, but yes, I'll agree to that. The money chests and all their contents go to India, plus the sixty-forty split."

"Agreed," Fletcher said, holding out his hand to Kalam. "I suggest we join forces and send an equal contingent of your men and mine to recover what is on the map. I recommend ten men from each side. As I mentioned before, I have a good idea regarding the general location indicated on the map. It is high on top of Bear Mountain. It's not more than a few hours' sail from here to Salisbury Island, followed by a half day's hike up the mountain."

"I will have my men ready tomorrow morning," Kalam said.

"My officers will be ready by then too. Due to the depth of the river, it may be more beneficial to use one of my ships than yours."

"That is probably for the best."

"So, shall we have our men meet at, say, eight tomorrow morning on the dock?" Fletcher asked.

"We'll be ready."

"I would like to join you all on this adventure; however, I am afraid I have a day packed with official meetings and will be tied up the entire day. I'm hoping we will meet later tomorrow evening with good news that you have found a sizable cache of what was taken from the emperor's ship."

"Yes, we understand. Hopefully, our journey will prove fruitful."

"Feel free to take your money chest today, or you may leave it here, whichever you prefer."

"Thank you. If you agree, I will arrange for six of my men to come get it in one hour and bring it back to the *Ganj-i-Sawai*."

Fletcher stood and held out his hand. "Very well. Mr. Herndon will assist your men when they arrive. Have a good evening, gentlemen."

# 44

FINN GAVE UP standing outside Fred's Tavern at five thirty in the afternoon and walked down the street. He noticed a well-dressed man leave the governor's mansion and head toward a house. The man looked like someone of importance to Finn, so he decided to follow him at a safe distance to avoid being seen. He hoped he might overhear something that would prove helpful. The man walked into the house, and Finn snuck up and hid behind a bush underneath the dining room window. His stomach growled as he could smell meats and pies wafting from the half-open window. He could faintly hear the man and woman talking about the day's events.

"I don't think I told you, but the governor decided to give the Barretts twenty-five percent of the money they found, and whatever is found on that map," the man said.

"I'm glad," the woman said. "They deserve every bit of what they get. They could have kept it all for themselves."

"The governor's a good man. A lot of people presume he's hard and loves the glory of being the governor, but he tries to do what's right by folks. He's even allowing the men from India to go up on the mountain with our officers in the morning. They're hoping to find the rest of the treasure, or whatever else is possibly hidden at the 'X' on the map the Barretts gave the governor."

"You're not going up there are you?"

"No. Governor Fletcher wants me to be here with him. We have a lot of meetings tomorrow. The men should be back later tomorrow evening with whatever they find up there."

"I'm glad you're staying here. It's dangerous up there. They don't call it Bear Mountain for nothing."

Finn had heard enough. Looking around to make sure no one could see him, he slid out from behind the bush and inched his way slowly to the street. Then he ran as fast as he could toward the dock to take the last ferry of the day up the Hudson River. *I've got to get back to the captain before those men reach the cave to get his treasure.*

It was eight o'clock in the evening and almost completely dark when the ferry arrived at the stop where Finn exited earlier that morning. Finn bit his lower lip. *What do I do, what do I do? I can't wait for Fig to pick me up tomorrow afternoon. The men will already be heading up the mountain.*

Finn walked toward the small town in the distance so as not to draw any suspicion. Once out of eyesight, he ducked into the woods. He decided to stay in the forest for the night and not try to make it up the mountain in darkness. It was a difficult enough hike during the day. He hoped he could remember how to get back to Fig's camp.

Finn slept restlessly and woke up a few minutes before the first rays of light peeked through big fluffy clouds. It looked like it was going to be a gorgeous day, but he didn't have time to enjoy it. He had to make his way up to Avery. He wasn't sure what time it was, but he knew the men would be sailing early that morning and be close-by in a few hours. It would take him at least an hour to find Fig's place.

Finn made it back to the trail Fig used to bring him to the ferry and started the walk up the mountain. He felt good he remembered so much from his trip the previous day, but then he came to a fork in the trail. "Which one do I take?" Finn covered his eyes. *God only knows where I'll end up on this stupid mountain. They'll catch the captain and he'll end up in jail or dead. It's all my fault.*

There was a rustling in the shrubs, and Finn saw a deer run off on the rougher looking trail. He remembered Fig having to push aside tree limbs on the way down. *This has got to be it.*

Finn half-jogged fifteen minutes when he stopped and scratched his head. He plopped on the ground and wiped the sweat from his brow. He cupped his hands and yelled, "Fig…Fig." No reply. He got up and walked another five minutes. "Fig…Fig," he yelled again.

"No need to scream." Fig pushed through deep thickets. "I wasn't expecting you for another day. Everything all right?"

"No. I need to tell, um…"

"Sedgeport? Already forgot what name he was using, huh? Sounds like you had a difficult time of it. Let's get you to camp. You made it far on your own. It's only a few minutes up to the right. I was out lookin' for herbs and heard you yelling. Glad I did. You may have missed the turnoff here and ended up near the *Mhuwe*."

"You have any food on ya?" asked Finn. "I'm starved."

"Got some mushrooms and deer jerky. You're welcome to it."

"Thanks."

"Well, here you go."

# 45

THE TWO WALKED in silence as Finn scarfed down the mushrooms and tore at the jerky. "It's us, Sedgeport," Fig said.

"Us?" Avery asked. "Who's with you?"

"The boy."

"Finn, you back already?" came Avery's voice from inside the hut.

Fig stood outside the hut. "I'll leave you two to discuss what he found out in town. I'll be right outside. Sounds like we may have trouble."

"What happened?"

Finn picked at his fingernails. He wasn't sure how Avery would react. The captain wasn't always pleasant to be around when he received bad news. He once threw a crewmember overboard when he told Avery he couldn't repair one of the sails. Finn decided to tell Avery all he discovered as quickly as he could.

"Wait a minute. Slow down. The captain from the *Ganj-i-Sawai* is here in New York?"

"Yes. That's what Isaac said. But, there's a new captain of the *Ganj-i-Sawai*. Said his name was Kal...something. Doesn't matter."

Avery furrowed his brow. "Kalam?"

"That's it. You know him?"

"Yes, but we'll get to that later. Tell me what else happened."

"Well, Isaac got caught too. I saw officers grab hold of him and bring him to jail. I think a couple of our crew were able to get away, but I can't tell you where they are now."

"This is bad."

"Sorry, sir, but it gets worse." Finn relayed everything he learned. "Sorry, Captain."

Avery put his hand on Finn's shoulder. "You did great. You'd make a good spy."

"Thanks."

Fig poked his head into the hut. "You two finished talking?"

"Looks like we got a problem," Avery replied.

"Is it about what the kid told you, or do you want to keep it a secret?"

"No, you should know. I could sure use your help, but you may not want to after I tell you what's going on."

"Haven't been on an adventure in quite some time. What we up against?"

"Finn found out a whole lot. You were right about us. We aren't quite who we said we were."

"I know. I told Finn I figured it out a while ago."

"I'll let you in on everything later, but I've got things buried in a cave up the mountain where those creatures got to us. The governor's officers and crew from India are going after it. Should be here some-time this afternoon."

Fig stroked his long white beard and scrunched his face. "Hmm. Got yourself in quite the pickle. Quite the pickle indeed." Cucumber, Pickle, Sweetie Pie starting barking. "No, not you, baby girl."

"I can't let them get all my money. That's all I got left. That was from all I did over the years. Not just that one big job."

"So, what do you want to do?" Fig asked.

"Not sure yet. But I deserve to keep all of it." Avery ranted on about not being made captain. His face got redder the more he talked.

"You're a great captain," Finn said, trying to ease Avery's temper.

"Sure am," Avery said, throwing his cup of water across the hut. "They robbed me of a chance to be a captain in the Royal Navy. I'll show them. Nobody disrespects me."

"Sorry all that happened," Fig said. "But we should get back to taking care of the business at hand. There'll be a bunch of men coming up this mountain soon."

"You're right," Avery said. "It just gets me all mulligrubs about what the Navy did to me."

"So, pay them back," Fig said. "Don't let them take what you earned, no matter how you got it."

"True. I've already got my revenge. I have the record for the largest heist ever. I've got more money than anyone else. It's just not with me right now. I don't need to prove anything. The key thing is to get my money back."

Avery walked over to Finn and Fig and put his hands on their shoulders. "I consider you both my friends, and a good man doesn't put his friends in harm's way. I'll take care of this myself." Avery walked back and forth, running his hands through his hair while trying to figure out what to do.

Fig put his hands on his hips and glared at Avery. "You can't get rid of me that easily, Sedgeport, or whatever your name is. I may be getting up there in age, and haven't been in a fight in a few years, but I can still take you or any of those landlubbers coming up here."

Avery cocked his head at Fig. "Landlubbers? You been a sailor?"

"You got my temper going, and I let it slip out. Guess we all got our secrets."

Finn put his hands on his hips too. "I'm not staying back either. I can fight too. You know...I don't want anything to happen to you either, Captain."

Avery froze for a second and looked at Finn. He looked at the ground and faintly smiled. "No, Finn. You can't. You're too young. I shouldn't have let you go into town and risk getting you hurt or arrested. You're staying here."

Finn walked over to Fig and stood next to him. They looked at each other and then stared at Avery with their arms folded across their chests. "Just try and stop us," Fig said.

"Aye," Finn replied.

# 46

AVERY SMILED AND shook his head. "Thanks. I really do appreciate it. Well, I guess since we're all in this together, I should come clean. Fig...my real name is Avery."

"Skull and crossbones Avery?"

"You heard of me?"

"People were talking about you in Tortuga a couple years back."

"So, you haven't been up here for years and years?"

"No, I just said that to throw you off."

"What were you doing in Tortuga?"

"I was bending the rules between privateering and purloining a bit for myself on the side. By the way, I'm Edward Nash."

"Don't be lying at a time like this."

"Tellin' ya the truth."

"You can't be him. He's dead."

"And I want people to keep thinking that, so keep it to yourselves."

"Why you up here in the mountains and not living it up on some island?"

"I got tired of it. Always trying to stay one step ahead of the authorities, and other pirates always trying to steal from me. Changed my name, shaved my beard, and got married. Wife's father had a plantation in Virginia, so we lived there. Not bad work. Had a couple of kids. They all caught small pox and...I just had to leave and ended up here in New York. My hair turned white almost overnight when that happened. Makes me look a lot older than I am."

"Sorry," Avery said.

"Life's that way sometimes, but let's get back to figuring out what to do with those scoundrels trying to get your loot."

Avery pointed to an area about fifty yards from their camp. "I see you have bottles and things that make a noise every time a deer or another animal passes by. We could use something like that to warn us when the men come up the mountain."

"It's my system for alerting me when intruders or something's gettin' close to my camp. The *Mhuwe* used to set them off all the time and it would scare them. Got my heart goin'. I think they just stay away from them now. Plus, like I said, they leave me alone 'cause I give them some deer once in a while."

Avery stood and walked around the hut, thinking. "The Mhuwe may end up helping us after all. Maybe they'll attack the men when they go into the cave after the treasure."

"Not bad thinking. We let them enter the cave, the *Mhuwe* attack them, and then we shoot the rest as they come out. Might work."

"I shot one of the young ones, and that set them off."

"Finn told me."

"Maybe shooting a bullet in the cave, while we hide out in the woods, might remind them of what happened before and cause them to attack the men."

"Might work, but you'd have to wait until all the men—or most of them—are in the cave. I have a feeling the Mhuwe aren't going to allow anyone near their cave anymore after what happened before. They're really smart."

"You're probably right. But if the *Mhuwe* don't take the men out…" Avery stopped.

"What?"

"Don't think I'm weak or anything, but I don't like killing anyone unless I have to. I was hoping the *Mhuwe* would take care of most of them or we could scare off the rest. But if I got to do it, I got to do it. The only one I don't mind killing is Kalam."

Finn wrinkled his brow. "Who's Kalam?"

"We used to work together for a time, until he stole my girl and my money. I swore if I ever saw him again, I'd kill him right then and there. I was hoping he was on the *Ganj-i-Sawai* when we took it over, but no such luck. Hopefully, he'll be one of them coming up the mountain. There's a bullet with his name on it."

Nash looked up at the sun and frowned. "Looks like it's almost noon. Those men will be nearby soon. How about I set up noisemakers several hundred yards from us, in case they end up getting close to our camp? I have a great lookout post where I can spot them about halfway down the mountain. Finn, can you do that."

"Lookout was my job on the ship. We got to come up with a way to tell you when I see someone without them hearing me."

Nash smiled and shook his head up and down. "Yesiree. We can do what the *Mhuwe* do. Take two tree limbs with you and bang them together if you see the men. We'll look up, and you can tell us which direction they're coming."

"Great idea," Finn said. "Just hope those *Mhuwe* don't hear it and come runnin'."

Avery stood and wrinkled his nose. "What do we do for weapons? We've only got a few rifles, pistols, and some shot Finn brought back from the beach."

"Give me a second. I'll be right back." Nash turned and headed toward a large tree with a hole in the bottom of it. "Will these do?" Nash smiled and held up three rifles and several boxes of shot. "Never know when they might come in handy."

"That'll take out just about anything."

"That's the idea. Now how about I go set up some noisemakers. You may want to check out those guns. Been a while since I used them. They'll need cleaning and priming. Got a few rags on the top shelf."

# 47

THE GOVERNOR'S SHIP set sail sharply at eight o'clock a.m. with eighteen officers and two captains onboard. Captain Martin headed up New York's contingent, and Captain Kalam led India's crewmembers. Kalam ordered Ibrahim to stay back with the *Ganj-i-Sawai*.

Martin's men spent their time double checking the supplies they'd be taking up the mountain and prepping their weapons. They carried muskets, pistols, swords, and knives. Kalam's officers prepared similarly. They checked their supplies, primed their guns and pistols, and sharpened their swords and knives. The ship arrived at the foot of Bear Mountain three hours later.

Captain Martin stood in front of his men. "Gather around. You were all briefed before we left. But, to reiterate, our instructions are quite simple. We are to follow the map, get whatever is located there, and bring it back. We maintain the "X" on the map is a reference to a cave up the mountain. I have been informed that pirates tried to bury their treasure in the cave but were overrun by huge animals. Most likely bears. Apparently, there was some kind of fight with the animals in the cave. We may find dead bodies. Nothing you haven't seen before. Each one of you has been picked for your fighting skills and discretion. This mission shall remain secret. You are not to tell anyone what we find, nor where we found it. Not even your families. Everyone understand?

"Yes, sir," Martin's men said in unison.

"Hitchcock and Matthews, stay with the ship and safe guard it until we return. Captain Kalam, would you like to address your men?"

"Thank you, Captain. I will be brief, since I also gave my sailors instructions earlier." Kalam addressed his men in their native language as they stood at attention. When he was finished, less than one minute later, they all bowed in unison. "We are ready, Captain Martin." "We shall follow behind your officers unless you wish otherwise."

"That will be fine."

The men offloaded their supplies and weapons and stood together on the beach waiting for their orders. Martin held up his sword and looked behind him. "Captain Kalam, I would be honored if you'd come up front with me. Gentlemen, fall in line."

They walked for two hours with military precision without saying so much as a word. They were serious and professional, knowing Captains Martin and Kalam demanded nothing less. The trail they followed was clear, and the men were in excellent shape. No breaks were taken, and only occasionally did they drink from their canteens.

FINN WAS HIGH in the tree when he squinted and saw a small outline of something making its way about halfway up the mountain. He wasn't sure what it was yet. *Could be people but may be a herd of animals.* He watched it for several minutes and could tell it was a line of men, some in uniform, walking in pairs. They were now about an hour away. He grabbed the two sticks he'd brought up the tree with him and banged them together. Nash and Avery looked up from priming their weapons to see Finn pointing east.

Avery tapped beneath both his eyes, giving their predetermined sign asking how many? Finn made a fist with each hand and opened them twice. He also held his hands out in front of him as if he were carrying a rifle. Avery tapped beneath his eyes again. Finn made a fist with each hand and opened them twice again. Avery waved him down.

Avery looked over at Nash. "There are twenty men. Each one has a rifle. I'm sure they have pistols and knives too."

Nash didn't look up from cleaning his rifle. "Wouldn't be a fair fight for them, unless they had seven men to each one of us. *Mhuwe* will be helping us out, so we got this one. No doubt in my mind. I kind of feel sorry for them. They won't know what hit 'em."

"I wish I was as confident as you."

Nash put down his rifle and slowly tied back his hair. He reached into the plain wooden chest he had brought with him and grabbed several items. Nash put on a crimson coat and a shoulder belt with hoops where he inserted two pistols. He looked at Avery. "We've got this. Trust me, my friend. Trust me."

# 48

MARTIN, KALAM, AND their officers were making their way up the mountain when they saw the same bent-over trees in the woods, and tree trunks lying across the trail as the pirates had earlier. None of them paid it any mind. They simply climbed over the logs and ignored the trees.

Martin stopped and held up his sword for the men to stop. He leaned over to Kalam. "Strange how I keep hearing tree limbs cracking, but there isn't any wind blowing. Did you hear that? Like someone is banging on a tree trunk."

"I hear it too," Kalam replied. "Do you think it's people sending messages to each other or just animals walking through the woods?"

"Not sure. Could be the Haverstraws. Let's tell everyone to keep an eye out. I heard chattering noises too. Weird. Almost sounded like kids talking to each other speaking gibberish."

"What do you mean?"

"Made-up speech little babies say to each other as if they're trying to talk to each other."

"Oh. I understand."

Martin stood on a fallen tree across the trail and spoke in a hushed tone. "Be on the lookout for anyone that may be watching us. Could be Haverstraws, perhaps someone else. Be alert. We're almost there. According to the map, it looks like we should be at the cave in another half hour or so."

Kalam said the same thing to his men in Hindi and Bengali.

The officers adjusted their rifles and pistols, ensuring they were ready if needed. They looked left and right through the trees and farther up the trail and even behind them for anything out of the ordinary. A deer ran across the path in front of them, and many of the men pointed their weapons.

"Just a deer, men," Martin said with a chuckle, looking at Kalam. "Seems our officers are on edge."

"Yes, this part of the woods feels different from below. Smells much worse too."

"Yes, there must be skunks close-by. The smell comes and goes."

Martin looked at the map to see how much farther they had to go when he heard something heavyset run across the trail in front of them and crash through the brush to their left. He didn't see what it was. Then the same loud noise came from behind the last two men in line.

"*Mande Barung. Mande Barung,*" one of Kalam's officers shouted as he pointed his rifle down the path. Several of Kalam's men backed up.

Kalam glared and yelled, "Stand your ground. There are no such things as *Mande Barung,* you fools."

"What are *Mande Barung*?" Martin asked.

Kalam rolled his eyes. "Some of our people believe there are gigantic, hairy, ape-like creatures that live high in the mountains of India. I've never seen one. But people who live in the mountains say they see enormous footprints in the snow and in muddy areas. The footprints don't appear to be bear tracks, but more human, only much, much larger. The villagers say there are loud yells at night that don't sound like any other animals that live there. Tiger, bear, leopard, and even elephant calls can be heard on the mountains, but they say these sounds aren't from those animals."

"I see," Martin said, shaking his head.

"Hey!" one of the Martin's officers cried out. "Somebody just threw a rock and hit me in the leg. Came from over there," he said as he pointed his rifle to a patch of thick brush twenty feet away.

"Meyers, take three men with you and see if anyone's there," Martin ordered.

The four walked slowly toward the brush with their rifles aimed and ready to fire. They pushed the thicket aside at the spot from where the officer thought the rock was thrown. They didn't see anything. "No one's here, Captain. But it smells like a dead, wet animal was in the area. Vultures and wolves must have taken care of it. Strange. I don't even see any bones."

"*Mande Barung*," several of Kalam's men muttered to themselves.

"Quiet!" Kalam demanded.

Martin scratched his chin and looked around to see if he could spot anything unusual. "Back in line, officers. I see a cave up ahead. That must be it. Rifles at the ready."

Green bottle flies buzzed the area, and the smell worsened the closer they got to the cave. Some of the men covered their noses with their forearms. They were thirty feet from the cave when a huge tree limb fell across the path in front of them. Five of the men were pelted with rocks.

"Back up," Martin yelled as he pointed down the trail behind them. The officers retreated twenty yards from the cave. "Gather around," Martin said. "It is unclear how many there are, but it looks like there are some people who don't like us being here."

"*Mande Barung*," cried one of Kalam's men, pointing at the front of the cave.

"Silence," Kalam yelled as he smacked the man. "Please go on, Captain."

"As I was saying, somebody doesn't want us here. Maybe pirates ended up surviving. I don't know and I don't care. A few rocks being thrown at us isn't going to stop us from completing our mission. At ease, men."

Martin looked at Kalam and nodded to his right. "Captain Kalam, may I speak with you in private?" The two men walked a few feet away and stood by a tree.

"Appears this may not be quite the simple task we thought. I was going to order five of my officers and five of yours to go into the cave and to report back what they find, but I didn't want to give direct orders to your officers."

"Thank you. That sounds like a good plan. I propose we gather our men and give them our orders."

"Excellent."

Martin collected his officers and told them the plan, while Kalam did the same with his.

Kalam stood straight and stared at his men. "Five of our men—Panguluri, Tenali, Naidu, Chowdary, and Dolma—will be going into the cave with five of their officers to investigate what is inside. The rest of us shall stand guard. Once the treasure is found, you will come out and inform us. We will all then go in and retrieve it. I also want to make one thing perfectly clear—I do not want anyone mentioning *Mande Barung* again. You will not be bringing up old myths while we are on this mission. Is that clear?"

"Yes, sir," the men said.

"Good to hear. Now, let's go get our treasure back."

AVERY, NASH, AND Finn laid hidden in tall grass fifty yards from the cave, intently watching the officers' approach. They chuckled when they saw the men get unnerved when the *Mhuwe* threw rocks at them.

Avery looked over and smiled at Finn. "I remember when the

*Mhuwe* were throwing rocks at us. I couldn't figure out for the life of me what was going on. Drove me crazy."

Nash poked his head above the grass to get a better look. "I'm hoping the *Mhuwe* will take care of them and we won't have to do anything. Maybe we don't need to fire a shot in the cave after all. I suggest we wait and see what happens when they go in there. By the way, is your old friend one of them over there?"

"I wouldn't call him a friend. At least not anymore. But, yes, he's there. Funny how we used to be the best of friends. Now I want him dead."

"You might get your chance. Just got to see how things work out."

# 49

THE TEN OFFICERS slowly walked toward the opening of the cave, with their rifles drawn. The others formed a semi-circle around the entrance. Another hail of rocks was thrown from far above the cave. The officers crouched, aiming their rifles up the hill.

Martin held up his hand. "Hold your fire. It's just rocks. Save your bullets for something more dangerous. They'd have shot at us by now if they had any weapons. Go inside and tell us what you find."

The officers stooped as they entered the cave. The smell was terrible, and they held their arms over their noses. Flies were buzzing around several of the decomposed corpses lying on the ground. They counted what appeared to be five dead men, but some of the skeletons were scattered about the cave as if they were thrown against the walls and ceiling. The officers couldn't be sure how many had died. They walked farther inside when several large rocks were thrown at them, hitting one of the men in the head and knocking him out. No one could see where the rocks came from, only that they were thrown from deep inside the cave where it was totally dark. Two of the officers lifted up the unconscious man and carried him toward the front of the cave, while the rest stayed and inspected the cavern.

"What happened?" Martin asked as they carried out the officer now sporting a bloody gash on his head, which was already swelling.

"Sir, someone threw rocks at us from deep inside the cave and hit him in the head."

"Did you see any of the treasure?"

"No, not yet, sir. We will need torches, sir. It's pretty dark in there."

"Bannister, you take O'Sullivan's place." Martin pointed to a group of torches on the ground. "Take ten. Need anything else?"

"No, sir."

"Good. Go back in there and tell us what you find."

"Yes, sir."

Bannister joined the other men and handed each one a torch. He lit each torch with his. The officers could now clearly see the blood-stained walls and floors. They looked at each other, wide-eyed. They walked farther into the cave waving their torches while holding onto their rifles with their other hand. The men heard scuffling sounds as if several large animals were moving around in the dark part of the cave. They could also hear grunts and chattering. Every few seconds a rock flew out of the darkness at them.

"Who's there?" one of the men yelled. "Speak or we'll shoot."

Only the sound of grunts answered back. The men inched deeper into the cave when they spotted one corner of what looked like a buried money chest poking out of the ground. They also saw several broken bags of gold and silver coins lying on the floor. They lifted the chest out of the ground and stared at each other. The lid was covered with jewels.

One of the men grabbed a rock and broke open the padlock. "Let's open it and see what's inside." He lifted the lid and the men gasped. It was filled with diamonds, rubies, and jewelry.

"Let's retreat and tell the captain what we found," Bannister whispered.

The officers rushed out of the cave, looking back to ensure they weren't followed. They were nearly out of breath from the smell as they bent over with their hands on their knees.

Martin and Kalam ran over to see what happened.

"Sir," Bannister said, trying to speak while catching his breath. "Sir, there' a money chest inside filled with jewels. There's also broken bags of coins scattered about the cave. Plus, and I know this sounds crazy, we heard grunting noises toward the back of the cave. Then whoever or whatever made those sounds threw rocks at us."

"Get yourself together, man," Martin said. "Animals can't throw rocks."

"Yes, sir. But I really do think that's what happened. I don't think they were people, sir. Animals were throwing rocks at us."

"What about the loot? Did you see any?"

"We saw several bags of coins scattered on the floor, and what looked like one corner of a buried money chest sticking out of the ground."

"Were there any bodies?"

"Yes, sir. We saw the bones of multiple dead people in there. Not sure how many, sir. There's blood everywhere. Even on the ceiling."

"I see," Martin said, while motioning for his and Kalam's officers to gather around. "Gentlemen, line up and prepare to enter the cave. We may have more rocks thrown at us, so be careful. We don't want anyone else getting knocked out. Fredericks, you stay outside with O'Sullivan."

"Yes, sir."

"We will go in, get the treasure, and leave. You will also see the bones of several dead men inside. Nothing more we can do for them now. Be respectful and walk around them. Keep your torches lit and your rifles at the ready. No one is to fire unless given the command by me or Captain Kalam. Everyone line up." Martin did a quick inspection of the men. "We will go in two at a time and fan out inside the cave. Captain Kalam, would you prefer to go in first or take the rear of the line?"

"I will go in first, Captain."

# 50

THE *MHUWE* LEADER sniffed the air and rubbed the stumps on his hand. He opened his enormous jaws and snapped them shut. The other creatures looked at him for direction.

He knuckle-walked back and forth in the rear of the cavern. The beast snorted and shook his head as he stared at his dead family members lying on the cave floor. He pounded his fists on the ground and then quickly stopped. He cocked his head when he sensed something. He peered around the side of the wall and grunted.

The others moved in around him and stopped.

The leader pointed toward the opening of the cave. He opened his jaws and chattered. He heard the humans getting closer, and crouched.

The other creatures followed his actions and squatted on the floor.

He glared at each one and grunted. He picked up a large rock, sniffed at the air, and waited.

MARTIN STOOD AT the cave's entrance as Kalam lowered his head and inched inside. It took less than one minute for Kalam and his officers to get inside and fan out.

Martin and his officers followed, filling the entrance of the cave. Shadows danced against the walls from the reflection of the lit torches. The men walked carefully around the bones strewn across the ground.

There were some animal carcasses, but most appeared to be human remains. Others looked too big to be from a person.

Martin waved over Bannister. "Where did you see the coins and money chest?"

"One hundred feet or so in the cave, sir."

The men slowly walked with their weapons pointed toward the darkest part of the cavern. As they crept along, the grunting sounds became louder. More rocks were thrown at the officers with a few hitting their arms and legs but not causing any significant injury.

"Remain steady," Martin commanded. "We'll get the treasure and then be on our way. No one fire unless Captain Kalam or I tell you."

The men walked a little farther and stopped at the torn bags of coins scattered on the ground. Kalam knelt next to the money chest and opened the lid when a deafening roar echoed throughout the cave. It was so loud the men covered their ears. The officers looked around, wide-eyed, pointing their guns toward the ear-piercing noise. The growls appeared to be coming from everywhere, bouncing off the walls of the cave. Shadows appearing like gigantic men darted across the ceiling.

"Fire," Martin yelled, pointing deep inside the cave. The officers shot their rifles and began reloading as creatures came running at them from all directions. Some came from deep within the cave, while others came at them from outside. The sound was deafening. The men screamed as they were hit with massive arms and stomped on with enormous feet. The creatures grabbed several of the men and threw them against the wall.

Martin shot at one after seeing it rip a man's arm off and throw it against the cave's ceiling. He froze as he watched another man get hit over the head with a rock. Crimson blood flowed from the man onto the cave floor. Martin covered his ears from the cries of the officers being killed, and the haunting screams of the creatures. He'd never seen such carnage.

Fourteen *Mhuwe* were running at the men, jumping on them and biting them on their necks and back. Several of the officers ran toward the cave's entrance, glancing back, trying to get off a shot as best they could.

It was then Martin saw red eyes coming toward him. The eyes looked as if they were coming from the top of the cave. He saw blood dripping from its mouth as it ran toward him. It was enormous. Martin didn't have time to aim as he shot at the beast.

The creature screamed and fell to the ground. It groaned, shook its head, and stood straight up. Blood was gushing from its shoulder and chest. The beast grabbed its shoulder and looked at the blood on its hand. It glared at Martin and roared. Martin could barely breathe. He tried to move but his legs wouldn't budge.

The creature stumbled toward Martin, reaching for him with every step. Martin stared in horror as it moved within inches of him. The creature was about to grab him when a shot rang out. The beast fell sideways against the wall. Martin slowly looked over in the direction of the shot. Kalam's rifle was still pointed at the creature, smoke flowing from the chamber. Martin got up and nodded thanks when he noticed Kalam's leg. It was bent and obviously broken.

Kalam collapsed, and Martin dragged him toward the entrance of the cave. He realized there were only two officers still fighting the creatures. The rest of his men looked dead. One officer fired at a beast but only made it angrier. The shot didn't slow it down. The creature grabbed the man and threw him against the wall. There was a loud crack, and the officer slid to the ground, blood spilling out the side of his mouth.

Martin was at the cave's opening when he looked back. Three creatures ran toward the last of his officers in the cave. Martin closed his eyes and turned away when he heard the men scream. Then all was quiet. No grunting. No screaming. Martin felt something hit the back of his leg. He turned around and looked down to see a man's hand. No body—just a hand.

# 51

"IT'S A MIRACLE you and I are still alive," Martin said, pulling Kalam under a tree. Martin then lit two grenades he had in his pouch and threw them as far as he could toward the cave. Four seconds later, there was a loud explosion. Boulders flew in all directions as the grenades exploded near the cave's entrance, killing several creatures and injuring many others. Some ran up the mountain to escape the falling debris, while others limped into the woods chattering to each other.

Martin stared at the brutes fleeing when he noticed a shadow on the ground. It was a *large* shadow. A shadow that looked like a human with extremely broad shoulders. Martin slowly looked up. A nine-foot, seven-hundred-pound creature jumped down from high in the tree and slammed onto Kalam's back, breaking it, and paralyzing him. It glared at Martin and inched toward him.

Martin shot at the creature and hit it in the arm, slowing it for a second. The beast bared its bloodstained teeth and stared at Martin as if he were looking through him. Then it jumped on him with one leap, hitting Martin on the head with one massive fist, killing him instantly.

AVERY, FINN, AND Nash watched the scene unfold before them. Several *Mhuwe* returned to the cave throwing boulders over their shoulders left and right trying to get to their own underneath the fallen rocks. It appeared as if half of the side of the mountain collapsed at the opening of the cave. They heard the creatures scream in anguish as they carried off their dead and injured into the woods.

An hour passed before Avery decided it was safe to leave their hiding place. "Let's get closer and see if we can get to the treasure before any of the *Mhuwe* come back."

Nash looked at Avery and frowned. "Are you sure you want to go over there after what happened to you and what you just saw?"

"You bet. I still want to get at least some of my loot. It's been quiet for a while now. I don't think they're coming back anytime soon. I don't want to force anyone. You two can stay back if you want."

"I'll go," Finn said.

Nash shrugged. "Me too. But let's make it quick. They can still smell you, and you're not their favorite person."

"Thanks. We won't be long."

They slowly walked toward the cave, keeping an eye out and listening for any sign of the *Mhuwe*. They stopped often and dropped to the ground every time they heard the faintest sound. It took them fifteen minutes to reach the cave's entrance. Avery and Finn pointed their rifles, while Nash had a pistol in each hand. Their heads were on a swivel, looking to make sure no *Mhuwe* were coming at them.

Nash walked over to Martin, felt his neck, and shook his head no to Avery and Finn. Avery marched over to Kalam.

Kalam's eyes grew wide. "I thought you had died in the cave."

Avery pointed his rifle at Kalam's face. "You wish."

"If I could move, I'd rip your head off and feed it to those creatures."

Avery spat on the ground. "I wish you could move. Nothing I'd like better than to tear you limb from limb. Give me one good reason I shouldn't kill you right here and now."

"You owe me."

Avery laughed. "I owe you?"

"You stole Mary and my share of the money," Kalam coughed out.

"What? You're cracked. You're the own who stole Mary and my money!"

"Now who's crazy?"

Avery picked up a rock and held it over Kalam's head. "Even on your death bed, you can't admit to being the scoundrel you are. Fred was right."

"He sure was."

"What's that supposed to mean," Avery said, dropping the rock and jabbing the gun into Kalam's stomach.

"You really are a scoundrel through to your bones. Fred told me you'd gone to our hiding place with Mary."

Avery kicked Kalam's leg. Avery leaned over Kalam and screamed at him. "I looked for you and Mary, and both of you were gone."

"You're a liar," Kalam sputtered.

Avery's face got red and he threw his rifle down and grabbed Kalam's shirt. He could hardly get the words out. "I...went...to... our...hiding...spot. Fred was right. You couldn't even remember where we buried the loot. You dug a million holes in the ground before you found our loot, you idiot."

"What? You're cracked, you knave. Fred told me what a terrible man you were and how he wished his sister never met you."

Avery smacked Kalam. "Take that back, you picaroon."

"Never. He couldn't understand why she had run off with you. He said how much better I was for her than you. Why d'ye take all the money? Couldn't have left me my share, could you? Had to have it all. Typical Avery. Had to be the big man. Had to have all the money and the girl."

Avery glared and pointed the rifle at Kalam's face.

Kalam coughed up blood. "I saw where you dug all the holes. Couldn't remember where we hid it, could you, Avery?"

"Wait a minute," Nash said. "You both were after the same girl, and each of you believes the other stole her and the money? Her brother came to you and told you that?"

"I don't think...I know he stole Mary and took all the money," Avery yelled.

"Quiet, before the *Mhuwe* hear you," Nash told Avery, and then looked at Kalam. "How about you, mister? You think the same thing?"

"Absolutely. Swore I'd kill him when I got the chance."

Nash shook his head and chuckled.

Avery scowled at Nash. "What's so funny?"

"You two are a couple of idiots! You both were taken by the oldest trick in the book. I bet one or both of you told Mary where you had hidden the loot. That's why there were so many holes. She and her brother weren't sure where it was, so they had to keep digging until they found it."

# 52

AVERY AND KALAM stared at each other. Avery furrowed his brow and then smacked himself in the head. "We were duped by Mary and her brother to get our money!"

"I can see it now," Kalam said as he shut his eyes.

"I've hated you all these years for something you didn't do," Avery told Kalam.

"Me too. I can't believe how cracked we've been," Kalam said as he closed his eyes in pain, as he choked and coughed up blood. "Well, old friend, looks like they got the best of us. But you still got a good bit of jewels and money in that cave. If you can get to it without those creatures killing you."

Nash looked to his right when he heard a bang on a tree. He turned to his left when the sound came from the other side. He sniffed the air and looked at Avery and Finn. "We've got to get out of here now." He pointed to a tree above the cave's entrance. "Look, there's one up there. They don't come out in the open much where people can see them. This isn't a good sign. Let's grab your friend and go back down the trail."

"I can't leave my loot again," Avery said.

Nash held his nose up in the air. "You don't have much choice. We'll have to regroup and make a plan to come back and get it, but now isn't the time, unless you want to end up like those men in the cave."

Kalam choked. "Leave me here. I'll just slow you down. I can't move anything below my neck. I don't have much time. Go ahead and leave before it's too late."

Avery looked into Kalam's eyes. "We aren't leaving without you." Avery waved over Finn and Nash. "I'll grab his legs. You two pick him up under his arms. one…two…three…lift."

The three carried Kalam back down the trail, while looking around to make sure the *Mhuwe* weren't following them. They made it thirty yards when Kalam started coughing up blood and choking again.

"Turn his head to the side so he doesn't choke," Avery told Finn. Kalam opened his eyes wide, staring at Avery as he tried to stop coughing.

Avery looked back at Nash and Finn. "Hurry, let's get him to Nash's place. You've got herbs for him, don't you, to stop the coughing?"

"I'll cook something up," he said. "But maybe we should let him rest in the shade under that tree over there," Nash said, pointing to a large oak tree.

Kalam was coughing more and was drifting in and out of consciousness. "Avery, we had a lot of good times, didn't we?"

"We sure did. We'll pick up where we left off. You just got to rest for a little bit. You'll be good as new in no time."

Nash touched Finn on the arm. "Let's give them some time alone."

"Remember that time we were with Captain Redhand and we raided that British ship outside Tortuga?" Avery asked, chuckling. "Those sharks swimming around? He thought they were going to eat him alive."

Kalam coughed up blood. "Don't make me laugh."

Avery forced a smile. "That was a great idea you had to blindfold him and tell him we were making him walk the plank. The crew could barely keep from laughing when he was only a foot above the deck on a box. He sang like a sparrow when his foot dangled over the edge. We'd have never found where he stashed all that money if you hadn't come up with that idea."

"He hid it in the flour jars."

"Expensive biscuits," Avery said, laughing.

"Hey, your friend over there looks an awful lot like Edward Nash. Is that him?"

"Aye, but no one's supposed to know."

"What's he doing up in the mountains? Are you teaming up with him?"

"Long story. He went straight and ended up in Virginia. Got married and had kids, but they died of smallpox. Looks like he kind of gave up after that and moved up here to be alone. He comes across as crazy, but he's anything but that."

"Can you trust him?"

"I think so. He helped me get better after one of those creatures almost did me in. I owe him."

"That's good." Kalam coughed, grimacing. His voice was barely more than a whisper now. "Who's the kid?"

"He was our cabin boy and lookout. He's great. I wouldn't have lasted this long without him."

Kalam smiled. "Glad we were able to work things out. By the way, your map is in Captain Martin's coat pocket. He was the one with me outside the cave. One of the money chests is on the *Ganj-i-Sawai*. The other is still in that cave. It was good to see you…" Then he took his last breath.

Avery bowed his head for a second then punched the ground.

Finn came over and stood next to Avery. "Sorry, Captain. I'm glad you two were able to be friends again."

"Me too. He was the best. Just wish things had turned out differently. I want to give him a proper burial. Kalam would like it here."

"I'll go back and get a shovel," Nash said.

Nash returned an hour later to find Avery and Finn sitting in silence. He put the shovel on the ground and handed Avery his map. "Sorry, it took me a while. I went back and got this off that captain. Figured you might want it. I heard your friend mention the captain had it."

"Thanks. You never know. With any luck we can figure out how to get the treasure after all."

# 53

AVERY ATE A few bites of stew and tossed the pot aside. "How am I going to get the treasure out of that cave?"

Nash stroked his beard. "I don't know. Those *Mhuwe* are spooked with people going into their cave twice now. No one will be able to get near the place for a while. Plus, most of the entrance is covered with boulders.

"There's got to be a way. I should start concentrating on getting my money back from that man and woman who were on the beach. What was their name again?"

"Barrett," Finn said.

Avery looked up at the sky, contemplating his next move. "Probably out of the question trying to rob the governor's mansion. Most of the gold and silver they found has got to be there somewhere."

"That's risky," Nash said. "You'd need a whole crew and time to set it up. There are a ton of officers around the place. It would take at least fifty men, and a lot of weapons and grenades to bust your way in there."

"Maybe the money's in the bank," Finn said. "I saw a lot of men standing guard in front of it."

Avery threw a rock at a tree and folded his arms. "I haven't done a land attack in years. I'll sleep on it and decide what to do tomorrow."

FLETCHER BIT HIS lower lip as he looked at Herndon. "They should have been back by now. Go ahead and head home. It's almost ten o'clock. They should be here in the morning. Probably had a hard time finding the cave and decided to stay on the ship until tomorrow. If they aren't back tomorrow by noon, I'll send a party out there to find them."

Herndon nodded. "Good night, sir."

Fletcher put his feet on top of his desk, lit a cigar, and took a sip of whiskey. Something didn't feel right to him. Thoughts kept racing over and over in his head. *All the pirates are dead, so the officers didn't get attacked by them. Even if a few survived, they couldn't have taken on and killed twenty of my men. The only thing that could have given them any trouble are the Mhuwe or if the Haverstraws decided to keep it all for themselves. No. They wouldn't do that. This doesn't feel good at all.*

# 54

AVERY WOKE WELL before sunrise, unable to sleep. He made a pot of tea. He still hadn't figured out what the best option was for getting his treasure back. But he did decide to ask Finn if he'd be willing to return to town to see if he could find out anything about the Barretts. Plus, he wanted to try to locate where the governor kept the treasure they found on the beach. Avery couldn't go into town. Too many people had seen him before.

Avery had decided earlier he wouldn't order Finn and Nash to do anything. He'd ask them, since they were a team. He was in charge, but things were different now. He was changing—not softening so much as being more like a manager in charge and not their captain.

Even though there were always pirates around the *Fancy*, it was lonely being the captain. Avery felt like he had to continuously prove he was a good leader to the crew and himself. He didn't have to with Finn and Nash. Nash understood what it was like being a captain, and Finn was almost like part of his family. Something Avery never had before.

Finn and Nash awoke shortly thereafter, unable to sleep well either.

Avery handed Nash and Finn each a cup of tea. "Looks like none of us got much sleep."

"No, I couldn't get the *Mhuwe* out of my head, and all those men dying," Finn said.

"I couldn't sleep good either," Nash said. "It's been a while since

I planned out any robberies, so I'm a little rusty. Sorry, hopefully, I'll come up with a good idea later today."

Avery put down his drink and tapped his finger again and again on his chin.

"What ya thinking about?" Nash asked.

"I have an idea, but I don't really like it."

"Let's see what you got."

"I was thinking…if Finn was up to it…he could go back into town and do some more spying. See where the Barretts were keeping their share of the money, and where the governor is storing the rest of it."

"You're right," Nash said. "It is a bad idea. Each time the kid goes into town is another time somebody can get suspicious and put two and two together."

Finn narrowed his eyes at Avery and Nash. "Wait a minute. Don't I get a say in any of this?"

Avery and Nash raised their eyes at each other.

"Kid's got guts," Nash said. "Got to give him that."

Avery nodded. "True, he's tough…but like you said…it's a bad idea."

Finn stomped his foot. "Oh, come on. Nothing bad happened last time. And look what I found out. I can go in, spy around, and be back in two days. Be here before you know it. I want my share of the treasure too."

Avery and Nash looked at each other and shrugged.

"Now that I think about it, the kid may be right," Nash said. "I wouldn't be surprised if the governor and most of his officers in town are wondering why their men aren't back yet. He'll probably send some more officers to see what happened. They won't be focused on what's going on in town. Could be a good time to go back in."

Avery looked sternly at Finn and pointed his finger at him. "No more than two days. If anyone so much as looks funny at you, you get out of there and come on back. I'll be in the woods, close to the ferry stop, in case you return early like last time." He reached into his pocket and pulled out some coins. "This should be enough for the ferry back and forth and for food. You probably should sleep out in the woods near town. Folks might wonder what a kid was doing trying to get a room for the night."

"I'll be fine. I can catch the afternoon ferry."

Nash stirred the deer and potatoes he had cooking in a pot over a fire. "You better eat before going down the mountain. You never know when you might miss a meal or two."

After eating, the three of them walked an hour to the top of the hill above the ferry stop. Avery looked around to make sure no one saw them. "Nash and I shouldn't get any closer than this. Don't want anyone seein' us. I'll be here at this same spot and wait for you to come back. No more than two days...that's it."

"Ferry should be here soon," Nash said. "Got your money?"

"Aye. I'm all set. Hopefully, I'll be back with good news. See ya soon." Finn turned around and headed toward the ferry.

Avery frowned at Nash. "Think he'll be all right?"

"Yes. But, if anybody bothers him, we'll just go into town and... tear their heads off."

# 55

THE FERRY RIDE into New York Town was uneventful. No one spoke to Finn, other than the fare taker asking for his money. He tried to blend in with the crowd when he was in town. *Keep your head down and don't look anyone in the eyes,* he told himself over and over. *Look like you're going someplace.*

The crowd thinned out, and Finn decided now was the time to try to find where the Barretts lived. He saw an old lady walking slowly by herself. "Hi, ma'am. Sorry to bother you, but I was wondering if you might be able to tell me where the Barretts are?"

The lady jumped and put her hand to her chest. "You startled me, young man."

"Sorry."

"No bother. It's just that I can't hear good, and I was daydreaming. What did you ask me?"

"I was wondering where the Barretts are?"

"Do you mean the store or where they live?"

*I better not say where they live, or she'll ask me a ton of questions.* "Um, the store."

"Well, you can follow me. I'm going over there now. Where are your folks?"

"They're doing business in town and told me to get some supplies."

"What's your family's name?"

All these questions were starting to worry Finn. *Did she suspect something, or was she just a nosey old lady?* He wished he'd asked someone else about the Barretts. He told her the first name he could think of—the head mistress at the orphanage back in Derry. "Um, the Runions. I'm Finn Runion, ma'am."

"Never heard of the Runions."

"We're from up the river pretty far. Just get into town every now and then. Where's the Barretts' store?"

She pointed up the street a block. "Right up there, sunshine."

Finn started to walk faster and away from the lady when she grabbed his arm. "Aren't you going to help an old lady to the store?"

"Sure. Sorry, but I need to get back soon."

"I always say life is better when you slow down and enjoy it. You know, I used to be a preacher. I was famous. People didn't walk to hear me preach—they ran. My sermons were legends around here. Had to have five services on Sunday."

Finn looked away and rolled his eyes. "That's great. Looks like we're here. Have a good day."

"Aren't you coming in?"

"Not yet, I just remembered something. I'll come back later. See ya," Finn said as he rushed down the street.

The old lady shook her head. "Crazy kids nowadays!"

Finn didn't want to attract attention while he was in town, and this lady was all about getting attention. *She'd have me handing out church fliers and singing "Amazing Grace" on the street corners if I'd stuck around any longer.*

He walked farther down the street and snuck into the woods behind the back of the stores. He planned to sit up high enough and follow the Barretts home when they closed up shop, then shadow them from a distance and figure out later what to do once he got to their house. He'd, of course, have to check around their place to see how many people lived there and what he and Avery might be up against. It was like being a lookout on a ship. Nothing would happen for long periods of time, and it was boring. Then, all of a sudden, there'd be a lot of action.

He walked up higher on the hill so he could get a better look at the bank. He saw five guards out front and five around back. *Hmm...there weren't that many before. Somebody must have put in a bunch of money since I was here. Why didn't they just put up a sign saying, 'We got a lot more money here now.' I should go inside and see how many guards are in there.*

Finn noted the sign on the front door of the Barretts store said "close at five p.m." He'd still have an hour to walk to the bank, scope it out, and be back in time to follow them. Hopefully, they would go straight home and not out for the night. If so, he'd just have to go with it.

FINN GAVE A quick smile to the guards at the bank's front door. Each carried a rifle and two pistols—one in each holster, the same as the guards behind the building. Finn walked up to a man sitting behind a desk reviewing paperwork. "Excuse me, sir."

"What can I do for you, young man?"

"I, um, I was wondering how much money I had to have for the bank to let me keep my money here?"

"You want to open an account with us?"

"I'm not sure, but I got money when my Uncle Henry passed away. It might be good to keep it here. Looks like you have a lot of guards keeping watch over things. My money should be safer here than me putting it in a jar and buryin' it in the ground."

The manager grinned. "That's very wise, son. How much money do you have?"

"£5."

"That's enough. Yes, we can open an account for you here. Since you're a minor, your parents would have to sign with you. We could do the paperwork now if you want to get your folks."

"Can't right now. They're busy, but I could come back soon. What time are you opened and closed?"

"We open at nine in the morning and close at five in the afternoon, Monday through Saturday."

Finn pointed to a room with bars in front of it. "Would you keep my money in that big room back there?"

"Yes, it will be very safe in there. Only a couple of us have the key."

"And I can get my money out whenever I want it?"

"Yes, you can."

"Thanks. I'm just nervous giving my money over to a stranger. Mother and Dad have never kept their money in a bank. Why do you have all those guards out front?"

"No need to worry, son. Your savings could not be any safer than right here. I'm not supposed to say, so promise not to tell anyone, but..." He looked around the room.

Finn leaned in close. "I won't say a word, promise."

The manager lowered his head. "We're holding a lot of treasure taken from pirates who died in a battle outside of town. Governor's storing it here until they send most of it back to England. One couple is also keeping a ton of their money here too. Boy, are they rich now."

"Wow. I mean if the governor and those rich people keep their money here, I should do it too. Who are they?"

"Oh, I can't say. I shouldn't have told you about them nor the treasure. The governor will be sending it to England in a week or two anyway. Promise you won't tell anyone?"

"Never. Your secret's safe with me," Finn whispered. "I'll talk with my parents, and, hopefully, they'll let me keep my money here. Thanks!"

# 56

FINN LEFT THE bank and went back up the hill to wait for the Barretts to leave their shop. He smiled, knowing where they kept at least some of their money, and where the governor kept the treasure before it would leave for England.

The Barretts locked up the store at five o'clock sharp and climbed aboard their horse and wagon. They strolled down the street at a leisurely pace, while Finn followed twenty yards behind them, keeping close to the storefronts until they made it out of town. He stuck to the tree line from then on. It took the Barretts fifteen minutes to make it home. They unhitched the horses and led them to a fenced pasture. Afterward they went into their small house. Neither saw Finn hiding behind a tree fifty yards away.

Finn smelled the farm—the pigs and chickens and hay. It didn't smell anything like the sea or the stink belowdeck on a ship. He liked this smell. Finn looked around and took it all in. *This must be what living in a regular house is like. Not bad. Not bad at all.*

Finn scratched his head. *Do I leave and go tell Avery what I already learned? It will be too difficult to rob that bank with all those guards, and the money's going to be gone soon.* Finn started breathing faster and sweat was forming on his forehead. *What do I do?*

Finn walked away and stopped. *There's no way we can rob it. There are too many officers. I've got to at least try to get some of the money back from these people.*

Finn watched as Sam and Emma Barrett came outside and walked to the pig and chicken pens. "Now's as good a time as any," he whispered out loud.

He pulled his shoulders back and marched toward them. "Are you the Barretts?"

"Yes, we are," Emma said as she brushed the dirt off her dress. "And who are you, young man?"

"None of your business," Finn said. "I want my money."

Emma took a step back. "Money?" Emma asked? "Why would we have any of your money?"

Sam, jaw clenched and face red with anger, stomped over to Finn. "Listen here, boy. You come onto our property uninvited and demand money. Who do you think you are? I'll give you two seconds to get out of here, or I'll throw you out on your backside."

Emma put a hand on Sam's shoulder and gave him a stern look. "Control that Irish temper of yours, Samuel Barrett."

Emma looked at Finn and smiled. "Why don't we all just calm down and talk civilly to one another? We'll figure out why you reckon we have your money. When was the last time you ate anything, young man?"

"What?" Sam asked. "You want to feed this scoundrel?"

"Settle down, Samuel. So, when did you eat last?"

Finn looked at the ground. "Yesterday." Then he glared at Sam.

Emma touched Finn on the shoulder. "Now, why don't you sit over there under the shade tree, and I'll fetch some chicken from the house. It's cold, but it's still pretty tasty. I'll bring you a tall glass of water too." She gave a warning glance to Sam to be nice.

Sam watched Emma walk to the house and close the front door. He turned to Finn and stood over the boy and whispered in an Irish brogue, "My wife's a lot nicer than I am. Any false moves and I'll ring your hide, boy." Sam turned and smiled at Emma looking through the window. She wagged her finger at him.

A minute later, she came out with a big plate of food. Finn licked his lips. His eyes grew big as she handed him the plate. He grabbed a chicken leg, then a thigh, and gobbled them up as Sam and Emma looked at each other in amazement at how quickly he ate.

"I have more chicken and apple pie if you want," Emma told Finn.

Finn looked at Sam, noticing he seemed to soften up a bit.

Sam nodded yes to the boy.

"I would love more chicken. I've never eaten apple pie, but I'd like to try it."

Emma put her hands on her hips. "Never had apple pie? Well, we'll take care of that right now. I don't wish to brag, but I do make a pretty good pie."

Emma came back outside with more food, and Finn ate it as fast as the first plate. "Any more?" she asked.

"No," Finn said. "It was good. Thanks."

"Now why don't you tell us why you came here, and why you think we have your money?" Sam said.

"First things first," Emma countered. "My name is Emma Barrett and this is my husband, Samuel Barrett. What's your name?"

"I'm Finn," Finn said, giving a faint smile.

"Where do you live, and who are your parents?" Emma asked.

Sam rolled his eyes. "Can we get to that later? I want to know why he's here."

"Of course, of course," Emma said, nodding.

Finn sat there for a few seconds before saying anything. He realized he hadn't planned this through very well. *What if the Barretts tell the authorities about me? Would I be arrested? They seem nice. They fed me. Maybe*

*I should tell them the truth and hope for the best. Possibly I could get them to like me and they would tell me where their money is if it isn't all in the bank.*

"Well?" Sam asked.

Finn took a deep breath and let it out. "I was hiding on the mountain when our crew was fighting that pirate ship on Salisbury Island. I saw you, but you didn't see me, and I didn't want to come out of my hiding place. Captain Avery was a tough man, but he was good to me, and so were most of the other crew. Captain always told me to hide when any fighting was about to take place. He didn't want me to get hurt. I hated seeing my friends killed." A lump formed in his throat.

"Wait a minute," Sam said, wide-eyed. "You were on Captain Avery's ship? He's the pirate people say robbed the *Ganj-i-Sawai*. Is that true?"

"Yes, but how d'ye hear about us robbing that ship?" Finn asked.

"It was all anyone talked about at Fred's Tavern. A fortune was stolen from the emperor," Sam said.

Emma frowned. "Sam, you know I hate it when you go to Fred's. There are too many fights, plus *those* kinds of women are there."

"Sorry," Sam said. "But that must be why we found all that treasure."

Finn nodded. "That's not half of what was taken. There's more from what we took from the *Ganj-i-Sawai* and a bunch of other ships we robbed," Finn bragged. "I got a half share, plus a little more staying with the captain, and some of the shares of our crew who died in that fight. That comes out to around £1,000."

Finn took a sip of water and puffed out his chest. "I followed you home when you left your store today so I could get my money and leave."

"Let's say what you told us is true," Sam whispered. "What would a boy do with that kind of money? You could buy a large plot of land with that. No one would believe you got the money honestly. You'd be arrested immediately."

"I'll figure something out," Finn said.

Sam put his hand on his chin and questioned Finn like a lawyer. "How can we be sure you were a crewmember of that ship and hiding on the mountains? You may have overheard it somewhere. You could have been hunting and just happened to see what was going on. Then you decided to try to get what wasn't rightly yours. Why should we believe you?"

Finn rubbed the back of his neck. "There was a map Suggs gave you. It had an $X$ on it that marked where we buried one of the money chests in a cave on the mountain. Huge creatures attacked us as we were burying it. They killed some of our crew. I barely escaped. I have never seen animals that big. And they smelled terrible. Like rotting dead animals, or a bunch of skunks." Finn shuddered as he told the Barretts about the creatures. "The captain didn't make it. He told me to run, and I took off as fast as I could. The captain must have given the map to Suggs. He had slash marks on his chest similar to these on my back." Finn lifted up his shirt and turned around to show the claw marks.

Emma and Sam both gasped.

"Looks like you're telling the truth," Sam said. "So, Emma, what do we do now?"

Emma shrugged. "I don't know."

She straightened her dress and looked directly into Finn's eyes. "It'll be getting dark soon. Where have you been staying? We'll take you there, and we can talk more about this in the morning."

"I've been sleeping in the woods around town."

"What?" Emma asked. "That won't do. You're staying with us."

"Wait…wait a minute," Sam said. "Let's talk this over, sweetheart."

"Give us a second," Emma said as she and Sam walked a few feet away.

Sam pleaded with her. "We can't have a pirate boy staying at our house. He'll rob us and maybe even kill us if he has a chance. Who knows what he learned on that ship? Those were really bad men, Emma."

"I understand, but we can't let him live in the woods," Emma whispered. "He's just a boy. It will only be for a day or two. We can set rules, and if he does anything wrong, we can tell the authorities."

"We should inform them about him anyway. All that money was stolen. I don't like it. I don't like it one bit, but I'll go along with this for one night, and one night only."

Emma smiled as she walked over to Finn. "You will be staying with us until we can figure this all out. We will not be having you staying in the woods. You can help us with some of the chores around here."

Finn looked at Sam. "Are you good with that?"

Sam narrowed his eyes at Finn and leaned into him. "You can stay one night. If you do anything to make me question our good intentions, I will haul you down to the authorities and see to it they throw you in jail where you belong. Do we have an understanding?"

"That'll do, Samuel," Emma demanded. She put a hand on Finn's shoulder. "You won't cause any trouble, will you? It'll be nice having another man around here to help out."

"I would like to stay until I get my money," Finn said. "I won't cause you any trouble."

"There, that's settled," Emma said. She took Finn's hand and walked him into the house.

# 57

EMMA DID HER best to make Finn feel welcome and at home. She fixed up the second bedroom. She put on clean bedsheets. She placed a small rushlight on the side table for him to see at night. She placed a basin, a pitcher of water, and a sponge and clean rag on the other bedside table for him to use if he wanted. Emma put a slice of apple pie on a plate and handed it to Finn. "Here's another piece for you, in case you get hungry. You let me know if you need anything tonight. Here's a glass of water too. We can talk a little more in the morning. Get a good night's sleep."

"Thank you, ma'am."

Sam shook his head as Emma sat down beside him. "Aren't you kind of overdoing it?"

"Just being friendly. You could be nicer to the boy."

"Letting him stay the night is friendly enough," Sam said as he put his hand on a loaded pistol on the table next to him. "I'm keeping my eye on him. He's young, but I'm sure he wasn't a choir boy living on that ship. No doubt he learned a lot of bad habits living among those thieves."

"Put the gun away, Samuel."

"Just a little insurance. I'm certain he saw it as he went into the bedroom. Don't want him thinking we're Quakers."

"You're ridiculous. This will be the best night's sleep he's had in a long time. He won't give us any problems."

"I hope you're right, but this won't be the best night's sleep I've ever had."

"Come to bed. We'll talk with him more in the morning."

Sam was up at dawn and peeked into the second bedroom to make sure Finn was still there. Finn was sound asleep with the covers pulled tightly around his neck. He looked, to Sam, like any eleven-year-old lying there, not at all like a pirate boy involved in robbing ships around the world. Sam quietly closed the door and stepped outside on the porch. *How could a kid get involved with pirates? Maybe Emma's right. I could ease up on him a bit.*

Emma walked outside and sat on the rocking chair next to Sam. "I looked in on Finn. He's sound asleep."

"Me too. Wonder how long he'll sleep?"

"Should we wake him?"

"How about in an hour or so if he's still sleeping."

Emma smiled at Sam and gave him a kiss on the cheek. "Thanks for not being too hard on him. You're a good man."

Sam smiled back. "You're making me soft. In the old days I'd have kicked him off our property in a second."

The door opened and Finn walked onto the porch.

"Good day," Emma said. "How'd you sleep?"

"Fine."

Emma patted her stomach. "Want any breakfast?"

"I guess."

"How about you help Sam feed the pigs and chickens, while I fix us up something to eat? How about bacon and eggs and biscuits?"

Finn looked at Sam. Sam nodded. "I'll have whatever you're having. Thanks."

Sam winked at Emma and tapped Finn on the shoulder. "Follow me. Ever feed farm animals?"

Finn lowered his head. "No."

"It's easy. Grab a handful from the bag over there and toss it to the pigs. Do that a few times, and I'll do the same for the chickens."

Finn nodded.

Both Sam and Finn eased up some around each other. Neither spoke for a few minutes, and then Sam broke the silence. "So, how'd you get involved with pirates?"

"Um, I don't know."

"You don't know, or you aren't sayin'?"

Finn had never been around a family before and wondered if this is what it would have been like if he had ever been adopted from the orphanage. He decided to tell Sam what had happened. "I ran away from an orphanage in Ireland and hid out on a ship. They let me stay on as a cabin boy. It started out being a privateering vessel but ended up being a pirate ship."

"That's some adventure. You said you were in an orphanage in Ireland?"

"Yes."

"Which one?"

"St. Anthony's."

"St. Anthony's in Derry?"

"Yes, you heard of it?"

"I was there too. Why'd you run away?"

Finn's eyes lit up. *Maybe Sam wasn't that bad after all.* "The head lady didn't like me very much. She overheard me saying something about her and whacked me in the head one too many times. I took off, and that was that."

Sam looked over his shoulder at the house to see if Emma was near. "Big, fat lady?"

"Yes, Mrs. Runion. Was she there when you were there?"

"She was, and nobody liked her. What'd you say that got you in trouble?"

"I made up a rhyme about her and was telling it to my friends when she walked in."

"You've got to tell me what you said."

Finn chuckled. "Mrs. Runion is no funion 'cause she weighs a tonion."

Sam laughed so hard he had to hold on to his knees. "That's great. I bet she was really mad."

"Sure was. I was saying it over and over and everyone was giggling. She came in and heard me and smacked me pretty hard."

Sam said the rhyme over and over, and both he and Finn laughed loud enough that Emma came outside.

"What's going on with you two?" Emma asked.

Sam gathered himself and straightened up. "Oh, nothing."

"Sounds like you're getting along. Come inside. Breakfast is ready."

Emma made enough food to feed five people.

Finn began to eat when Emma cleared her throat. "Let us pray. Lord, we thank you for this food and for Finn joining us. Also, thank you for this wonderful day. Amen."

"Amen," Sam said.

"Amen," Finn mumbled.

Both Finn and Sam were digging into their food when Emma interrupted. "So, what were you two laughing about?"

"Turns out Finn used to be at St. Anthony's orphanage in Derry like me. He was telling me a funny rhyme he made about that mean headmistress I've told you about. I don't think you'd like it though."

"I'm not an old lady. Go ahead and tell me."

Finn looked at Sam, who nodded to go ahead. "Mrs. Runion is no funion 'cause she weighs a tonion."

Emma chuckled then burst out laughing. Before long all three were laughing and smiling at each other.

Finn looked at Sam and Emma and realized how nice they really were. He felt badly about rudely demanding his money earlier, but he still wanted to get as much of it as he could. He just didn't want to harm them to get it. He decided to leave well enough alone and go back up the mountain and tell Avery and Nash what he learned in town. Maybe he would tell them about the Barretts, maybe not. He hadn't worked it all out in his head yet.

Finn pushed his plate forward. "I should go."

"You leaving already?" Emma asked.

"I shouldn't have come. I'll leave you be. Thanks for the food and letting me sleep here last night."

"What about the money?" Sam asked.

"I do want it back. Do you have it here?"

"Come on…I wouldn't tell you even if I did. Think about it. Avery and his crew stole that money. We couldn't just give it to you, even if we wanted to. Plus, what would you do with it? The authorities would be after you for the rest of your life. You can't live that way."

"Don't worry about me. I'll be fine."

Emma walked over to Finn and put her hand on his shoulder. "But where will you go?"

"I met some sailors in town who could use a good cabin boy. I'll go work with them. Thanks for…everything."

Sam shrugged and shook Finn's hand. "Just so you know, we don't have any of the money here. It's all in the bank. If you ever want to come back…"

"Thanks," Finn said, and then walked out of the house. He walked a few feet and turned around. Sam and Emma waved. He waved back, turned around, and continued to walk toward town.

# 58

HERNDON TOOK A deep breath and then knocked on the governor's door. "Sir, it's twelve o'clock and we haven't seen nor heard from the officers."

Fletcher sighed and drummed his fingers on his desk. "Something must have happened. They should have been back by now."

"Yes, sir."

"Inform Officer Scouse to gather ten sailors and come to my office."

"Yes, sir."

Fifteen minutes later, Herndon returned.

"Come in," Fletcher said.

Herndon opened the door and stepped inside. "Governor, the men are here."

"Send them in."

The officers walked single file into the room and stood at attention. Fletcher walked in front of his desk and put his arms behind his back. "Gentlemen, what I am about to tell you must remain confidential. It is not to leave this room. Yesterday morning, Officer Martin sailed with ten men and an equal contingent from the *Ganj-i-Sawai* up the Hudson. Their plan was to hike up Bear Mountain to retrieve, what we surmise, is a treasure buried in a cave by the dead pirates we found on Salisbury Island. Officer Martin and the others have not returned. We are concerned something may have happened to them.

They should have gotten back last night. Your mission is to go find them. Their ship should be close to the base of Bear Mountain near Salisbury Island. Any questions?"

"No, sir," the officers said in unison.

"Very well, then. Godspeed."

IT TOOK SCOUSE and his men three hours to sail up the Hudson River before they spotted the ship anchored where the governor told them it should be.

Scouse shouted at the two sailors who remained behind to guard the vessel. "Officers, the governor sent us to see if there's been a problem. You were expected back yesterday."

"Officer Scouse, good to see you, sir," Hitchcock yelled. "The captain and the others haven't returned. They left yesterday morning, but we haven't seen them since. Don't know what happened."

"I've brought ten men to find them. I understand they went up the mountain looking for a cave?"

"That's correct. If you don't mind, we would like to go up with you to look for them."

"I understand. I'll leave four of my men back to watch our ships. Which direction did they go?"

Hitchcock pointed up the hill. "Sir, they walked straight up there."

Scouse nodded. "They should have left a pretty easy path to follow with all those men. Let's see if we can find them. Hopefully, we'll run into them on their way down."

Scouse and the others followed the trail left by Martin, Kalam, and their men for several hours, not finding any trace of them when Scouse cocked his head and held up his hand. "Stop. Did you hear that?"

"No, sir, I didn't hear anything," Hitchcock replied, looking around.

"It sounded like someone was banging on a tree," Scouse said. Then, pointing to his right, he shouted, "There it is again, over there."

"I heard it that time. Do you think it's the captain trying to signal us?"

"Only one way to find out. The first five in line come with me, and the rest stay here."

Scouse and the others pushed through the thick brush, slowly walking toward where they heard the knocking. They came to an enormous oak tree but didn't see anyone or anything. The forest surrounding them was quiet. No birds were chirping. No small animals were running around. The officers looked at each other and shrugged.

One of the men leaned in toward Scouse. "It's almost too quiet, sir. You know what I mean?"

Scouse nodded, cupped his hands, and yelled, "Captain Martin." Hearing nothing, he yelled again, "Captain Martin."

"I don't think anyone's around here, sir," Hitchcock said.

"I keep getting the feeling someone's watching us."

"Yes, sir. I do too."

"Let's head back to the others."

They returned to the trail to see the five officers left behind kneeling and pointing their rifles in all directions.

"Rogers, what's going on?" whispered Scouse as he and the others with him pointed their rifles here and there.

"Somebody's been throwing rocks at us, sir," Rogers whispered. "Must be a bunch of them 'cause they've been coming from all over the place. But we haven't seen anyone. Some of the rocks are pretty big too. One hit Fredericks in the head." Rogers pointed to a red maple tree. "He's knocked out over there."

"Did you see Captain Martin or anyone in the woods?"

"No, sir. This place is getting stranger and stranger by the minute. We thought someone was watching us when we tried to find where that banging sound came from." Scouse looked around. "Can't be the Haverstraws. They don't come up here. They're afraid."

"Afraid of what?" Rogers asked.

"Creatures. Haverstraw call them something that sounds like 'muh-hoo-way.' They believe they're kind of like cannibals. My father told me about them. Said he saw one once. It was huge."

"Sir, may I have a word with you in private?" Rogers asked Scouse.

They walked away from the other officers.

"Creatures?" Rogers whispered. "No time for jokes. I'm your best friend and can put up with your silliness. But if you continue to talk like that, the men will think you're crazy."

"I'm serious. There are creatures up here. But enough of that for now. Let's get back to the business at hand."

Scouse gathered the officers. "We're going to follow the path Captain Martin left, but keep an eye out. I need a volunteer to stay back with Fredericks."

Bradley, raised his hand.

"Thank you. Fire a shot if you have any trouble. We should be near the top of the mountain soon."

The officers walked another fifteen minutes when they all covered their noses and waved their hands across their faces.

"Smells like a skunk or…" Scouse said, and then paused. He raised his eyebrows at Rogers. "Dad said they stink too."

They walked twenty yards and saw Captain Martin lying on the ground not far from a cave. Scouse ran over to him and put three fingers on his neck. He looked at his officers and shook his head. He took off his hat, said a quick prayer, and crossed himself.

Scouse stood and faced his officers. "Keep a sharp lookout."

He pointed to two men. "You go to the left of the cave."

Scouse pointed to two others. "You two go to the right. The rest of us will spread out across the front. Now, slowly advance. Only fire if I give the command."

The officers inched up to and around the cave as a hail of rocks were thrown at them.

"Retreat, retreat," Scouse shouted.

They ran back twenty yards.

"Stop," Scouse yelled in a panicked voice. "Gather around. I told you Rogers. They're enormous. Look part man too."

"I'm not…going back there!" one of the officers stuttered, his eyes on a swivel. "They'll kill all of us, like they killed the captain and the others."

"Let's all calm down," Scouse said as he steadied himself. "We're no good to anyone if we don't think this through. Now, what have we learned? The captain is dead. The front part of the cave is blocked with stones. We didn't see any of our officers, nor Captain Kalam's. There is a great stench around the cave. Hate to say it, but it smells like death."

"Sir," Rogers said. "I don't think we can get close to the cave without a big fight on our hands. We have half the men Captain Martin had, and it looks like they were all killed."

"We don't know for sure whether they're all dead or not," Scouse said. "But I understand what you're saying. I don't want to leave without knowing for sure about our fellow officers. I didn't see anyone but Captain Martin's body. Even though I am in charge, I will not command anyone to go back to that cave. I'm going in there. We need to find out whether anyone's alive. Are there any volunteers who'll go with me?"

One man raised his hand, then another, then another, until they all had their right hands lifted above their heads.

"Thank you, men. Make sure your rifles and pistols are primed. I saw some of the creatures above the cave and in the woods. I'll go first. Hopefully, we'll just get rocks thrown at us. We'll fan out once we're near the opening to the cave. Let's go."

# 59

THE NINE-FOOT TALL, seven-hundred-pound *Mhuwe* crouched on all fours in the back of the cave. It lifted its head and sniffed the air. Human scent again. It quietly grunted and moved its head left and right. Four other *Mhuwe* backed out of the way as the giant creature walked toward the front of the cave. It crouched and looked at the other *Mhuwe*. They crept back. It scowled as it peered through an opening in the boulders and saw humans walking toward the cave.

The men crept up the trail, coming closer to the cave's entrance. They looked at each other and shrugged. They didn't hear anything other than a slight rustling of the leaves. No rocks were being thrown at them, and they didn't see any of the creatures above the cave nor in the surrounding woods.

"Where'd they go?" whispered Scouse to no one in particular. "Keep a sharp lookout. I'm going to climb over the boulders and get a look inside."

Scouse pulled himself on top of several boulders. He looked at a gap between two boulders just large enough for him to put his head through. He turned back toward the men. "I'm going to take a look inside. Fire if any of the creatures start to attack." He held his breath and stuck his head between the two boulders.

The rest of the *Mhuwe* in the cave backed up mimicking their leader.

Scouse could barely see inside so he waited a few seconds for his eyes to become accustomed to the dark. He noticed all the dead bodies of his fellow officers and those from the *Ganj-i-Sawai* near the opening of the cave. He pulled his head back out and looked at his officers. "They're all dead. I'm going to take another look to see if I spot any of the treasure. Everything quiet out here?"

"Yes," Rogers replied. "Need any help?"

"No, I'm good. Just going to take another quick look."

The biggest *Mhuwe* quietly grunted at the others, and they slowly followed it to the front of the cave. It crouched on its hind legs as it raised its enormous hands.

Scouse put his head between the two boulders and started to scan the cavern when the *Mhuwe* grabbed his head. The creature let out an enormous roar that rattled the walls of the cave.

"Help, help," Scouse screamed.

Rogers ran to his friend. Several officers tried to pull Scouse out, but the beast was too strong. Growls came from within the cave, and then Scouse's body went limp. Another howl came from the top of the hill above the cave, followed by rocks being thrown at the men from all directions.

"Fire," Rogers yelled as he aimed his rifle at a creature atop the hill, his hands trembling.

The men shot aimlessly into the forest and above the cave, hitting nothing.

Trees swayed as creatures swung from limb to limb, howling at the men below. Several of the beasts ran out of the woods toward the men. Dust kicked up, preventing the officers from seeing clearly. Several pointed at the creatures, desperate to scream, but their voices failed them. Three *Mhuwe* jumped from trees fifteen feet above and landed on top of three of the officers. They pulverized the men with their massive fists and stomped on them with their massive feet.

"Run," several men yelled as they ran back down the path, rocks still being hurled at them. They didn't stop running until they were a good half mile from the cave. Out of breath, the officers leaned against trees and one another as they tried to make sense out of what just happened.

"My God, what were those things?" one of the men cried out.

"I don't know," another yelled.

"They're those muh-hoo-way Scouse told us about," Rogers said, looking at the ground. "The muh-hoo-way."

Rogers said a quick prayer to himself for his friend. He crossed himself, shook his head, and then spoke barely above a whisper. "How many of us are left?"

"Four, sir," one of the officers said.

"Well, there's not going to be any more of us dying today. Let's head back."

An hour later, four ashen-faced officers walked the path with their heads down, and their rifles dragging on the ground when they met up with Fredericks and Bradley.

"What happened?" Bradley asked. "You look like you've been through a war."

"Where are the others?" Fredericks asked.

"Dead," Rogers said. "We're going back to the ship. Tell you what happened on the way. How's Fredericks?"

"Still out, sir."

"We'll take turns carrying him. Two of you grab him and let's go."

The officers heard a loud roar, and trees toppled over in the nearby woods.

The men looked at each other and then ran down the path. They kept looking back, expecting creatures to jump out at them. They tried to prime their rifles as they ran but kept tripping over rocks and branches.

The howls got louder, and sticks and rocks were thrown at the men. It felt as if the ground were shaking from the weight of the enormous creatures. The sound grew louder and louder. The rocks and sticks landed closer to the officers.

Then...silence. The noise stopped as quickly as it began.

"Keep running," Rogers screamed. "Don't look back. Keep running."

# 60

HERNDON RUBBED HIS eyes. He held his breath and knocked on Governor Fletcher's door.

"Come in," Fletcher said.

"Sir, I have more bad news. I should let Officer Rogers tell you what happened."

Fletcher shook his head, put down the pen on the papers he was signing, and sighed. "Have him come in."

Rogers stood at attention as he tried to gather his thoughts. "Sir, I don't know how to tell you what happened. They're all, they're all…"

"Say it, man," Fletcher demanded.

"They're all dead, sir. Captain Martin and all the others are dead, sir. Officer Scouse is dead too. Only a few of us made it back. There were massive creatures, sir. Larger than anything I've ever seen."

"*Mhuwe.*"

"You've heard of them, sir?"

"Yes, but I figured they were just bears."

"The *Mhuwe*—they're the ones who killed everybody, sir. Sir, they're gigantic. Half-ape, half-human looking, seven to nine feet tall and weighing over six-hundred pounds if not more."

"Are you sure those weren't men dressed up with animal furs?"

"Couldn't have been, sir. They were too big to be men. And they were throwing boulders at us like they were pebbles. They jumped down on us from high up in the trees. They killed men instantly with just a swing of their huge arms and fists. No man is that strong or can

238

jump down from that high. Impossible. It's difficult to believe, sir. I wouldn't unless I saw it myself."

"No one is alive except those of you who made it back?"

"It sickens me to say it, but that's correct, sir. And I think it would take a small army to take on and beat those creatures."

Fletcher shook his head in disgust and slammed his fist on his desk. "It's like that treasure in the cave is cursed. Nearly everyone who comes near it meets with death." Fletcher threw his glass against the wall, smashing it into tiny pieces.

Herndon took a step back. "Sir?"

"I apologize for my outburst. Those officers are dead on my watch. Rogers, please feel free to take a couple of days off to be with your family after such a tragic day. I thank you for your service." Fletcher shook Rogers' hand and put his hand on his shoulder.

"Thank you, Governor," Rogers said. He saluted and left Fletcher alone with Herndon.

Fletcher turned to Herndon and pointed for him to sit in the chair in front of his desk. "My God. Treasure, pirates, *Mhuwe*, and all in a few days' time. I hate to think what'll happen next. I have no idea what to tell Mr. Ibrahim. He might believe we're trying to keep all the treasure for ourselves and Mother England."

"I'm sure he won't think that, sir."

"You're right. He might if only *his* men were dead, but ours are dead too."

"What do you want to do, sir?"

"I'm not sure, to be perfectly honest with you. The treasure is not worth all of those men's lives. I will not send another contingent of my officers to that cave. Ask Mr. Ibrahim to come see me. I'll tell him what happened."

"Yes, sir."

# 61

"WHAT IN THE world were you thinking?" Avery shouted at Finn. "You're lucky you didn't end up in prison."

Finn continued to stand behind Nash, looking at the ground. "I'm...I'm...sorry. There were a lot of guards around the bank. I didn't think we could ever get the money. I was hoping the Barretts might have their share of the treasure on their property, and I could at least get some of it for us."

Nash put a hand on Avery's arm to calm him and then turned towards Finn. "Looks like you're no worse for wear and didn't end up in jail. Doesn't appear anyone followed you either, or we'd know by now. Why don't you tell us what you learned?"

"There are five guards in the front of the bank, and five in the back. Each is carrying rifles and pistols. I pretended I wanted to open an account, and a man who worked there gave me some good information. He said the governor was storing the money from the treasure in there before it's sent to England in a week or two. Also, the Barretts are keeping their money there too. None of their money is at their place. And, the money chest is back on the *Ganj-i-Sawai*."

Avery unclenched his jaw and forced a smile. "Excellent work, Finn. Sorry I got so mad earlier. I guess I was just...worried about you."

"Thanks, Captain."

Avery nodded. "How many guards are inside?"

"I counted three, but I'm not sure if there are any in the back room with the money."

"That sounds about right. I doubt there are any in there, but you never know." Avery tapped his finger on his chin.

"What're you thinking?" Nash asked.

"It's pretty farfetched, but do you know what happened to the British soldiers at Bacon's Rebellion?"

"No."

"First, is there any jimsonweed up here on the mountain?"

"Never heard of it."

"It's called by a lot of different names—Devil's snare, Devil's weed, Jamestown weed, stinkweed…"

"D'ye say Jamestown weed?"

"Yes."

Nash nodded. "There's a ton of it not too far from here. But what…ohhh, I see where you're going with this."

"What are you two talking about?" Finn asked.

Avery laughed. "Back in 1676, the British soldiers accidentally poisoned themselves with that weed. They were trying to hold back Bacon's Rebellion in Jamestown, Virginia. The stupid British soldiers put the weed in their salads. They didn't know what it was and started hallucinating and acting crazy for a while. The soldiers ended up lying on the ground seeing things. A few even took off their clothes, and others acted like monkeys. Some blew kisses at people. It apparently was hilarious. That's why some call it Jamestown weed. It would be a whole lot easier to break into the bank if we could get the men guarding it to somehow either eat or drink some of it."

"Sure would," Nash replied. "It'd be easier, too, if we could rob them before they move the money. But we've got to learn when they're moving it. Not an easy task. They aren't just going to tell us, and we can't sit around waiting for them to move it and then drug the guards. We have to find out ahead of time."

Finn held up a hand like he was in school. "I bet I can get information from that bank manager. I told him I was going to ask my folks if I could put my money there. People may be on the lookout for Captain, but they probably don't remember you, Nash. You could go with me as my grandfather, and…"

"Hey, I'm not that old," Nash said. "I'm Avery's age. I've just been through a lot."

"Sorry, you know what I mean. You can sign as an adult for me on the account. I'll tell him we want to see what the vault room looks like to make sure my money will be safe. We can trick him into telling us something about when they'll be moving the money. He loves to brag."

Nash smiled and looked over at Avery. "You taught the kid well. He sure does think like a pirate."

Avery frowned. "I taught him a little too well. Most of us are either dead or in prison. The *Ganj-i-Sawai* was supposed to be our last robbery and then we were going to make a fresh start."

"Come on, Captain," Finn pleaded. "We can plunder one more place. "We get back the loot and go somewhere where nobody knows us."

Nash held his hand up like Finn did earlier. "Aren't you two forgetting about the money chest on the *Ganj-i-Sawai*? You just going to let all them jewels get away?"

Avery shrugged. "Not sure what to do about that. They're a fortune all by themselves. I don't want to let the chest just slip away, but it'll be tougher to get it off the ship than stealing the money in the bank. Who knows how many sailors are on that ship? We can't simply drug all of them, and then board the ship like it's our own. I'm sure they'd shoot me at first sight, especially Captain Ibrahim."

# 62

IBRAHIM PUT HIS hands on his head and squeezed his eyes shut. "They're all dead? How can that be? Twenty men went up the mountain."

"This may be difficult to believe," Fletcher said. "It was hard for me to accept at first, but what I'm about to tell you really happened."

"Yes, Governor?"

"There is a cave on Bear Mountain where the pirates put part of the treasure they stole from you. Most of them died because of…" Fletcher could hardly get the words out. He wiped his forehead with his hand as he recounted what occurred.

Ibrahim nodded and sighed. "I have heard of such creatures. We have them in India too. We call them *Mande Barung*. Ours live high in the mountains. Most people say they are only a legend, but my father saw one when he was on pilgrimage alone on a mountaintop."

"Well, I must say I am glad you believe me. I was concerned you'd think I was making it all up."

Ibrahim sat and shook his head. "I believe you. The creature my father saw roared at him, and my father ran. He said it made the hair on the back of his neck stand up. Father, too, talked about how large it was and how it looked like a man and an ape."

"I've been on Bear Mountain but not as high up as the cave. Can't say I have ever seen or heard them."

"Villagers who reside near our mountaintop say similar things about these animals. They live hidden in the woods and are rarely seen. But when they are accidentally stumbled upon or startled, they become extremely territorial and aggressive. They are also said to have gigantic feet."

"It's simply incredible."

Ibrahim frowned. "I'm sorry all those people have died trying to regain our stolen treasure. I am of the belief there isn't any amount of money worth a person's life. However, between us, I am not sure my emperor feels the same, especially about his treasure."

"I understand. But I cannot send any more of my officers to that cave. It is too dangerous, and I won't risk any more lives."

"Will you agree to allow my men to go on the mountain without any of your officers?"

"If you wish."

"I'll speak to those onboard the *Ganj-i-Sawai* and leave it up to a vote. Of course, we will split the findings with you according to our agreement."

"That'll be fine with me."

"Thank you, sir. I am sure many of the crew want to retrieve the emperor's treasure. I'll be back shortly with our answer, and at that time request information from you as to where to find the cave."

"Very well, Mr. Ibrahim. I await your return."

# 63

"LET'S GO OVER our stories one more time," Nash said.

Finn dropped his head and kicked at a rock. "Really. Do we have to? We've gone over it a million times already."

"Just once more. We need this to come off as naturally as possible."

"So, you're my grandfather. My parents couldn't come with me because of a personal matter. You are here with me to sign on my account as a relative. My parents and you have given me permission to put my money in the bank if it meets with your approval. Our names are both David Cussler, since I was named after you. We are depositing £5. You have the coins in your coat pocket. You would like to go in the back where they'll be putting my money. You came to make sure it looks secure enough before you will sign. You'll ask why there are so many guards outside the building and try to get him to tell us when they're taking the money out to go to England. I am to let you do all the talking, unless the manager asks me something directly. We'll be polite, and if he becomes suspicious, you will say you have to think about it some more and will be back with your decision in a day or two. How'd I do?"

"Perfect. You ready to go in?"

"Let's do it."

Finn and Nash walked toward the bank. Nash tipped his hat at the ladies as they passed. They tried to blend into the crowd, walking without drawing any attention to themselves. At the same time, they took a mental picture of everything they saw in case it would come in handy later.

Nash had on his best clothes, which made him look less like a mountain man, but barely. Finn had on the same pair of pants he wore when he first went to the bank, but he had put on a different shirt so he wouldn't appear as only having one pair. Nash nodded at the five guards standing at attention in front of the building and held the door open for Finn to walk inside.

They stood in the entrance looking for the man Finn spoke with earlier. Nash tapped Finn on the shoulder when he saw a man wave at him.

"Hi. Come on over," the manager said.

"Good day, sir," Nash said as he shook his hand. "My name is David Cussler, and I understand you have already met my grandson, David."

"Yes, I met David the other day. My name is Gareth Pope. I hope you are here to open an account for this fine young man."

"We'll see. I am here with my namesake, since his parents were called away due to a personal matter."

Pope puffed out his chest. "I can assure you, sir, we have the finest bank in all the land, if not the world."

"That's mighty high praise, sir. My grandson deserves the very best place to keep his money. Before I sign for him, I wish to see where his money will be kept. I have always found it is best to see things for oneself."

"I completely understand. Please follow me."

They looked around the vault room, taking it all in. Nash winked at Finn.

Pope opened a cabinet. "As you can see, we have areas of the room sectioned off with cabinets and shelves with customers' names on them."

"Wow," Finn said.

Pope smiled. "Your name will be on one of these shelves, if you put your money in our bank."

Nash scrunched his eyebrows. "May I ask if all those guards out front are always there?"

"Well…" Pope whispered as he leaned toward Nash, and he nodded at Finn. "I can see your grandson has not told you my secret about why we have so many guards here. I'm sure I can trust you too."

Nash put his hand over his heart. "You can trust me without reservation. You have my word."

Pope leaned even closer to Nash. "I have no doubt. We normally only have the three guards you have undoubtedly seen inside the lobby. They leave when the bank is closed at five. The guards out front, and I assure there are five more in the back, are here because of the large amount of money the governor is keeping here.

"I see," Nash said.

"I don't mean to brag, but I wouldn't be surprised if I get a promotion out of this. I'm being entrusted to secure much more money than is usually kept in our fine bank."

Nash glanced at Finn. "Please go on."

"I mustn't. I've said too much already. Can't let my ego get ahead of me. It's just so exciting. I will tell you this though—it'll be gone late next Tuesday evening. I'll be here to let the guards in. Things will get back to normal after that."

Nash looked around the room as if others might overhear him. "What happens next Tuesday?"

Pope grinned. "See that cabinet over in the corner?"

"Yes."

"That money is going to England. To the king himself."

Nash put his arm around Finn and nodded. "Well, if the governor keeps England's money here…that is a very good sign. I conclude your money will be safe here too, David."

"I assure you we will take excellent care of your grandson's money,"

Pope said as he raised his chin and stood straight. "We have taken extraordinary measures to ensure this bank is safe."

"I can see that. I'll sign the paperwork."

"Outstanding, sir," Pope said, smiling. "Please follow me back to my desk."

After signing the forms and depositing the money, Nash and Finn walked quickly to the ferry.

"Next Tuesday doesn't leave us much time to get prepared," Nash whispered to Finn as they leaned against the railing of the ferry.

"I know. I hope the captain was able to get some Jamestown weed. We only have one week before they move the money."

"Not to step on Avery's toes, but we'll also need an escape plan. Getting the money is one thing. Taking it out of there without getting caught and hiding the money is another. I have some ideas, but Avery's in charge, so I'll see what he's decided."

"Captain's always two steps ahead. I bet he's already figured out what to do next."

"You going to stay with him after we're finished robbing them?"

"I sure am. He's never done me wrong. He can also teach me what to do with the money I'll be gettin'."

"If you ever run into trouble you can always come back up the mountain and hide out with me."

"Thanks. You never know. I may need to take you up on that."

"Looks like our stop's up ahead. It'll take us a couple of hours to hike back up to camp. I bet Avery can't wait to hear what we learned."

# 64

"I FILLED THREE bags with Jamestown weed," Avery said and then laughed. "That should be enough to knock out a horse. So, tell me… what'd you learn?"

"You've been busy," Nash replied. "Well, we have good news and bad news. The good news is they're only having the ten guards move the money to their ship in the middle of the night. We think the banker we spoke to will be alone letting the guards in. Bad news is it's happening one week from today."

Avery nodded. "I guess those ten guards are the five outside in the front and five out back?"

Nash reached down and scratched Cutie Pie behind her ears. "I'm sure they are. So, you got any plans on how we're going to move the money and hide it once we get it?"

"Here's what I'm thinking," Avery said as he began drawing on the ground with a stick. "Here's the bank. Finn walks over to the guards in the back with a bucket of tea with the weed in it. He says his mother told him to give the guards something to drink. Then he goes and does the same thing to the guards in the front of the building, and then gives some tea to that manager inside."

"Not bad," Nash said.

"That'll be easy for me to do," Finn said.

Avery stirred the Jamestown weed tea in the pot. "I hope they're in the mood for tea. We need to test how long it'll take to work." Avery grinned at Nash. "I'll do it, unless you feel a great urge to try it."

Nash shook his head and held up his hands. "No, you feel free to go ahead and drink that stuff."

Avery shrugged. "I'll test it. I'm probably bigger than those guards, so it should work quicker on them. Make sure I don't do anything too crazy."

Finn and Nash smiled at each other. "Sure thing," Nash said. "We'll make sure you don't do anything too foolish."

"You promise?"

Finn snickered. "Absolutely, Captain."

"We'll also need to get a horse and carriage. Once the guards and banker are knocked out, we grab the key, get the money, and take off. I'm guessing we'll have about a half hour before the captain of the ship will wonder why the guards aren't there. By then we should be long gone."

Nash stroked his beard. "Got any ideas where we'll hide out?"

"I was hoping you might know a place for us to sneak away for a few days."

"There used to be a small abandoned cabin about three miles out of town. I haven't been there in a few years, and even then, it was falling apart. But that might be a good place to hide out for a while. Where'll we be going after that?"

"We'll need you to go back into town and buy a small boat for us to sail upriver. If it's all right with you, I was hoping we could stay with you on the mountain for a while until things settle down."

Nash nodded. "No problem. Stay as long as you want."

"Of course, we'll split the money three ways, between you, me, and Finn."

"I get a full share?" Finn said, wide-eyed.

"You deserve it." Avery smiled. "I'll help you figure out what to do with it once we get settled."

"That's great. Thank you, Captain."

"My pleasure," Avery said as he put his hand on Finn's shoulder. "So, how does the plan sound to you, Nash?"

"Not bad. Not bad at all. I appreciate you splitting the money three ways. Any plans for the money chest on the *Ganj-i-Sawai*?"

"No, to be honest with you. I've been thinking and thinking trying to come up with something, but I can't figure out how to get on that ship while it's in port. If we were out at sea and we had a crew, I could take it then. But I don't see how we can rob it with only the three of us. Plus, who knows how long it will stay in New York?"

Nash scratched his chin. "That's a tough one. Not sure how we're going to get it off their ship."

Avery shrugged. "Let's focus first on getting the money out of the bank. Guess I should drink some of this Jamestown weed. I'm hoping it works fast."

Avery slowly sipped the concoction from the cup. "Tastes like a normal cup of tea. Finn, you start counting to see how long it takes for me to start acting funny."

A minute later, Avery frowned. "Would you take off that silly looking hat? And where d'ye get that bird on your shoulder? Looks like the parrot Seeds kept."

Finn and Nash looked at each other and snickered.

"Looks like it's already working," Nash said.

Avery sat on a log and yawned. "I'm going to take a nap for a little bit. Would you two mind leaving my room for a while so I can get some rest? And tell those children to stop playing outside my house. They're making enough noise to wake up the dead."

"All right, Captain," Finn said, smiling.

An hour later, Avery came out of the hut holding his head. "I've got a splitting headache. I don't remember what happened after I drank the tea. Did I do anything crazy?"

"You weren't too bad," Finn said, laughing. "You started seeing things and wanted to sleep. It only took a minute or so before it began working. Must be pretty strong."

"How long was I out?"

"About an hour," Finn said. He looked at the ground, digging his toe into the dirt. He didn't look at the captain. "Captain, I was wondering…Um…I was wondering…"

"What is it?"

"Well, the Barretts were great and didn't report me to the authorities. I was wondering if we could leave their money in the bank. I'll give up half of my share to cover it."

"You'd do that?"

"Yes, sir. Mrs. Barrett was really nice, and Mr. Barrett was in the same orphanage I was in, so I know he had it pretty hard like me."

"I'll think about it," Avery said. "Not making you any promises, but I'll think about it."

# 65

IBRAHIM WALKED INTO the governor's office with his head held high. "Governor, all the men aboard the *Ganj-i-Sawai* requested to retrieve the money chest."

"I see. That is very brave of them."

"With your permission, we would like to leave immediately, so as to be on the mountain by early afternoon. I'd appreciate if you'd be so kind as to provide me with directions and a map."

Fletcher handed Ibrahim the copy of the map. "Of course. Mr. Herndon has already recreated the map for you. Just curious—How many men will you have with you on the mountain?"

"I plan on taking sixty-five heavily armed sailors with me. That should be enough to take care of any *Mande Barung* we may encounter."

"I recommend you anchor your ship around Salisbury Island and trek up the mountain there. I understand you'll find a trail that will lead you eventually to the cave. The officers who went before you most likely have cleared the path, making it easier to follow. I wish you luck."

"Thank you, sir," Ibrahim said. He bowed and left the room.

Fletcher pointed to the chair in front of him for Herndon to sit. "That many heavily armed men should be enough."

"I don't know what to think anymore, sir. Like you said, that money chest seems cursed. I hope they're able to retrieve it and not lose any men. I just don't have a good feeling about it."

"Me neither, but Ibrahim wants to bring back both money chests to the emperor. I'm sure he feels guilty for letting the *Ganj-i-Sawai* be looted in the first place and needs to redeem himself in the emperor's eyes."

"I can understand that. I hope he doesn't lose his life and any more in the process."

"Agreed. Changing subjects on you—are we set for moving the money out of the bank next Tuesday?"

"Yes, sir. As you ordered, the guards at the bank will move the gold and silver at precisely eleven o'clock p.m. to our ship. The street should be deserted at that time. Mr. Pope will let the guards in and bring them to the vault, and hand the money over to the guards for transport."

"Excellent. Captain Drinkwater will be waiting onboard with his crew. The ship will sail for England on Wednesday morning. I'm sure the king will be tremendously happy with what we send him."

"Indeed."

IT WAS RAINING hard and lightning crackled as Ibrahim stood on top of a wooden crate and pointed to several men. He was, once again, fully in charge of the ship. "The four of you stay here with the *Ganj-i-Sawai,* while the rest of us retrieve the money chest. We should be back by nightfall. I'm sure no pirates would dare try to take over the *Ganj-i-Sawai* here. They will expect a large crew onboard. Nevertheless, be alert at all times. Fire a cannon if you run into any trouble, and we will return immediately. As I told you earlier, the cave and the surrounding area have many *Mande Barung.* They have killed numerous men who were trying to retrieve the emperor's money chest. But I am sure they will be no match against all of us. Nevertheless, always be at the ready. Have your weapons primed and be alert. I'll let you know when we are close to the cave. It looks like, from the map, that it will take us two hours or more to get there." Ibrahim raised his sword high above his head. "I say, let's take back the emperor's money chest and return it to India."

A loud cheer rose among the crew. The men followed the trail in pairs for two hours without a single word spoken until Ibrahim raised his hand. He wiped the rain off his face as he pointed to the right of the trail. "The governor told me we will be close when we start to see trees bent over like the ones over there. The *Mande Barung* may start throwing stones at us. Be prepared."

"THERE ARE SIXTY, maybe seventy men coming up the mountain," Nash said, out of breath and soaking wet as he ran back to Avery and Finn. "They look like they're from India. They're each carrying a rifle and have pistols on them. I was out looking for more Jamestown weed, and I saw them about one hundred yards to our east and about five hundred yards from the cave."

"They just don't give up, do they?" Avery replied. "But this could work in our favor. They can't have too many crew back on the *Ganj-i-Sawai* with that many men coming up the mountain. The odds are better now for us to get that money chest off the ship. We won't have their entire crew to deal with. We'll need to head down to the water. Nash, do you have any bullets left?"

"Absolutely," Nash said with a grin. "Got bullets and even a couple more rifles stashed around these woods. Never can be too safe. Grab the rifles in the hut, and we'll get a couple more and extra bullets on our way."

THE CREW FROM the *Ganj-i-Sawai* crept along the trail looking for any sign of *Mande Barung*. The path was muddy and the men were drenched. Some were whispering prayers.

"HELP!" screamed six of the men at the back of the line as several bulky creatures thundered through the woods in a blur holding a man in each arm. The *Mande Barung* ran with the men to the other side of the trail and threw them on the ground. They stomped on them, killing them instantly. They glanced around and immediately ran off deeper in the forest.

"Fire," Ibrahim yelled as he ran toward the back of the line. The men turned around and shot hopelessly in the direction of the fleeing beasts.

"*Mande Barung*," several at the front of the line screamed before they were carried off and killed.

"Fire," Ibrahim yelled again as he ran forward. "We're surrounded," he shouted, and then fell over after a large rock hit him in the head.

Boulders and tree trunks rained down on the men as they fired aimlessly into the woods. The *Mande Barung* growled and jumped on the officers. They threw them against trees and stomped on them until all were dead. It took only two minutes for the creatures to kill everyone.

Streams of water mixed with the men's blood flowed down the trail. Rain fell harder and lightning struck a tree nearby.

Several of the creatures sniffed the air and moved aside as their leader walked amongst them. It snarled at the humans and let out a blood-curdling wail that could be heard throughout the mountain.

# 66

"WHAT WAS THAT," Finn asked, wide-eyed.

"That was a *Mhuwe*," Nash replied.

"I don't hear any more gunshots," Avery said. "That means either the men killed the *Mhuwe* or the *Mhuwe* killed the men. It sounded like one of our battles at sea. We better hurry, in case any of the crew are still alive and try to make a run for it back to the ship."

Nash pointed to a tree. "I've got three more rifles and a ton of bullets wrapped up and hidden in the trunk in that dead tree over there. Let's grab 'em and go."

Two hours later, the rain let up as Avery, Nash, and Finn were almost at the river. "Stop," Avery said as he held his arm out. "There's the *Ganj-i-Sawai*. I see four men with rifles. One aft, one at the bow, and the other two are near the middle of the ship. I don't see anyone else. Nash, you go to the right and Finn go to the left. I'll head straight toward them. If we fire a shot from the two rifles we each have, we'll make them think there's more of us than there are. Finn, I don't want you shooting at anyone. You shoot the mainmast and sails. Let's see if we can scare them into surrendering."

The three got to their places and Avery mouthed *one, two, three, shoot*. Shots ricocheted off the ship as the crew ducked and peeked over the railing trying to see where the shots came from.

"You are completely surrounded," Avery yelled. "You have ten seconds to throw your weapons overboard and come off the ship. If you don't…"

The officers shot wildly toward the woods, hitting only trees.

Avery, Nash, and Finn shot one round and then another at the ship before stopping.

The four sailors on the ship raised their hands. "We surrender, don't shoot." Then they threw their rifles overboard and climbed down.

"Hands on your head and slowly walk towards my voice," Avery yelled.

"Where are you?" shouted one of the men.

"Keep walking," Avery yelled back.

"Stop, that's good enough," Avery said. "Keep your hands on your head and get down on your knees."

The officers did as they were told.

Avery stepped out from behind a tree. "Men…out of the woods."

The crew shook their heads when they saw Avery, Nash, and Finn. "There is only three of you and one's a boy?" a crewmember asked.

"Got ya," Avery said as he pointed a rifle at the man. "Where's the money chest? I know it's on the ship. The rest of your crew aren't coming back. The creatures got them all, so you might as well hand it over. No need to try and be a hero."

"It's you," one of the officers said. "You robbed us in the Arabian Sea. My emperor will have your head."

"Maybe, but he's got to find me first. Where's the money chest?"

"We're not telling you."

"Very brave and very dumb of you," Avery said, and then slapped the crewman in the face.

"Let's just kill them all now," Nash said and winked at Avery. "We don't need them alive. They'll only slow us down."

"You're right. Say good-bye, men." Avery shot at the ground between two of the crew.

"No...no. Don't shoot us. It's on the third level next to the captain's quarters."

"Nash, you keep watch over them while Finn and I get the money chest," Avery said. "Here're two more rifles. One for each of them if they get any ideas."

"You got it," Nash said, pointing two of the rifles at the men and laying the other two next to him. "No sudden moves, gentlemen."

Avery and Finn admired the ship as they made their way to where the money chest was stored.

"This ship truly is magnificent," Avery said. "I didn't get a chance to look around when we were looting it before. It's enormous. No expense was spared when they built this."

"I know," Finn said. "You could keep it for yourself."

"I'd love to, but there's no way I could get this out of here without a fight once we got to port. I'd need a large crew just to fend off the governor's officers. They'll realize soon enough what happened here. I wonder if we're in the right place. I don't see my money chest." Avery pointed to the corner of the room. "Look under the tarp over there."

Finn removed the canvas. "Yes, this is it."

"Look for the key in the captain's desk. That's where I'd keep it."

Finn opened a draw but didn't see a key. He opened another small drawer but didn't see anything but papers in it.

"Find it?' Avery asked.

"No, just a bunch of documents."

"Pull out the drawers and see if it is hidden on the bottom of one of them. We can just break off the padlock if you don't find it."

Finn flipped over the drawers and saw a key wedged into one of the corners with candlewax. "I found a key. This has got to be it."

Avery looked around the room to see if there was anything else he might want. He found five bags of coins and put them on the desk. "Hurry up. We don't have much time."

Finn stuck the key in the padlock and gave it a turn, unlocking it. He lifted the lid of the money chest and gasped. "This is it. It's full of jewels. There are gold necklaces, rings, silver, pendants, rubies."

Avery raised both fists in the air and had a huge smile on his face. "Yes. Let's carry it out of here and head back to Nash's camp. I'm not a hundred percent sure the *Mhuwe* killed all those men. They could be coming back. I found some bags of coins."

Avery and Finn were carrying the chest and the coins up the stairs when they heard gunshots.

"Leave 'em here," Avery shouted as he grabbed his pistol from around his waist.

Avery and Finn ran onto the deck. Avery saw Nash with blood flowing down his head, and the four men from the *Ganj-i-Sawai* lying facedown on the beach next to him. Avery ran to Nash. "What happened?"

"They ran at me and jumped me," Nash said, out of breath. "I got off two shots and got two of them before another one hit me on the head. Lucky for me, I had my pistol ready and got him before he could hit me again. I shot the last man with one of the rifles you left me when he came charging at me."

"I'll check to make sure they're dead," Avery said as he walked over to each man.

"Are you hurt?" Finn asked, running.

"No. My head hurts a bit. Nothing I haven't felt before. Been hit in the head plenty of times. It's hard as a rock."

Avery walked back to Nash and Finn. "They're all dead. You good?"

"I'm fine. Did you find the money chest?"

Avery nodded and smiled. "Yes, plus five bags of coins. You sure you feel well enough for us to go back and get it?"

Nash rubbed the back of head. "Sure. I'll just sit here and rest for a second."

"We'll be right back," Avery said. "I'd like to go through the ship and see what else we can take. We'll make it quick. I'm sure the rest of the crew will be back soon, if they didn't get killed off."

"Good idea," Nash said. "Not sure if we should bury these men or leave them where they are.

"How about you drag them to the woods over there and cover them with leaves," Avery said. "Will take less time."

Nash nodded, holding his head.

Fifteen minutes later, Avery, Nash, and Finn were walking up the mountain using a parallel trail just in case the men from the *Ganj-i-Sawai* were returning to their ship. They took turns carrying the money chest and coins, still marveling at how many precious jewels were inside. It took them two- and one-half hours to get to Nash's camp where they were greeted by a barking Cucumber, Pickle, Sweetie Pie.

"D'ye miss us, girl?" Nash asked as he scratched her head. She kept turning around and looking in the direction of where the men from the *Ganj-i-Sawai* met up with the *Mhuwe*. "Did the gunshots spook 'ye? Don't worry. It's over. They're not shooting anymore."

"Is she all right?" Avery asked. "She seems nervous."

"She'll be fine in a few minutes. She hates gunshots. I think it hurts her ears."

"I'm going to go scout out what happened," Avery said. "They could have made it to the cave and gotten the money chest out and are heading back to their ship."

# 67

AVERY PUT HIS hand over his mouth as he walked up to the gruesome scene. Dead bodies were scattered on the trail and nearby woods. He didn't see any *Mhuwe*, but he knew it was they that killed these men. He walked closer to the cave and noticed more dead men. He heard whistling noises coming from both sides of the path and sensed it was time to return to camp.

"So…what d'ye find?" Nash asked.

"I counted fifty-one dead men. All looked like they were from India. It was if a herd of buffaloes ran through the bunch of them. There were bodies everywhere. Buzzards are already flying above them. I'm guessing no one was able to make it back to the *Ganj-i-Sawai*. We didn't see or hear anyone going down the mountain when we were coming back here. I also went closer to the cave, but the *Mhuwe* were whistling, so I rushed back here."

"I better hunt some deer and give it to them," Nash said. "It appears they're getting a deep dislike for man. I need to keep on their good side if I'm going to continue living up here."

"Not a bad idea," Avery replied. "So, we've got five more days before they move the money. I made the tea too strong. We don't want any of the guards passing out before they've all had a drink. You say it took a minute before I started acting weird after drinking it?"

"That's about right," Finn said.

Avery scratched his chin. "I'll cut it in half."

"That should be perfect," Nash said.

"Have you thought any more about taking the Barretts' money?" Finn asked, looking at the ground while standing behind Nash.

"You really like them, don't you?" Avery said.

Finn kicked at a rock. "I do. They were very nice to me. Being with them, even if it was just for a little while, was kind of like being in a family I never had."

Avery shook his head. "I understand they mean a lot to you, but it's way too much money to pass up. If we leave their money in the bank, they may assume you or they were involved."

Finn picked up a rock and threw it at a tree. "I can't believe you won't let them keep it. You're just like all the other pirate captains. Money is all you think about."

Nash put his hand on Finn's shoulder. "Calm down."

"No, I won't calm down."

Avery's eyes narrowed. "It's my money and jewels. I get to say what happens with it, not you."

Finn glared at Avery. "Well, I'll give them my money when it comes to me. You can't tell me what to do with my share."

Avery threw his cup on the ground. "I don't care what you do with your share."

Nash clapped his hands. "Enough, you two. I'm going to get a deer and give it to the *Mhuwe*. Finn, want to go with me?

"No, I'm going to go for a walk." Finn stomped off. "Maybe I won't come back."

Avery shrugged his shoulders. "Fine with me. See how long you last alone in these woods."

Finn ran off.

Nash stood next to Avery. "You were a little hard on the kid."

"He needs to remember I'm still in charge."

"He knows that. He just wants to help out those folks who were good to him. Like he helped you 'cause you were good to him."

❖ ❖ ❖

IT WAS DARK by the time Finn came back in camp. He grabbed a blanket and walked out to the nearest tree and plopped down.

Nash walked over. "You all right, boy?"

"I'm fine. I just want to go to sleep. The faster I sleep, the faster we get to robbing the bank and I get my money."

❖ ❖ ❖

FLETCHER SAT BEHIND his desk with his hands over his eyes as Herndon relayed the news Ibrahim and all his men were dead. "That's it. No one else is ever going after that treasure again. And you said the officers looked throughout the *Ganj-i-Sawai* and the money chest and their share of the money is missing too?"

"Yes, Governor," Herndon said.

"This is terrible. I bet the pirates who roam the Hudson got it. Both those money chests must be cursed. Hopefully, whoever stole it will meet the same fate as the men on the *Ganj-i-Sawai*."

"Yes, sir."

"We'll have to send word to the emperor that many of his officers have died and his ship is here." Fletcher rubbed his temples and shook his head. "My head's killing me. This is a total diplomatic nightmare."

# 68

## THE BANK ROBBERY

AVERY, NASH, AND Finn hid behind a large oak tree. Avery put his hand on Finn's shoulder. "Before we start, I want to let you know I've changed my mind."

Finn furrowed his brow. "About what?"

Avery smiled. "We won't be taking the Barretts' money. They can keep it. We'll just be taking the money set to go to England."

There was a big grin on Finn's face and he pumped his fist in the air. "Thank you, Captain. You're the best."

"And you can keep all of your share."

"I really appreciate it, sir."

Avery smiled. "You're welcome."

Nash lightly punched Avery on the arm. "You're a good man."

Avery nodded and turned away. "Let's get back to stealing that money bound for England."

Nash nodded, tented his fingers, and cracked his knuckles. "I'm ready."

"Me too, Captain," Finn said.

Finn walked toward the men at the back of the bank with a bucket of tea laced with Jamestown weed. He rehearsed his lines over and over.

He stood in front of the guards and took a deep breath. "Good evening, officers."

"What are you doing out here at this hour?" one of the guards asked.

"I was out with my parents after a late meal. My mother told me to bring you tea. She said you might be thirsty standing out here so long in the hot weather."

"That's very nice of you, young man," the guard in charge said. "We've been here four hours and no one's brought us anything to drink."

Finn scooped out tea for each of the men. "I'll go bring some to the guards out front."

"Thank you. They'd appreciate that. Also, there's an employee inside and he might want tea too."

"I'll give them all some," Finn said. He started to walk away, then turned around. "Have a nice evening, officers."

It took two minutes for the guards behind the building to collapse on the ground. Avery and Nash ran over.

Avery asked Nash for the rope and rags they brought with them. "I'll tie these three up and gag them, while you take care of the other two. They should be out for about an hour. Long enough for us to get what we came for and get out of here. I'll drag the guards behind the oak tree. No one will see them there. Grab their guns and run them over to the carriage. Don't want anyone waking up and shooting at us."

"Got it," Nash said as he hustled to tie up the men and gag them. "I'll take the guns to the carriage and be right back."

Finn walked to the front of the bank and went through his same routine. "Good evening, sirs. I was out with my folks after a late meal when my mother told me to bring you tea. She told me you might be thirsty standing out here so long in the hot weather."

"Thanks!" one of the guards said.

Finn gave each a ladle full of tea. "Looks like someone is still work-ing inside. I'll see if he wants any tea too." He knocked on the door, and Mr. Pope walked over to see who it was.

"David, what are doing you doing here so late?" Pope asked.

Finn repeated the same story he'd told the guards. "Want some tea?" .

"No thanks."

Finn began to sweat and tremble. But then he remembered what to say if someone didn't want a drink. "Umm…my mother will be mad at me if I bring back the bucket with any tea left. She said not to take no for an answer. She says men are stubborn and need to drink tea for their health. She says people need to drink tea for their health."

Pope chuckled.

"Men need it for their health," Finn screeched.

Pope rolled his eyes. "I got it the first time you said it. I need to drink tea for my health. Give me a ladle full."

It took only fifteen seconds for Pope to fall on the floor. Finn tied him up, gagged him, and dragged him behind his desk. He pulled the vault room and cabinet keys from Pope's pocket chain and ran to the front door. Finn opened it just as Avery and Nash were carrying guards up the stairs to hide them inside.

"No one else in here?" Avery asked.

"I haven't seen nor heard anyone, but I haven't gone in the back yet," Finn said.

Nash walked toward the rear of the building with his pistol drawn. He raised his gun as he skulked into the vault room. He had a big grin on his face as he looked back at Avery and Finn. "No guards. Let's drag our friends in here. Finn, you got the keys?"

"Here," Finn said as he handed Nash the keys.

"So far, it's working as planned," Avery said. "Finn, go get the horse carriage and bring it around back. Remember, if you run into anyone, and they start asking you questions, tell them your father had too much to drink and you're bringing the carriage around to pick him up."

"Yes, sir. I'll be back in a few seconds."

Finn saw one person as he was riding back to the bank, but the man was too drunk to ask him any questions or try to stop him. Finn pulled up the carriage to the back door.

"Run into any trouble?" Nash asked.

"No. Just some drunk, but he was too far gone to bother me."

"Good, help us load the carriage and let's get out of here," Avery said.

It took the three of them a full five minutes before they were able to load all the bags of coins onto the carriage. They walked back inside to double check they hadn't left any money behind.

✢ ✢ ✢

FLETCHER PACED ON the dock waiting for the guards to bring the money from the bank to the ship. "They should be here by now. Herndon, get three officers and go see what's taking them so long."

"Yes, sir," Herndon said and called out the names of three men standing near the railing of the ship. "Come with me."

Herndon and the men quickly walked the four blocks to the building. They rounded the corner to the front of the building when Herndon grabbed his head. "Where are the guards? No, no, no. Hurry, get inside."

Avery, Nash, and Finn froze when they heard the commotion outside.

Avery put his finger up to his mouth. "Shh. Let's get out of here. Once we're around the corner and down the street a little bit, we'll speed off to the cabin."

# 69

HERNDON DREW HIS pistol, while the officers pointed their rifles and crept into the bank. He pointed to the officers. "Highgrove, you go to the left. Samuels, to the right. Fredericks and I will go to the vault."

Herndon and Fredericks walked cautiously. They saw the guards tied up and gagged on the vault room floor. They were untying the men when Samuels yelled from the front. "Mr. Pope is tied up behind his desk."

Herndon smacked the wall. "The guards are tied up and gagged back here too. Looks like they were drugged. They're out of it. I didn't see anyone out front. They must have left out the back door."

Herndon slowly opened the door and peeked around the corner. He saw a carriage moving down the alley. "There they are," Herndon screamed. "Stop or we'll shoot."

❖ ❖ ❖

"TIME TO GO," Avery said calmly. Then he let out a sharp cry, "Yah, Yah," and yanked on the reins.

"Fire," Herndon shouted.

Bullets whizzed by Finn as he dove to the floor of the carriage.

Nash turned around and shot back. He fired a shot from a rifle and another from one of the pistols he had tucked into his belt. He reached for another pistol just as a bullet hit his arm. "I'm hit," he howled.

Avery looked back. "Finn, use a rag and tie it off until we can get to the cabin."

Nash looked at his arm and winced in pain. "It grazed me, but it hurts like crazy. They aren't playing around. Take the next turn and go up that hill. We'll be at the cabin in a half hour or so."

"Hold on," Avery yelled as he yanked on the reins.

Nash peeked over the carriage rail. "We're out of range now. They'll think we headed straight for the water. Nobody knows about the cabin anymore. Hurry though. Man, it hurts."

"Sorry you got hit," Avery said. "You all right, Finn?"

"I'm fine, Captain."

Nash winced. "This jostling around hurts my arm even more. You can slow down a little bit. Don't want to kill the horses, or me."

Finn held on to the back of the carriage while he was lying down. He looked up occasionally to see if anyone was following them. "I see dust on the trail about a mile behind us."

Both Avery and Nash looked back.

"Looks like we may have company," Nash said. "Wait…there they go. I was right. They're turning toward the river. We aren't kicking up enough dirt with only two horses. It's too dark for them to see us."

"Let's stop and think for a minute," Avery said as he pulled on the reins making the horses come to a stop. "They're going to look for our tracks and follow us straight to the cabin."

Nash nodded. "I hate to say it, but maybe we should unload the coins and come back and get them. It's a long trek up there—a mile away. Send the carriage off in another direction so they follow those tracks."

Avery shook his head. "I don't want to leave the money and get it later. I already lost the money once. I can't lose it again. How many bags we got back there?"

"There's one, two, three...ten bags total," Finn said.

Avery looked at Nash and held up his hands. "You able to carry a couple of bags?"

"Absolutely," Nash said. "I'm insulted you even asked."

"Sorry, I wasn't sure how badly you were hurt."

"I'm good to go. A little pain just lets you know you're alive."

Avery nodded. "I'll take five. Can you carry three, Finn?"

"No problem."

They tied the bags of coins over each shoulder and took one last look in the carriage and cleared the area to make sure they didn't leave a trail.

Avery looked at Nash and Finn. "We set?"

"Yes, sir," Finn replied.

"Ready to go," Nash answered.

"Good," Avery said. "On the count of three, I'm going to smack the horses and send them running. I'm hoping they'll head back to their home. Finn, I never asked how you got the carriage."

"It was too late to buy one. I walked around and saw an old couple walking to the hotel, and I took it while they were going inside. It'd be funny if the authorities thought they stole the money."

"Good job. Nash, is that old rowboat you had stashed away ready?"

"Got it tied up behind a tree about half mile upriver. We're all set."

"You steal it?"

"I left it in the same spot years ago. Checked it out last time Finn and I were in town and it still looks good. I reckoned it would come in handy one day."

Avery looked at Nash and frowned. "How's the arm? You aren't dripping any blood, are you? Don't want them to track us."

"I'm fine," Nash said with a *humph* and a furrowed brow. "Quit asking me. And, no I'm not bleeding on the ground. I got it covered nice and tight."

Avery gave Nash a thumbs up and then smacked the horses. "Let's get out of here."

The horses ran off like they were in a race. They galloped a quarter of a mile and turned off the trail.

One half hour later, Avery, Nash, and Finn saw the cabin fifty yards away and stopped.

Nash leaned into Avery and Finn. "The cabin was deserted last I checked."

"Excellent, but we've got to make sure no one is in it now," Avery said.

They dropped the bags behind a tree twenty yards from the cabin and drew their pistols. Finn stayed behind to watch the money, while Avery and Nash slowly walked up to the cabin. There wasn't any smoke coming from the chimney, and they didn't see any candles flickering inside.

Avery pointed to one window and whispered, "You look inside that window, and I'll look in the other one."

Nash nodded.

Avery peered in the window and back at Nash. He shook his head left and right. Nash did the same.

Avery waved Nash over. "You open the door, and I'll run inside. On the count of three. One...two...three."

Avery ran inside with Nash following closely behind. Several mice scurried out of the room. The cabin looked deserted. It was a simple one-room house with a small fireplace. There was no furniture or food in sight. The cabin looked as if it had been abandoned for several years.

Nash shrugged. "It isn't much to look at, but it will keep the weather off of us. I don't think anyone but me even remembers it's here. We should be fine for a day or two, until things settle down in town."

Avery nodded. "It's good enough."

# 70

GOVERNOR FLETCHER, HERNDON, and Officer Monroe, who was in charge of guarding the money at the bank, sat in Fletcher's office. They tried to figure out how the money was stolen and how they'd get it back.

Monroe looked at the floor. "I'm sorry, Governor. The tea the boy gave us must have been drugged. We all passed out after drinking it."

"Did you see anyone other than the boy?" Herndon asked.

"No, sir, and I hardly remember what he looked like. It's like a bad dream."

Fletcher shook his head and glared at Monroe. "You got duped by a little boy. How stupid can you be? You had one order. Stand watch over the money, and you failed miserably. Now who knows where it is? The king will be furious."

"I'm sorry, sir," Monroe said without looking up. "You will have my letter of resignation in the morning."

Fletcher slammed his hand on his desk. "No, you will organize a team to locate the money. You will report on your progress to Mr. Herndon daily. I am reducing your rank until the money is found. If—no, when you recover the money, I will decide whether to restore your rank and pay. Is that understood?"

"Yes, sir. You are most generous."

"Now get out of my office," Fletcher yelled.

Monroe saluted and promptly left.

"What an idiot," Fletcher said, red-faced, to Herndon.

"Should I get another man to work on it?"

"Let's wait. Monroe has his reputation and his salary on the line. That should give him the incentive he needs to get the job done."

"Yes, sir."

"You say they took off in a carriage?"

"Yes, Governor. Looked like there were three of them. We lost track of them about a mile or two out of town."

"Has the carriage turned up anywhere?"

"Yes, sir. The horses ended up back at old man Smith's place. He reported the carriage was stolen, so we went to his house to see if it was the same one used in the robbery. It is. Even has bullet holes in it from where we shot at them."

"Did he notice anyone lurking around their carriage?"

"No, sir. He has no idea who took it. He and the missus were out for the evening, and they got a ride back to their place from a friend. When they arrived home, they saw their horses running back to the barn. I'm positive they had nothing to do with the robbery."

"I'm sure they didn't. Anybody could have stolen their carriage. It doesn't take a genius to figure out there was something important in the bank, with all the guards around. What did the manager say?"

"He said he thinks the boy who gave him the tea was a David Cussler. He had talked to him a few days earlier about opening a small account, but he wasn't sure. He said his mind is pretty fuzzy. The boy had come in with his grandfather about opening an account."

"Let's bring them in and talk to them."

"We asked around town, but no one has seen nor heard of them. It's late. Perhaps someone will give us useful information tomorrow."

"They have to be involved."

"I bet they are, sir, but we've come up empty so far."

"Have you talked to any of our usual informants?"

"Yes, sir, and they haven't heard of them either."

"Great. Well they couldn't have vanished into thin air."

"We're inspecting all the ships leaving port, in case they try to leave town."

"Keep me informed, and keep an eye on Monroe. He had better come through."

# 71

MR. POPE WALKED into the Barrett's store. "Good morning, Mr. and Mrs. Barrett. May I have a word with you in private?"

Sam furrowed his brow and looked at Emma. "Of course. No one is in the store right now, but let's go in the back, in case someone walks in. Is everything all right? You look upset."

"May I get you some hot tea to drink?" Emma asked.

"Oh, no thank you, Mrs. Barrett. I may not have tea for a long time after what happened last night."

"Why?"

"You will understand what I mean after I tell you about the incident."

"Please go on, Mr. Pope," Sam said.

"First, I want to let you know your money is still safe in the bank."

"What happened?" Emma asked. "Was it robbed?"

"Yes. Late last night, the guards and I were drugged. We believe it was from the tea a young boy gave us to drink. We're still unclear on the particulars, since none of us can remember much. Not to cast aspersions, but I remember a young boy from a transaction I had with he and his grandfather a few days earlier. I'd never seen the boy nor his grandfather before. They aren't from around here. We're assuming they, and who knows who else, robbed our fine establishment of the money found with the dead pirates that was slated to go to England."

Sam and Emma gave each other a quick glance.

"What's the boy's name?" Sam asked.

"He said he was David Cussler. The grandfather had the same name too. Do you know them?"

"No. I was just wondering because a lot of people come through our store, and I thought perhaps we may have seen them. The name doesn't sound familiar. We haven't seen anybody new around here."

"Well, I wanted to explain what happened. You and the other townsfolk who keep their money with us were lucky. The thieves only took the money slated to go to the king."

"I see," Sam said.

Pope stared off for a few seconds, shaking his head.

"Mr. Pope?" Emma asked. "Mr. Pope. Is everything all right?"

"I'm sorry. I'm trying to understand how this happened. We can't figure out how they knew the money was in the bank. Conceivably having so many guards gave it away." Pope wiped his brow. "Yes, that must be it. We usually don't have that many guards. I'm sure that's how the thieves knew we had more money than usual."

"That's probably it, Mr. Pope," Sam said as he squeezed Emma's hand.

"We are taking extra precautions to ensure your money and the rest of the bank's patrons' money is secure. Of course, I cannot divulge what those measures are, due to the sensitivity of the matter. I pray you still wish to keep your money with us."

"Thank you, Mr. Pope, for coming to tell us what happened," Sam replied. "We hadn't heard anything about a robbery. We feel fortunate we still have our money."

Pope bit his fingernails. "Please keep your money in the bank. I don't mean to beg, sorry, it's just—"

Sam interrupted Pope. "I think it's still safe enough to keep our money there. How do you feel, Emma?"

"I have faith you will protect our money."

Pope shook their hands. "Thank you…thank you very much."

Sam and Emma walked Pope to the front door.

"Please let us know if they catch those who did this horrible act," Emma said.

Pope shook their hands again. "Thank you for being so understanding. I will keep you informed if any new information arises. I hope you have a pleasant day."

Pope turned around and left.

SAM MOTIONED EMMA to the far end of the store. "Do you think it was Finn?"

"I hope not."

"Any new families in town would have stopped by here to gather supplies," Sam said. "I haven't seen anyone new, have you?"

"No, I haven't either."

"Finn didn't mention he was with anyone. Maybe it's just a coincidence. Hopefully, it's another boy. We should keep knowing Finn to ourselves. No need to get the authorities wondering if we had anything to do with the robbery."

"You don't suppose they believe we were involved, do you?" Emma said, biting her lip.

"No, they didn't take any money other than what was meant for England. Could be they're like Robin Hood and steal from the rich and give to the poor."

"Are we wrong in thinking our money is still safe in the bank? What if they get robbed again and we lose it all?"

"That's a chance we'll have to take. It's safer there than us hiding it at home. Mr. Pope said they're taking extra security measures. I guess we'll just have to pray there'll be no more robberies."

# 72

"RESTLESS DOESN'T COME close to describe how I'm feeling," Avery said, and then smiled. "But it sure beats sitting in jail."

Finn walked in the door and shook his head. "I climbed up that big oak tree and didn't see anybody. You picked a great spot, Nash."

"Told you. No one knows about this place. It's not captain's quarters, but it will have to do for another day or two. The longer we stay here, the better off we'll be."

Avery frowned. "I'm sure you're right. Finn can keep checking every couple of hours to see if anyone is coming. I guess the jerky and water we brought with us will last another two days. I don't want us to shoot anything for food. Might draw attention to us."

"Two more days should be enough time for things to quiet down," Nash said. "Then it should be all right for us to go to the boat and head upriver. But we should go at night. Now there's something I wanted to bring up for a while now, but I don't think Finn will like it."

"I'm not going to like what?"

Nash grinned. "Well…you're the only person they might connect to the robbery because you gave them the tea. They'll be on the lookout for a boy."

"So, there are a lot of boys in town."

"True, but they know most, if not all, of them. You're the newcomer in town."

Finn folded his arms. "What are you gettin' at?"

"I brought a wig with me and hid it in one of my coat pockets. How'd you like to be a girl?"

"What?" Finn cried out. "No way. No way you're going to get me to dress up like a girl."

"You don't have to wear a dress, just a wig."

Avery started laughing. "Oh, I think Finn wearing a dress is a great idea."

Finn stormed toward the door, turned around, and yelled, "You two are sick. You're both completely out of your minds. You must have had some of that Jamestown weed. I'm going outside to see if anyone is around."

Avery and Nash looked at each other and laughed hysterically.

Finn glared at them. "Be quiet. Someone might hear you." He stepped outside and slammed the door.

Avery looked at Nash. "You know, it really isn't such a bad idea for him to wear a wig. Let's keep it on hand in case someone sees us on the water or here in the cabin. He can always put it on at the last minute."

Nash chuckled. "He wasn't too big on the idea, was he?"

"No, but he'll get over it. Why do you have a wig?"

"Well, when I was starting out, I didn't have a beard, and I didn't have a big crew. From time to time, I needed to make a quick escape. No one was looking for a woman, so I was able to get out of a few pretty tough situations with that wig. It's surprising how little people really pay attention to what's going on around them."

"That's a great idea."

"They're looking for a particular person or someone who looks a certain way. They get fixed on that and ignore everything and every-one else. I never got rid of the wig. It kind of reminds me of how far I've come."

"Hey, I've got another question for you."

"Sure."

"Why did you come up with such crazy names for yourself and your dog?"

"My kids came up with those names. We used to play silly games and give funny names to our animals. They named the dog, and I gave myself the name of one of our cats. Folks thought I was nuts and they left me alone. They weren't sure I was altogether there."

# 73

THE NEXT TWO days went by without incident. Finn would go outdoors every two hours during the day and every four at night. He'd climb up the oak tree to see if anyone was close-by, while Avery and Nash stayed holed up in the cabin. The temperature was warm outside, so they didn't have to make a fire. They were getting restless and decided enough time had passed since the robbery for them to return to Nash's camp.

Avery paced back and forth in the cabin and looked out the window a few times to make sure he didn't see anything suspicious. He gave a thumb up to Nash and Finn.

"Thank goodness the only things we've seen were those deer and a nosey bear," Nash said. "Other than that, it's been just us."

Avery nodded. "Let's wait until later on tonight before we go to the boat. There shouldn't be anyone on the river at that time."

"Sounds good," Nash said. "Say the word, and I'll lead the way to where I hid the boat. Shouldn't take us more than an hour to get there, even carrying the money."

A light rain fell and fog covered the area. Avery, Nash, and Finn gathered the bags of money. They looked around the cabin to make sure they didn't leave any clues they were there. Then they quietly walked to where Nash had hidden the rowboat. It took them exactly one hour to get to the spot. They hid behind a large oak tree where the boat was stashed and looked to see if anyone was on the river. They hadn't seen anybody on their walk, and the river looked deserted.

"The fog is perfect cover," Avery said. "We couldn't have picked a better time. I don't see anyone. How about you two?"

"Looks clear," Nash said.

Finn agreed. "Looks clear to me too."

Avery circled his hand. "Let's head on out. No talking unless you see someone. When we get there, we'll scuttle the boat. How long will it take us, Nash?"

"Probably an hour...hour and a half. You two will have to do the rowing, since my arm is still hurtin' me pretty good."

"No problem. Just tell us when we get close."

They slowly rowed up the Hudson, not only due to the heavy fog, but also so no one would hear them if anyone happened to be on shore. It took them two hours to get to their exit point on the river. They formed a human chain by passing the bags of money from Finn to Nash to Avery, until all the money was on the riverbank. After the bags of coins and their few belongings were offloaded, Finn took the rowboat out thirty yards and pulled the plug from the hole in the boat they made. He waited until it sank, and then swam to Avery and Nash waiting for him on the shore.

It would take several hours before the sun would come up, but their eyes had adjusted to the darkness, so they decided to walk up the mountain. Boats would soon begin their journeys on the river, and it would be better to be deep in the woods before anyone could see them. They were tired and sweaty by the time they reached the halfway point.

Nash noticed Avery was getting tired, so he held up his hand. "How about we take a break for a few minutes. We're far enough in the woods where no one can see us."

"Good," Avery said, huffing. "I could use a break. How much longer we got till we get to your place?"

"Probably another hour. No need to rush it though. Looks like we're in the clear. We would have known if someone was following us. Sounds echo in these woods, and all I've heard are squirrels and a fox. The governor's men must be keeping an eye out near port."

Avery grinned. "It wasn't as hard as I thought to get that money. The only hiccup was you getting shot in the arm. You were lucky it only grazed you."

"It's going to take more than that to stop me."

"How's the arm feeling?" Finn asked.

"Not too bad. Still stings some. I'll put those herbs on it and it will be fine." Nash smiled. "Just one more scar I can show off to the ladies. I've rested enough to start back up, if you two are ready."

"I'm fine," Avery said. "How 'bout you, Finn?"

"I'm ready."

They slogged up the mountain another hour when Cucumber, Pickle, Sweetie Pie barked and came running up to Nash and jumped in his arms, licking his face. "Hey, Cucumber," Nash said. "How's my girl? D'ye miss me?"

Finn scratched her behind her ears. "Looks like it."

"I hate leaving her alone for too long. She's good at finding her own food, but I worry about them *Mhuwe* getting her. Camp's up ahead. We'll be there in a few minutes. I got a good hiding place for the money. We shouldn't leave it at the camp. You never know when somebody may come by. That old hollow tree where I hide my guns is a good spot to put the money."

"Thanks," Avery said. "Any thoughts on where we can hide the money chest?"

"There's a small group of rocks with a decent-size opening not too far. We can hide it there. It's not big enough for it to be a home for *Mhuwe* or bear. I should have thought of it earlier before we left." Nash pointed. "There's camp."

Avery shook his head. "I didn't think of it either." He walked in the hut and looked under the tarp. "Thank God it's here. All the jewels are still in it too."

AVERY SPENT THE next three weeks passing the time by resting and taking short walks, while Finn played with Cucumber, Pickle, Sweetie Pie, and explored the nearby woods. Nash gathered herbs and made his medicinal concoctions.

Avery grew a beard to hide his identity, in case someone came looking for him, and for when the time would come for him to leave camp. Nash shaved off his beard for the same reason as Avery grew his out.

"So, what are you going to do with your share of the money and jewels?" Nash asked Avery.

"Most likely stick to the original plan of going somewhere and starting a new life. Something on the straight and narrow. Buy land and have a bunch of cattle. I'll tell people I inherited it from my folks who passed away, and I wanted a change so moved here from Ireland."

Avery looked over at Finn. "Hope you still want to come and help me run the place, at least until you're old enough to have one of your own."

"That would be great," Finn said. "Where you thinking of going?"

"Someplace upriver. I bet the authorities will assume whoever robbed the bank will head south. They won't be looking for anyone going north. But I do like what you said, Nash, about Virginia. It sounds nice."

"Virginia's great, but no matter where you go, you'll need to buy a boat to get there. I could go into town and buy one for you. Especially now that I've shaved."

"How about we stay up here on Bear Mountain?" Finn asked. "Buy land and raise cattle up here. Sorry, Nash. Not sure how you would feel about that."

"I don't mind, just as long as I have some space to myself."

Avery stroked his newly grown beard and scrunched his nose. "I don't know. It's not too far from town. What if someone spots us?"

"So, we wait a couple of years. Things will calm down by then. I won't go into town. They've only seen me in connection to the robbery. If you think people will remember you, Nash can go into town and buy the property using whatever name you want, and it will still belong to you. We can go up north to buy the cattle."

Avery shrugged. "Maybe. You sure you're all right with that, Nash?"

"No problem. I was getting a little tired of being up here alone. I heard you had to buy land from the Holland Land Company. They own almost everything in these parts. I didn't want to go through doing that, so I came up here and hid out. Not positive they own the land, but they probably still do."

The next morning, Avery gathered Nash and Finn. "So, I thought about it some more, and why not? I can buy land up here and own most of the mountain. Someday I can go back to that cave and get the other money chest, but I'm going to put it on hold for a while. What do you think about the plan, Nash?"

"I'm good with it. Let me stay where I am now and give me, say, twenty acres of my own, and we're all set."

"Great. It's settled. One thousand acres should do it. I don't think the Haverstraws will object. They don't like it up here because of the

*Mhuwe*. I like your idea, Finn, of waiting a year or two. My beard will be grown out by then. No one will recognize me."

"So what name are you going to go by?" Finn asked.

Avery puffed out his chest. "Thomas Dendro."

"Why Dendro?" Finn asked.

"Dendro is short for Dendrobatoidea. That's the scientific name for the poison dart frog. I saw the locals use the poison from the frogs' skin when I was in Guatemala. They can be deadly. You'd never know it from them being so small. Most of them are colorful too. They come in blues, red, yellows, greens, and some of them have mixed colours. I always thought it might be an interesting name to use."

"I like it," Nash said.

"When it's time, I'll go to the Haverstraws and make sure they're fine with me buying the land. I'll give them what they want for it. No need to get on their bad side, especially since it originally belonged to them anyway."

Nash nodded. "That's smart. How about we go and hide the money chest and coins we each have? Probably best to hide it in three different places, rather than put all our money together."

"Great idea," Avery said. "Then, I guess we just wait."

EUGENE HOPKINS, THE owner of the bank, walked through the door and headed straight toward Mr. Pope, shaking his head. Pope nervously stood at attention. "Mr. Pope…I am relieving you of your duties. I am sending you to our bank in Connecticut where hopefully you will find it less taxing. I am confident you won't let a little boy dupe you there as you did here. You are to gather your effects and be out of here no later than the end of the day. I am giving you two weeks paid leave to find a home in Connecticut. Good day, Mr. Pope."

"But, Mr. Hopkins, I…I…" stuttered Pope.

"I hope you're not trying to defend your careless behavior or question my generosity, Mr. Pope."

Pope looked at the floor. "No, sir. I appreciate you allowing me to remain employed. You are most generous."

Hopkins huffed and headed out the front door. "Good day, Mr. Pope."

# 74

IT DIDN'T TAKE long for the people of New York Town to return to their normal activities. The rumors of pirate treasure on Salisbury Island and Bear Mountain had been interesting, but nothing more than that. Most had decided the talks about treasure were merely tales being told at the bar by drunken men trying to impress each other and the ladies.

The wives and children who had lost their husbands and fathers on Bear Mountain never knew the truth about what happened to their loved ones. They were told their husbands and fathers were killed by pirates and outlaws who were plotting to wreak havoc on the town.

The lost treasure had never been recovered, and it was assumed, by the governor and his officers, that the thieves had escaped to pirate havens in either New Providence or Tortuga.

Governor Fletcher retired six months after the tragedies and returned to England. Mr. Herndon also retired and moved with his wife to Massachusetts.

The new governor, Richard Coote, the First Earl of Bellomont was now the man in charge. Before Governor Fletcher left, he decided not to tell Coote what had actually happened. Instead, he told him local pirates had robbed and killed the crew from the *Ganj-i-Sawai* and had stolen the money from the bank. It was said they sailed with their stolen treasure to the Caribbean. The duped guards were more than eager to corroborate Governor Fletcher's story.

Sam and Emma Barrett bought three hundred acres in Peekskill,

New York and opened a store there. They kept the shop in New York Town but hired staff to run the day-to-day business for them. Even though the Barretts were now one of the richest people in New York, they hadn't changed much other than owning more property, building a bigger store, and living in a larger but not extravagant house.

Avery and Finn spent the next two years learning everything they could from Nash about living on the mountain and how to run a business and farm the land. Nash had learned the hard way that he couldn't run the family estate like he ran his pirate crew. He advised Avery and Finn on the dos and don'ts of having a successful, legitimate business.

AVERY TURNED TO Nash and Finn and stroked his now raggedly grown beard. "Well, gents, and I don't mean any disrespect, Nash, but I can't just hang out here any longer. I need to do something. Build something. Be in charge of something."

"I get it," Nash said. "You've been a captain and in charge of running things. Hiding out here for two years has got to have been boring for you."

"It's funny. I always imagined it would be enough for me to prove the Royal Navy and the privateering companies wrong by not making me a captain."

"You were—I mean, *are* a great captain," Finn said.

"Thanks. It was a thrill robbing them and beating them at their own game."

"You showed them," Nash said.

"Yes, but I want more. They'll never see me as a legitimate captain. I'll always be a pirate in their eyes. They probably figure I ended up being killed by other pirates or hanged somewhere overseas."

"Who cares," Nash chuckled. "You got more money than all of them combined."

"True, but now I want to do it the honest way. I want to prove, I guess to myself, that I can run an operation better than they can. Better than most anyone."

Nash smiled. "Sounds to me like you're ready to make this cattle ranching thing happen."

Avery nodded. "I've decided it's time I go into the city and buy the land and get our next adventure started."

"You might want to tidy yourself up a bit," Nash said. "Not sure anyone will want to do a land transaction with someone looking so scruffy."

"Scruffy?" Avery laughed. "I prefer the phrase 'man of the land.'"

"You can call it what you like, but no one is going to take you seriously, unless you present yourself as a rich businessman. They'll think you stole the money."

"You could always go to the Barrett's store and get the clothes you need," Finn said.

"It's probably not a bad idea for you to stay at the inn a night or two and take a bath and get yourself looking more presentable before you set up a meeting," Nash said.

"You got something I can trim this beard with other than a knife?"

Nash shook his head. "No. A knife's all I got. You can sharpen it up on a rock and trim it up so it's looking decent. Then go to the barber in town and he can fix you up."

"Sounds good. The barber can tell me who to meet with about buying the land too. They always know what's going on in their town, and who's in charge of what. I figure I'll leave here tomorrow morning. I'll take money with me to put down as a good faith hold on the land. Then come back for the rest later. Oh...I almost forgot...before

I go into town, I need to talk with the local Haverstraw chief to make sure they won't have any issues with me buying the land."

"You can head toward the water, and I bet you'll run into a Haverstraw who can take you to the chief," Nash said.

"I'll do that first thing in the morning. I'll clean up a little before I go."

# 75

THE NEXT MORNING, Dendro met up with a Haverstraw named Pishkw, meaning night hawk, canoeing up the river. He used hand gestures and spoke the little bit of their language he'd learned from Nash. Dendro was allowed in the canoe, and Pishkw took him to meet his chief.

Pishkw held up his hand, motioning for Dendro to stand beside several tents as he walked to get the chief. Several of the Haverstraw men came and stood next to Dendro. They stared at him, saying nothing.

Dendro looked around for an escape. *I shouldn't have come here by myself.* He smiled at them, trying to lessen the tension, and to show them he meant no harm.

After several minutes, a large man wearing a roach headdress came out of the biggest tent with four bulky Haverstraws by his side.

"My name is Sakima Maxkw," he said in perfect English. I am the chief of this clan. Pishkw tells me you wish to discuss buying land on the mountain."

"Yes. My name is Thomas Dendro. I wanted to speak with you before I went into town to purchase the land. I wasn't sure if the land was yours. If so, I wanted to see if you would sell some of it. I'd like to buy one thousand acres and use it to raise cattle and farm it for our personal needs."

"That is honorable of you to come to me first. Many people do not."

"Thank you."

"But I must tell you the Haverstraw people believe no one owns the land. It is everyone's to use. I have heard a man named VanderLinden has, as you say, bought most of the mountain."

"I see. So, you wouldn't mind if I work part of the mountain and bring in cattle?"

"Would you mind if my people live and hunt on the mountain like we have done for generations?"

"I have no problem with that. I see it as we are sharing the mountain and living side-by-side."

"Good, I have only one request—that the Barrett and Collins families be allowed to freely use the mountain as they wish."

"Why those two families?"

"They saved my son when he was being attacked by a bear, and I told them they could come onto the mountain anytime without asking me."

Avery scratched his beard for a few seconds and looked at the ground. He started to say something but noticed Maxkw narrow his eyes and decided it was best to agree. "I am fine with that. I'm guessing they don't want to live on the mountain, just hunt on it."

"That's my understanding, but I would let them build on the land if they wanted."

"Then I will do that too. Do you want any money for the property?"

Maxkw chuckled. "No, we have all we need. If we had wanted money and jewels, we would have already taken it from you before you buried it."

Avery's eyes grew big. "You must be mistaking me for someone else."

Maxkw clenched his jaw. "I am not." He walked closer to Avery. "You have lied to me. Lie again, and our agreement has ended."

Avery's face turned red and he held back his shoulders. "How dare you…"

Maxkw turned around and began walking away.

Avery put a hand on Maxkw's shoulder to stop him. Immediately, the four men grabbed hold of him. "Stop. You took me by surprise. I never saw anyone watching us. I won't lie to you again."

Maxkw waved the men off Avery. He stared directly into Avery's eyes. "Will you lie again?"

"No…never." Avery reached out his hand to Maxkw.

Maxkw smiled and shook his hand.

Avery drew a sigh of relief. "Thank you for meeting with me and for allowing me to live on the land."

Maxkw nodded. "Pishkw will take you back. I suggest you stay away from the *Mhuwe*. They are the ones who truly own the mountain."

❖ ❖ ❖

AVERY MADE HIS way up the mountain and was close to camp when he heard Cucumber, Pickle, Sweetie Pie barking and running out to greet him. Avery scratched her head. "Hi, girl."

"How did it go?" Nash asked.

"It went pretty good, I guess."

"What do you mean 'pretty good?'"

Avery told Nash what happened and shrugged. "I told him he must be thinking of someone else…"

"Oooh, bad move."

"I know. Where's Finn?"

"He told me he was going out for a walk. He probably wants to go into town with you. I'm not sure that's such a good idea. You look different with your beard. No one will recognize you. But Finn's appearance hasn't changed much."

# 76

THE NEXT MORNING, Avery and Finn paid the fare taker and walked to the railing. "I know you didn't want me going into town with you," Finn said to Avery. "But I promise I'll keep in the background and won't speak to anyone."

"It's not the best thing you coming along, but we've both gotten a little restless being on the mountain without much to do."

"Thanks."

"I've been thinking. You can come with me when I meet with VanderLinden to discuss buying the land. You can be my son."

"I'd like that."

"Who knows, it may soften him up having you along. How about we say your name's Thomas Dendro, Jr., and your mother died two years ago from the pox. We should probably tell folks we're from Ireland. There are more people here from England, and some may start asking too many questions about where we lived."

"Can you speak in an Irish accent?"

"Oh, I don't know," Avery said in an Irish brogue. "I think it's pretty good. How's that for ya?"

Finn smiled. "Perfect."

"Let's stop off at the barber shop first. Get us a haircut, and then see about getting decent clothes to wear. We want to put our best foot forward."

❖ ❖ ❖

"WHAT CAN I do for you, gentlemen?" the barber asked in a friendly, welcoming voice.

"How about a haircut and my beard trimmed for me, and a haircut for my son?" Avery said in an Irish brogue.

"I see you're from the homeland."

"Yes. We came here to buy land and make it our new home."

"Well, I wish you the very best. New York's a great place to make a new start."

"Tell me, how I can get hold of a Mr. VanderLinden? I understand he may own the land I would like to purchase."

"Mr. VanderLinden has an office near the governor's mansion. You can't miss it. It has a flag hanging near the front door with a big letter "*V*" on it. You'll need to get the sale recorded in the governor's office, but that's usually just a technicality. This new governor is pretty good about those things."

"We won't be working through the local bank in town?"

"Only to deposit your funds. They fired the previous manager a couple of years ago now. This administrator is pretty fussy about following proper procedures. But he's very accommodating to Mr. VanderLinden. I guess having a ton of money will make certain people jump through hoops for you."

"Thank you. You have been most helpful. Can you also tell us where we might buy some new clothes?"

"Barretts is your best bet. Most people go there. The store is still good, even though Sam and Emma opened another store upriver. They have a fine man running the store in town here."

"Thank you again. You and your partner have done a great job fixing me and my son up. I feel human again."

"Come see us again. Good luck with your land purchase."

Avery and Finn waved and headed to the Barrett's store.

"See. I told you he'd be a great source of information," Avery said. "Now we don't have to worry about you being recognized by that manager. Also, the Barretts probably won't be in town. Things are moving smoothly. But keep an eye out for them in case they're here. You stay outside. I'll come get you once I know they aren't in the store."

"You got it."

THE BELL RANG as Avery opened the door into the Barrett's store. Finn waited outside.

The man behind the counter waved and walked over. "Good morning, sir. Welcome to Barretts, the finest store in all the east coast."

Avery straightened and looked at the man walking toward them. "Good day. Might you be Mr. Barrett?"

"Oh no, sir. I run this store for Mr. and Mrs. Barrett. They are at their other store upriver. I promise to provide you with excellent customer service. How can I help you?"

"My son and I would like to buy some clothes. What might you have in the latest fashions? I am looking for business attire, and clothes for my…" Avery spun around, pretending to look for his son. "Where's that boy? He was right behind me. Wait one second while I get him."

Avery opened the door and winked at Finn. "There you are. Come inside."

The clerk stood next to a rack of clothes holding up a dark-blue suit. "Right over here, sir. I'm sure you will like this. All the businessmen around here are wearing them." He walked to the next row over. "And over here you'll find clothing for your son. I'll leave you to browse at your leisure. I'll be over at the counter. Please call me if you have any questions. I don't want to hover. The dressing room is over to your right."

"Thank you," Avery said. "We'll pick out a few things and try them on."

Finn frowned. "I hate all of these clothes," he whispered. "I feel stupid wearing them."

"Me too. They aren't my style either, but we've got to fit in and look like we're regular town people. From now on, we've got to dress the part. It's not that bad." Avery chuckled. "At least you don't have to dress up in girls' clothes."

"Very funny," Finn snarled.

After fifteen minutes of trying on shirts and pants, they walked up to the counter. Avery was wearing a new blue suit, and Finn was wearing a nice pair of Sunday church clothes and carried a pile of men's and boys' clothes.

"We'll take these," Avery said.

The clerk added up the cost of the clothing. Avery reached into his pocket and pulled out several silver coins. "Will this cover it?"

"Oh, that's too much, sir."

"Keep the change. You've been quite helpful."

"Thank you, sir. You are most generous."

# 77

IT WAS A typical hot and humid summer day in Cuba. Andrew knocked on the door. Carmen looked through the peephole the Boss had installed after Andrew sailed to the colonies.

She opened the door with a big smile. "The Boss is out but should be back soon. Did you find Avery?"

Andrew nodded. "I know where he is."

"The Boss is going to be happy. You did a great job, Andrew. Yes, the Boss will be most pleased with you."

"I hope so," Andrew said and turned around when the door opened and closed.

"I hope so…what?" the Boss asked.

Andrew smiled, and then looked at the floor. "I hope you will be pleased with me."

"Depends. What did you find about Avery?"

"He's in New York, sailing up the Hudson River."

The Boss strolled over and put his hand on Andrew's shoulder, making him wince. "No need to worry, my good man. You did outstandingly. Come…come. It's time to celebrate. Let's have a drink."

The Boss strolled to his bar and poured three glasses of his best whiskey. He turned around and smiled. "Andrew and Carmen, please have a drink with me. We have finally narrowed down the search for that lousy scoundrel. Avery will wish he were never born when I get through with him."

Carmen curtsied and took the glass. "Thank you, Boss."

Andrew furrowed his brow and cautiously looked at the whiskey "Yes, thank you very much, Boss. That is most kind of you."

The Boss held his glass up in the air. "To a job well done." Then he took a big gulp. "You two have been wonderful servants to me."

Andrew and Carmen held their glasses in the air and took a sip.

"Thank you, Boss," they both said in unison.

"Please, take a larger drink. You deserve it."

They both took another sip.

Andrew grabbed his throat and dropped to the floor.

Carmen's eyes went wide at seeing Andrew fall. Then she, too, grabbed her throat and collapsed on the floor.

The Boss walked over and put two fingers on their carotid arteries and felt no pulse. He held his glass up in the air as if giving a toast. "Yes, you two have been exceptional servants. But you must die, like the others who were no longer needed." The Boss took a long gulp of his whiskey and walked to his desk. He sat back in his chair and looked at the map of Cuba on the wall. "Good-bye, Cuba. I must go to New York."

"GOOD DAY. MY name is Thomas Dendro, and this is my son, Thomas, Jr. Are you Mr. VanderLinden?"

"No, sir," the smart-dressed man behind a mahogany desk said. "I am Mr. Jenkins, Mr. VanderLinden's business manager. How may I help you?"

"I understand Mr. VanderLinden has a tract of land on Bear Mountain. My son and I have recently moved to this country, and I would like to propose a purchase of that land."

Jenkins gestured to two nicely appointed chairs by the window. "Please have a seat. I will inquire to see if Mr. VanderLinden is available to meet with you. He is a very busy man."

"Thank you. It is much appreciated."

A thin man, reaching barely five feet tall, came into the room wearing impeccable clothes, with shoes shined as if they had never touched the ground. He walked over and shook both Avery's and Finn's hand. "I am Lars VanderLinden," he said in a heavy Dutch accent. "Mr. Jenkins has informed me you have a proposal for me."

"Yes. My son and I have just come over from Ireland to begin our new life here. I wish to purchase one thousand acres on Bear Mountain to start a cattle business. We were hoping you might be willing to sell to us."

VanderLinden puffed his chest. "As a businessman, I am always prepared to make a profitable business transaction. But it has to be for the right price. I would have to be convinced it is in my best interest to sell to you. Several people and businesses have provided offers to purchase land on Bear Mountain from me, but I have never sold. Their offers were always too low."

"I, too, am a businessman who understands you must make a good profit on your transactions. I have brought my son along so he can learn how to conduct business and one day take over for me. I won't be wasting either of our time with a low offer."

"I see. What is your proposal?"

"I am willing to pay £100 for one-thousand acres starting from the shore of Salisbury Island to the top of the mountain."

"I've turned down multiple offers for that amount. I simply cannot go below £140."

"How about we meet halfway? We both give in a little, and I pay £120 for the thousand acres."

VanderLinden sat back in his chair and looked at the ceiling. He stood up and walked back and forth behind his desk, calculating on his fingers. He breathed in deeply. "My good man, we have a deal."

Dendro stood up and shook VanderLinden's hand. VanderLinden called for Jenkins. "Jenkins, draw up the paperwork for the sale of one thousand acres from the shore near Salisbury Island to the top of the mountain to Mr. Dendro."

"Yes, sir. I will get right on it."

VanderLinden looked at Dendro and smiled at Thomas Jr. "I usually require a ten percent deposit as a good faith gesture on the buyer's part."

Dendro pulled out a small bag from his coat pocket and handed him £12. "Here you go, my good man."

"Excellent. How soon can you have the rest of the funds?"

"No later than the end of this week."

"Outstanding. How about we meet in my office this Friday at ten o'clock in the morning and sign the transfer of property paperwork? We will need to take it over to the governor's office for his signature. I have done many transactions with him. He usually signs off on it immediately. I will inform him of our transaction so there will be no delay. Afterward, we can go to the bank and transfer the funds."

"Excellent. It has been a pleasure, Mr. VanderLinden."

"Please call me Lars. It has been my pleasure too. Looks like you will own one side of the mountain, and I will own the other."

"Yes, see you on Friday."

Avery and Finn walked down the street with smiles on their faces. Avery put his hand on Finn's shoulder. "We did it. I shouldn't count our chickens before they hatch, but it looks like that part of the mountain will be ours. Guess we're going to live a normal life after all. I almost forgot. I have to open an account so I can put the money in for

Friday." Avery turned the corner and walked into the alley and started discreetly counting the money he pulled from inside his coat pocket. "I only have about fifteen pounds left. How about you?"

"I have ten pounds," Finn said.

"That should do it. I'll pay you back when we get back up the mountain."

"No need. Consider it a down payment. I guess I'll need to build a place to stay on the mountain."

"You can always stay with me, especially since we're telling people you're my son."

"That'd be great. Thanks!"

Avery winked at Finn. "Now, let's go open that account."

# 78

"HOW DID IT go?" Nash asked.

"It went great," Avery replied. "Couldn't have gone any better. We meet on Friday to do the paperwork and pay for the property."

Nash slapped his knee. "I can't believe this is really happening. Now starts the hard work of buying cattle, and bringing on people to help with all of that."

"You're right. I'll have to get the word out we're hiring. There's going to be a lot to do clearing the land. Then we have to fence off a large area for the cattle. Build a place to live, and on and on. But it'll be worth it once everything's finished."

Nash nodded. "You'll be one of the biggest land owners and businessmen in all of these parts."

"Nash, you need to go by a different name now. Who do you want to be from now on?"

"I was thinking about that. How about Michael Williams?"

"Sounds good. Why that name?"

Nash's eyes welled up. "They're the first names of my sons."

ON FRIDAY, AVERY and Nash, with Finn right behind them, carried an old chest filled with bags of gold and silver coins onto the ferry and headed into town. They each held a rifle under their arm and had two pistols hidden in their coat pockets. Their heads were on a swivel looking for any possible thieves, until they reached the bank. The men walked in a straight line with Finn in the middle, Avery out front, and Nash in the back.

Upon entering the building, the manager, Mr. Peabody, stood and greeted them as they walked through the door. "Mr. Dendro, it is a pleasure to see you and your son again. I see you've come to make a deposit."

"Yes. This is my business partner, Mr. Michael Williams," Avery said.

"Pleased to meet you, Mr. Williams."

"Pleased to meet you," Williams replied.

After shaking hands, Peabody straightened. "Please follow me to our safe room. Will you and Mr. VanderLinden be finalizing your business transaction today?"

"Yes, in one hour's time. I understand you must count it, but we have brought £25,000 to be deposited."

Peabody's eyes widened. "Oh my. That is quite a lot of money to be depositing without a security escort."

"We felt secrecy may be more advantageous for us. Word somehow always gets out once you hire a security outfit."

"Very well, sir. I will need to call one of my men to assist me in counting the gold and silver you've brought. You are more than welcome to stay and watch us count, or you may have a seat out front. Whatever you prefer."

"We will stay here with the money."

# 79

*SIX YEARS LATER*

NINETEEN-YEAR-OLD TOM DENDRO stood outside Barrett's store in Peekskill, New York. He had a wrapped gift box tucked inside his coat pocket. His hair was slicked back, and the tailored clothes he wore fit him perfectly.

Tom put his hand in his pocket and felt the box. He had bought it several years earlier for Emma Barrett. He thought of the Barretts constantly but didn't have the courage until now to visit them. Tom remembered fondly how Emma acted toward him. Like a mother. A mother he wished he had.

He fidgeted with the buttons on his jacket. *What if they don't remember me? Will they be mad at me for not keeping in touch all these years? Will they both regret not turning me in to the authorities? Will they be proud of the man I've become? Dad told them they're always welcome on the mountain. I wonder why I've never seen them up there?*

The bell above the door rang, notifying seventeen-year-old clerk Isabella Schillachi that a customer had entered the store. She hurriedly walked up. "Welcome to Barretts. How may I help you?"

Tom's mouth dropped, and his face turned red. "I…I…was wondering, um…um…if Mrs. Barrett is here?"

Isabella smiled. Her eyes shifted downward. "Mrs. Barrett is in the back. I will get her for you. Do you have an issue with a product you purchased from us? Is that why you wish to see her?"

"No, it's not that. I haven't seen her for a long time, and I was in town, and wanted to stop by."

"Please wait one moment and I will get her."

Emma Barrett walked through the curtain separating the store from the work area in the back. "Yes? How may I help you?"

"Good day, Mrs. Barrett."

Emma furrowed her brow. "Sorry, I don't recall…" She gasped, held her hand over her mouth, and hugged Tom. "I prayed I'd see you some day." She held him at arm's length and gushed. "Look at you. You're so grown up. And, by the looks of it, you're doing quite well."

"It's great to see you. I was in town and wanted to stop by. Sorry it's taken me so long to stop by. I've always wanted to thank you and Mr. Barrett for being so kind to me years ago." He reached into his coat pocket and pulled out the gift box. "This is for you."

"You shouldn't have. You didn't need to bring me anything."

"I saw this in a store window and thought you might like it." He leaned in and whispered in her ear, "No need to worry. I bought this with money I earned. Those other days are far behind me. I'm Tom Dendro now."

She opened the box and held up a beautiful necklace with a gold cross and a small diamond on it. "I love it, but this must have cost you a fortune. It's too much."

"What's too much?" Sam Barrett asked as he walked up.

"Look who's here."

"Sorry, but I'm afraid I don't quite remember where we've met."

"Look closer," Emma said.

Sam's eyes widened. He shook Tom's hand. "Well I'll be. I wasn't sure we'd ever see you again. Looks like you're doing well."

"Look what Fi…I mean Tom Dendro bought me with his own money. Isn't it beautiful?"

"Sure is. That was mighty nice of you."

"I wanted to thank you for being so kind to me way back when. You didn't have to. I really appreciate it."

Sam pulled over a few chairs and looked at Tom. "You wouldn't by chance be part of the Dendros who run that cattle business up on Bear Mountain, would you? They've been a big help to the area by hiring folks and giving a lot of money to local causes."

"Yes. I was adopted by Thomas Dendro five years ago. I help him run the business. It has been more successful than we could have imagined."

"I should say so. You all are the biggest business on the east coast. Mr. Dendro told us and the Collins years ago we were always welcome on his side of the mountain. We've been too busy with the stores to ever get there."

"Yes, please stop by anytime." Tom looked over his shoulder and watched Isabella taking clothes out of a box and putting them on the shelves.

Emma glanced at Sam and winked. "Excuse me one minute." She walked over to Isabella, grabbed her hand, and walked her over to Tom. "Isabella, please meet an old friend of ours. This is Tom Dendro."

"Pleased to meet you, Mr. Dendro."

"I'm…um…happy to…um…meet you too."

Sam smiled and nodded at Emma. "Isabella, please sit and join us while we catch up?"

"Oh, I couldn't, sir. I don't want to interfere with your reunion, and I have much work to do."

"Don't worry about that. There are no other customers at this time. Come sit with us."

"Yes, please join us?" Tom said, smiling.

Sam brought over a chair.

Emma held Isabella's hand. "We have been so lucky to have Isabella here. She came over from Italy with her family last year and has been a great help to us. I don't know what we'd do without her."

"Thank you, Mrs. Barrett," Isabella said, blushing. "You are too kind. It has been a blessing to work for you and Mr. Barrett."

Sam put his hand on Tom's shoulder. "So, Tom...how long are you going to be in town? Can you have dinner with us tonight?"

"I'd love to. I'll be here for two days. I need to purchase lumber for a new pasture enclosure we're constructing for the additional cattle we're buying."

Emma tapped Isabella on her shoulder. "You must join us."

"Thank you, Mrs. Barrett. I would love to, but I can't. My uncle just came over from Italy and we are having dinner as a family tonight."

Tom straightened his tie and looked at Sam, who nodded and silently urged him along. "Miss Schillachi..."

"Please call me Isabella."

"Isabella, I was wondering if you would like to have dinner with me tomorrow evening."

Isabella's face turned red and she looked at Emma, who nodded and mouthed the word *yes*. "I'd be delighted, Mr. Dendro."

"Great! Oh, and please call me Tom. How about I come by your house at six o'clock tomorrow?"

"That would be perfect. We live at the edge of town. We're the farm with the blue barn. I'm afraid you might be asked a million questions by my family. They are quite protective of me."

"I understand. I look forward to our dinner, Isabella."

Isabella smiled widely. "Me too."

Sam looked at Isabella. "I will speak with your father today and put in a good word for Tom to ease his mind."

"Thank you," Tom said, standing up. "Well, I should be going. I have a meeting with Mr. Heath in a few minutes about the lumber. What time should I come by for dinner tonight?"

"How about six o'clock?" Emma asked.

"Six would be great."

"We live up the road a mile in the house with a red-and-white barn." Emma gave Tom a big hug, wiped away a tear, and whispered, "I am glad you came by."

"I wish I had visited sooner."

"I understand. We never stopped looking out our window for you. I've missed you so much."

Tom hugged Emma back and quietly said, "I've missed you too."

# 80

"HOLD THIS POST for me, Tom," Williams said. "So…what's up with you? You've been out of it ever since you got back from the city. Don't tell me it's that girl you've been courting? What's her name—Bella?"

"Isabella," Tom said. "I don't know. We went out a few times, and I can't stop thinking about her. She's really nice, and we have fun together. She's a great cook too. I like her."

"Uh oh. That doesn't sound good."

"What do you mean?"

"Next thing…you're going to want to marry her and start a family. You're too young for that."

"I'm nineteen. That's not too young. And anyway, what's so bad about getting married and having a family? I've got a good job and plenty of money."

"Have you mentioned it to your dad?"

"No."

"Well, you should. Now hand me that post, and let's get back to work."

Dendro walked up, sweating from hammering in posts all day. "What are you two talking about?"

"I'll leave you and the kid alone," Williams said. "He's got something he wants to talk to you about. Talk some sense into him, will ya?" Williams walked off in a huff, muttering to himself, "Kids nowadays got no sense. No sense at all." He turned around and yelled, "Nuts, I say, nuts!"

"What's he talking about, Tom? What have you got to tell me?"

"Um, nothing really. He's crazy. We were talking about Isabella. You know, the woman I've been going out with in the city."

"Yes."

"I mentioned how nice she is and how I kind of like her."

"You do, huh?"

"Yes, but he has me going off and marrying her. Don't get me wrong, it's not a terrible idea."

"What's not a terrible idea?" Dendro repeated. "Marrying her?"

"I'm not going to ask her soon, but maybe someday."

Dendro nodded a few times and grunted. "Hmmm, I see. Well, you are at the age when men start thinking about such things. Why don't you bring her up to the house to have dinner with us sometime?"

"You'd be fine with that? And you wouldn't make fun of me in front of her, would you?"

"Sure, have her come over so I can meet her. And, no, I won't make fun of you. We'll send Williams off somewhere. Otherwise, she might not want to see you again," Avery said, laughing.

"Thanks. She's so nice. You'll really like her."

# 81

A MAN WALKED up to Tom and tapped him on the shoulder.

"God, you scared me," Tom said, putting a hand to his chest. "You're on private property. What do you want?"

"I'm sorry," the man said. "I was looking for Tom Dendro."

"I'm Tom Dendro."

The man cocked his head and smiled. "Is there an older Tom Dendro? The owner of the cattle business."

"You must mean my father. I run the day-to-day work."

"I heard you were a natural at running this operation. Why are you out here by yourself mending the fence? You're too important for that."

"Thanks. A bunch of our ranch hands went out last night in town and came down with food or alcohol poisoning. They're all sick. Is there anything I can do for you?"

"I was wondering if you would be interested in purchasing some cattle."

"You'll need to speak to my father about that. Did you make an appointment?"

"No. I was in town and speaking with local business owners. They said Tom Dendro was the man who might buy my cattle. I'm sorry. This is highly unprofessional of me. If it's not too much bother, please direct me to his assistant and I will make an appointment."

"No need. We usually don't conduct business with folks who simply walk up, but we try to keep things as casual as possible. Follow me."

"I appreciate it. Thank you."

Tom pointed behind him. "It's a half mile up to the right."

THE MAN LOOKED around. Seeing no one, he took out a rock he had in his jacket and hit Tom on the back of the head. Then he dragged him down a ravine. There were chains and a grenade hidden under leaves behind a boulder.

Tom started to come to. "What are you doing?"

"Be quiet," the man said, and stuffed a rag in Tom's mouth. He pointed a gun at Tom's head. "Any sudden moves and it's over for you. You understand, young Tom?"

Tom nodded.

The man tied Tom to the boulder and rigged the grenade's fuse with a flintlock mechanism to the chains.

"Now it's time to see your daddy. Better hope he likes you."

THE STRANGER WALKED up to the barn and saw Dendro tending to a nursing cow. He had waited what seemed a lifetime for this day. *Steady. Don't spook him. Smile nice and big.* "Excuse me, sir. Are you Mr. Thomas Dendro?"

Dendro stood up. "Yes, I am. May I help you?"

The stranger clenched his jaw. *You lowdown, dirty pirate. Just shake his hand and get it over with.* "Pleased to meet you, sir. I'm surprised to see you here alone."

"We're short-staffed today. What can I do for you?"

The stranger cocked his pistol and pushed it into Dendro's

stomach. *This is almost too easy*, he thought. "Tom will live, just as long as you do what I say." *Keep him off balance.* The stranger tilted his head and began whistling.

Dendro's hands clenched into fists as he glanced at his gun lying on the ground. "Where's my son?"

"He's alive for now," the stranger said, and then howled like a wolf. "And don't even think about going for your gun."

Dendro reached over to grab to him. "You're crazy," Dendro said.

"Easy, Thomas. Is today the day you want your son to die?"

"What have you done with Tom?"

"In due time, Thomas. In due time. It's a beautiful day isn't it?"

Dendro glared at him.

"You really should have security on your ranch. You never know when someone like me will come around. It's a shame all your people got sick. Wonder how that happened? Guess something they drank didn't agree with them."

"Listen, you demented…"

"Demented? Hmm, I used to be what people call normal. Then you did what you did, and things went a little off track after that."

"Stop fooling around and tell me where's Tom. If you've hurt him—"

"Then what?" the stranger interrupted. "What are you going to do? This didn't have to happen. It's your fault."

"What did I ever do to you?"

The man laughed. "Never thought you'd see me, did you, Avery? You don't notice any similarities?"

"Avery? I'm Thomas Dendro. You must be mistaking me for some-one else."

"We really do look alike, don't we?"

"Who are you talking about? Now give me my son."

"They say we had the same eyes."

"What?"

"Look at my eyes," the stranger screamed. "Look at them and tell me what you see."

"I don't know what you want. They're eyes."

"They don't remind you of anyone?" *How can he have forgotten?*

"No. Stop playing games and bring me my son. I'll give you whatever you want."

"You will address me properly," the stranger yelled, pushing the pistol deeper into Dendro's stomach. "You will call me *The Boss*, you dirty mongrel."

"All right," Dendro yelled. "Just settle down."

"Don't tell me to settle down. You ruined my life. Now I'm going to ruin yours. You took away what was most important to me. Now I'm going to take your son away from you."

"No…No…I'll give you anything. Please leave Tom alone. Whatever I did…I'll make it up to you. You can have whatever you want. Just name it."

The stranger shoved the pistol under Dendro's chin. "What I really want is you dead. You still don't understand, do you? You have to ask forgiveness for your sins. Then maybe I'll let your son live."

"Forgiveness for what? What did I do?"

"Down on your knees, sinner."

Dendro knelt. "I'm sorry."

"Sorry for what, you dog?"

"Sorry for whatever I did to you."

The stranger held the pistol against Dendro's temple. "You must address me properly."

"Fine…Boss…Boss? Wait a minute. You're the one who's been looking for me."

"That's right, dog. Do you get it now?"

Dendro stared at the man. He shook his head, not understanding. *How can he not know who I am?*

Dendro's eyes grew wide.

The Boss smiled. "You get it now, don't you."

"You do look like him."

The Boss wiped away a tear. "He was my world. He meant everything to me. You left him on that island to die like a rat."

"No…we left him food and water after we mutinied the ship. A boat should have come around in a day or two. We didn't want him dead. He could have remained with us, but he didn't want to."

"He was too good a man to run off and be a lowdown pirate like you."

"What happened?"

The Boss couldn't hold back the tears. His hands trembled, and his head kept shaking. "He barely stayed alive on the island. Survived one year, until a boat sailed by and saved him. He was a changed man when he came home."

"I'm sorry. We didn't mean for any of that to happen. Please give me my son back."

"He was an excellent father," The Boss said, staring off in the distance. "He never meant to be so mean to me. The whippings weren't too bad. But Mother told him he shouldn't keep hitting me over the head. Sometimes he'd yell out your name when he was mad at me."

"I'm sorry."

"He never wanted me to call him Father. It was always Captain Gibson."

# 82

DENDRO CAUGHT A glimpse of Williams as he snuck up and swung a large stick, hitting Gibson over the head and knocking him to the ground. Dendro jumped on Gibson, pointing his pistol at him.

"Don't hurt me, Captain Gibson. Don't hurt me."

Dendro looked at Williams and shook his head. "I'm glad you showed up. Thanks."

"I had a feeling I should stop by and see you and Tom today."

"I'm glad you did."

Williams put his foot on Gibson's chest and leaned back, looking at Dendro. "What's up with him?"

Dendro shook Gibson and slapped him across the face. "Where's Tom? Tell me where he is."

"You took Tom?" Williams asked, and then kicked Gibson in the ribs. "You're a dead man."

Gibson grabbed his ribs. "I'll take you to him, Captain Gibson. Just don't hit me."

"Start walking," Dendro said, hauling Gibson to his feet and pushing a pistol in his back. "Williams, get my gun."

Gibson started singing like a child. "He's in the ravine. He's in the ravine."

"You better not be lying," Dendro snarled. "If Tom's not there…"

Gibson hit himself on the head. "He's there. I wasn't going to hurt him. I just wanted to hurt you, Captain Gibson, like you hurt me. I mean Avery, like you hurt my father. My head hurts. Can I sit for a while?"

"No," Dendro yelled. "Keep moving. You better not have hurt him."

Gibson pointed to a boulder. "He's over there, behind the rock."

Dendro waved over Williams. "Keep an eye on him." Dendro ran to Tom.

He found Tom shackled to a boulder and gagged. A grenade was attached to the chains. "You hurt?" Dendro asked as he took the rag out of Tom's mouth.

"I'm all right."

"Bring Gibson here," Dendro yelled.

"You heard the man," Williams said, pushing Gibson forward.

Gibson smiled as he walked around the boulder. "I told you I didn't hurt him."

"Get Tom out of that lock now," Dendro demanded. "I don't know how you wired the grenade to that flintlock, but disarm it."

"I'd love to, but I'm not in a generous mood today."

Williams punched Gibson in the kidneys, bringing him to his knees.

Dendro walked over to Gibson and punched him in the face. "Free him now or I swear I'll shoot you in each knee until you do."

Gibson narrowed his eyes at Dendro. "My, my, aren't you the testy one? Give me your estate, and we'll call it even."

"It's yours. Just get Tom out safely."

"How can I be sure you aren't lying?"

"You have my word."

"You swear you'll never hit me again, Captain Gibson?"

"I swear," Dendro said.

Williams stood a few feet away from Tom, staring at the grenade.

"If you so much as twitch, I'll shoot you," Dendro said and pushed Gibson forward.

"I have the key in my pocket," Gibson said.

"Back away from Tom," Dendro said, standing between them. "Take it out slowly and hand it to me."

Dendro shoved the gun into Gibson's chest.

Gibson slowly reached into his pocket. In half a second, he pulled out a knife he had hidden in his jacket and spun around facing Dendro.

He pushed the pistol Dendro was holding up in the air.

Dendro pulled the trigger, but the bullet ricocheted off a tree.

Gibson swung the knife down, striking Dendro on the arm. Gibson reached over and grabbed Tom. He smirked as he held the knife to Tom's throat.

Dendro grabbed his bleeding arm with one hand while still pointing the pistol at Gibson. "Don't hurt Tom," Dendro pleaded.

"Put the pistols down," Gibson yelled, spit flying from his mouth. "Both of you. Do it now."

Dendro dropped the pistol and backed up two steps, holding up his hands. Williams did the same.

"See we're backing away. The pistols are on the ground. Let's talk this out. You can have the estate like I said. It's all yours. Please let Tom go."

"Why should I trust you…you…pirate? You left my father to die."

"No…no. That was a mistake. That should have never happened. We took over the ship because none of us were getting paid. Like I told you, your father didn't want to join us."

"Join a bunch of pirates? My father was too good for you criminals."

"I'm sorry. I know I can never make it up to you. But you can have my estate. The business. The cattle. It's yours. Tom had nothing to do with what happened to your father. Please don't hurt him."

Gibson put the knife between his teeth and unlocked the padlock attached to the chains holding the grenade in place preventing it from exploding. He held the grenade and flintlock mechanism up to Tom's face. "All I have to do is drop this chain and Tom and I die. I don't mind dying…again. You've already killed me once."

# 83

GIBSON DROPPED THE chain igniting the flintlock mechanism. He held the now lit grenade next to both his and Tom's faces. He started counting backwards. "Five...four..."

Dendro's eyes grew wide and he rushed Gibson, knocking him to the ground. The grenade fell a few feet from them. Dendro punched Gibson on the side of his face, knocking him out. Then he ran over and covered Tom with his body.

Three seconds passed, and nothing happened. Three more seconds lapsed, and still no explosion. Dendro turned around and looked at the grenade while still covering Tom with his body. He looked at Williams, who was taking cover behind a tree. "It didn't blow up," Dendro said, almost laughing with joy. "It didn't blow up."

"Be careful," Williams said from behind the tree. "It can still go off."

Dendro gradually walked over to the grenade and picked it up. He reached back and threw it as far as he could. It rolled down the hill thirty yards and kept rolling. There was a large explosion and a cloud of dirt flew up in the air.

Gibson moaned and slowly pushed himself up from the ground. Williams ran over and grabbed him. "Don't move."

Dendro glared at Gibson, fists clenched as he walked over and punched Gibson as hard as he could, knocking him out again. Then he walked over to Tom and pulled the rest of the chains off him.

Tom hugged Dendro. "Thanks, Dad. I wasn't sure I was going to see you again."

"That's the first time you've ever called me Dad."

"I should have done it sooner. Would you really have given up everything to save me?"

"Of course. I'd do anything for my son."

Tom hugged Dendro again. "Your arm. Is it all right?"

"It's fine. It's already stopped bleeding. Let's take Gibson and tie him up in the barn," Dendro said. "Guess we have to notify the authorities."

"What if he starts saying you're Avery?" Tom asked.

"I don't know. He's acting crazy, so they'll probably think he's daft."

"Hope so," Williams said.

Dendro walked over to Gibson lying on the ground and smacked him on the face a few times. "Wake up. Time to go to jail."

Gibson held his jaw and glared at Dendro. "Don't send me to jail," Gibson yelled. "I won't make it in prison. I promise I'll leave you alone. Just let me go."

Dendro pushed the pistol in Gibson's back. "Start walking."

Dendro watched as Tom and Williams walked ten yards ahead. Williams lightly punched Tom on the shoulder and put his arm around him.

"You haven't won yet, Avery," Gibson grimaced. "You'll never get the best of me. One day I'll have your head mounted on my wall."

"Everything all right?" Williams asked as he and Tom turned around and began walking back to Dendro.

"He's just getting ornery."

"Maybe another punch to the head will do him good," Williams said.

"Absolutely," Dendro said as he cocked his arm.

"Don't hit me, Avery. Don't hit me."

Dendro scowled at Gibson. "I'm not Avery anymore." He aimed his pistol at Gibson's head. "Stop calling me that."

They tied up Gibson in one of the stalls in the barn. Dendro stood there staring at Gibson. He prayed his past had disappeared. Now it came flooding back. He worked hard to be a respected, wealthy man in the community. *Was it all going to vanish?*

Tom and Williams started to walk to the house. "You coming, Dad?"

"Be right there. Go ahead. I'm going to close the back door."

Dendro walked over to Gibson and stood over him.

Gibson furrowed his brow as Dendro untied the ropes.

"You letting me go?"

"It's one thing to try and kill me, but kidnapping my son..." Dendro's face grew red and his hands were shaking. "I've never killed a man in cold blood before. That changes today." Dendro pulled the trigger.

# 84

WILLIAMS AND TOM heard the shot and looked at each other. They turned around and ran toward the barn. Williams pulled out his pistol and held it out as he ran. Tom got there first.

Gibson and Dendro were wrestling on the ground. Dendro was on top of Gibson and swung, but Gibson moved and the punch landed on the ground. Gibson kicked Dendro off him and rolled over and grabbed a knife he had in his boot.

Dendro was getting up when Tom rushed over and tackled Gibson. The knife went flying. Gibson kicked Tom in the ribs and punched up, hitting him under the chin. Tom fell backward and landed hard on his back. Tom was trying to catch his breath when Dendro ran over and grabbed Gibson.

Dendro spun Gibson around and hit him with a series of punches that left Gibson stunned. Gibson stumbled back and stepped on the knife. He picked it up and ran at Dendro, knocking him down. He stood over Dendro, knife raised.

A shot rang out.

Gibson dropped the knife and put his hand to his chest. He raised his hand and saw blood. Williams ran over and kicked the knife away as Gibson fell to his knees.

A tear rolled down Gibson's cheek. "I tried to hurt him for you, Captain Gibson. I really tried."

Dendro, Tom, and Williams looked at each other without saying a word. Gibson fell over and let out a deep sigh. Williams leaned over and put his hand on Gibson's neck, feeling for a pulse.

"He's dead," Williams said. Then he looked at Dendro and Tom and shook his head. "He was crazier than a cow that ate bat dung."

"I couldn't bring myself to kill him," Dendro said. "I shot at the wall behind him. I wanted to kill him for what he did to Tom. But I couldn't. I even felt a little sorry for him. Thanks for saving me, again."

"Anytime. How'd he know you were in New York?"

Dendro shrugged. "I didn't ask. Guess I was too worked up trying to get to Tom. Thanks again for saving my hide."

"No problem. Just buy me a beer, and we'll call it even."

# 85

TWO WEEKS LATER, Dendro and Tom sat to eat lunch after rounding up the cattle. They were almost inseparable after the kidnapping. Dendro didn't want to miss any opportunity to spend time with Tom.

There was a knock on the door, and the housekeeper, Mrs. MacDermott, poked her head in the dining room. "Sorry to bother you, but a man says it is urgent he speak with you."

"Who is it?" Dendro asked.

"He says his name is Paddy, sir. He says he is an old friend of yours."

Dendro's eyes grew wide, and Tom dropped his fork. Dendro froze for a second, and then smiled at Mrs. MacDermott. "Thank you. Please take him to the sitting room. We'll be right there."

"Yes, sir."

"It can't be Paddy," Dendro said to Tom. "I saw him being dragged to the back of the cave by a *Mhuwe*."

"What do we do?"

"Figure out who it is and what he wants. Is your pistol primed?"

Tom checked his gun. "Yes, and I have my knife in my boot."

Dendro pulled out his gun and looked it over. "Good, I'm ready too. Let's go see what this is about."

Both Dendro and Tom walked into the room with pistols drawn. There was a man with his back to them. He was leaning on crutches and had only one leg.

The man turned around and smiled. "Is that any way to treat an old friend—with your pistols drawn?"

Dendro and Tom looked at each other and then back at the man.

"Well aren't you two going to say anything?"

Dendro slowly walked up and stared at the man in front of him. "Paddy, is that really you? You look exactly the same, 'cept for the leg. Sorry."

"Aye, Captain. It's me. That can't be Finn can it?"

"Yes, but I'm Tom now."

"Man have you grown up."

Dendro pointed to a chair. "How'd you find us? It's been years."

"Just dumb luck, really. I was in a bar in the city last year and overheard someone talk about how a kid had helped rob the bank some years ago—not long after we got to New York."

"Why'd you think it was Finn?"

"I didn't really, until I ran into Isaac after he was let out of prison but before he sailed to the Caribbean. He told me he ran into Finn before he went to jail, and how you two were up on the mountain. I guessed you headed to Tortuga or somewhere down there. But I saw someone walking in town last week who looked a lot like you. Older, but..."

"Thanks."

"You know what I mean. So, I ask this man at the bar who's that fellow walking down the street, and he says it's Tom Dendro. And how you inherited all this money and came over from Ireland and set up a cattle ranch. I started to put two and two together. I wasn't sure, until I just seen you two now."

Dendro handed Paddy a glass of whiskey. "But I saw you get dragged far back into the cave by one of those creatures."

"One of them was pulling me out the other side of the cave and was about to tear me apart when—"

"There's another side to the cave?"

"Sort of. Way back in the cave there was a pool of water. The creature jumped with me into it—"

"I had no idea there was anything back there."

"It's like a small pond, but you come out the other side of the mountain."

"That must be how some of them got into the cave," Tom said.

"I guess, but then there was a big roar from one of those creatures, and the one holding me let go and rushed back into the water. I hobbled down the mountain as fast as I could. I was kind of out of it and in a lot of pain. All I ate for days was grubs and mushrooms. My leg got green and all swollen."

"How'd you survive?" Dendro asked.

"These three hunters heard me moaning. By that time, I was really hurting and not making much sense. I remember some of it but not much. They took me to a doc in town and he ended up cutting off my leg. Said I had the gangrene, and if he didn't cut it off, I'd die. So...."

"What have you been doing since then?" Tom asked.

"Odd jobs here and there. Lots of people don't have much use for a one-legged man."

"I wished I'd known," Dendro said. "You were one of our best crew. How can I help?"

Paddy gave them a big toothy smile. "Well, that's why I'm here. I deserve double my share of the treasure. Especially for what I've gone through, with the leg and all."

"I see," Dendro said, and then looked at Tom.

"And what about a job here on your ranch? You really don't want me hanging around town. May have too much to drink one night and talk about you and Finn—I mean Tom."

Dendro's eyes narrowed. He held out his gun and walked over to Paddy. "You wouldn't be bribing me would you, Paddy?"

"Settle down, Captain. I didn't mean it. Just got a little greedy that's all. I'd never tell anyone about you and Finn. Besides, they'd put me in jail too."

"That's smart, Paddy." Dendro turned around and winked at Tom. "Paddy…there's no money left."

"What do you mean? It's gone?"

"We spent it all on the ranch. We didn't know anyone else was alive."

"Sorry, Paddy," Tom said.

"You couldn't have spent it all. You just couldn't have."

"Remember those pirates we saw in Tortuga?"

Paddy nodded.

"Well, they found out we were in New York and came after us. There was a big battle on Salisbury Island. Everyone but me and Tom died. We were only able to get a small amount of the treasure before the governor got most of it."

"What about what you robbed from the bank?"

"That wasn't us. I don't believe anyone really robbed it. Probably was just a ploy by the governor to keep the treasure for himself."

"How'd you get this place?"

"We saved and worked hard. Bought a little at a time. Plus, we were lucky. Everything fell into place at the right time."

"I don't believe you. You're just trying to keep it for yourself." Paddy clenched his jaw and pulled out a gun. He ran at Dendro, knocking both men and their guns to the ground. Tom jumped on

Paddy's back and tried to pull him off Dendro. Paddy hit Tom with his elbow, knocking him to the ground.

Paddy grabbed his gun and pointed it at Dendro. Two shots rang out. Tom dove on Paddy, knocking him to the side. "Dad, are you all right? Are you shot?"

"He missed me," Dendro yelled.

Dendro and Tom looked at Paddy lying there, blood gathering around him on the floor.

"Why'd you do it, Paddy?" Dendro asked. "We could have worked something out."

Paddy coughed up blood. "Once a pirate, always a pirate, I guess. Never thought I'd die on land. Give me a good burial, will ya, Captain?"

"I will, Paddy."

Paddy gasped and then stopped breathing. Mrs. MacDermott came running in.

"I heard a gunshot, sir. Are you and Thomas all right?"

"Yes. He pretended to be an acquaintance of ours from a long time ago and tried to rob us. He grabbed my pistol and it accidentally fired."

"Thank God you are both are fine. I'll get a few men from the fields to take his body away."

"Don't worry about it, Mrs. MacDermott. Tom and I will take care of it."

"I'm so sorry I let him in the house."

"It's not your fault. He was a sharper."

"A sharper, sir?"

"Someone who pretends to be someone he isn't to try and get money from you."

"Oh, I understand. Some men are very good at that."

"Yes…yes, they are."

TOM STARED AT the grave. "Maybe it was a bad idea to stay up here on Bear Mountain. What if another one of the crew is still around?"

"Don't worry. Paddy said Isaac sailed to the Caribbean. There can't be anyone else around after all these years."

"You're probably right. I hate that our past has shown up again. I'd hoped we were done with that."

"I know. Hopefully, that's all we'll have to deal with from now on. We should look into getting security up here though."

"Good idea, Dad. Seeing Paddy again got me to thinking about the cave and what's in it. Ever think about going back there and getting it?"

"I do. I've never really stopped thinking about all that money and jewelry in there. But it isn't worth it anymore."

"What do you mean?"

"Can't believe I'm saying this, but it would be crazy to try to get the money chest and coins. Despite what happened with Gibson and Paddy, things are going great for us. Why risk it? You got to let it go, Tom. We both have too much to live for."

"You're right. It's too dangerous."

"Exactly. Let's head back home and try to put this out of our minds. Let's see what Mrs. MacDermott has cooked up for us."

# 86

DENDRO SAT ALONE under a tall oak tree and clasped his hands on his head. A fine mist filled the air. He looked out at hundreds of cattle grazing on the side of the mountain. The large estate he had built had smoke billowing from the two chimneys. Horses were neighing in the fields. He took a deep breath and smiled. *I've finally achieved what I've always wanted—respect from the community.*

Tom walked up. "What you doing under this tree, Dad?"

"Just thinking."

"Everything all right?"

"Just reflecting on how much things have changed for you, me, and Williams over the years."

"It is a lot different. I never dreamed it would be this good."

"No more looting and risking our lives. And having you as a son. It's more than I ever hoped for."

"It's what I've always wanted too, Dad."

"Even having Williams as a friend and business partner. I wouldn't have guessed that in a million years."

"He can be strange at times, but I'm glad we met him and he's here with us."

"I got something I've been meaning to tell you. Um…"

"What, Dad?"

"Well, when I die…"

"Don't talk like that."

"It'll happen one of these days."

"Not for a long time. Let's talk about something else."

"No. I got to say it. Tom, you're a great young man. I couldn't be prouder."

"Thanks, Dad."

"So, when I die, this is all yours. I went into town and drew up a Will."

"All of what is mine?"

Dendro pointed left and right. "Everything. The land, the cattle, the house, the business. It's all yours."

"Dad, I don't know what to say."

"No need to say anything. I know you'll take great care of everything."

"Thanks. I'll do my best to run things like you do. But none of that is going to happen for a long time."

"There's something else I've been thinking about. I just keep coming back to it."

"What?"

"I want to do something meaningful while I'm still around. Kind of a legacy thing. What people will remember about me when I'm gone."

"I see. So, what do you have in mind?"

"I'd like to give some of our money away. Sounds crazy, huh?"

"No, not really."

Dendro put his hand on Tom's shoulder. "We've got more money than we'll ever need. We could do a lot of good with it. I know we've already given money to help those in need around us, but I was hoping you and I could create an organization where we can give away a bunch of money to worthwhile causes."

"That actually sounds fun."

"I was hoping you'd like the idea. But it's your money too, so… let's sleep on it and talk more about it later this week."

"Probably a good idea to think it over, but I can tell you now…I love it."

Dendro scrunched his nose. "I hate to admit this, but part of me wants to do it for selfish reasons too."

"What do you mean?"

"They must never discover who I really am, of course, but can you imagine the looks on those Royal Navy higher-ups if they learned how much money I made over the years? And now giving a lot of it away?"

"They'd fall all over themselves just to shake your hand," Tom said, laughing.

"Now that would be funny. Success really is the best revenge."

# ABOUT THE AUTHOR

James Gallahan is a multi-genre writer living in Northern Virginia with his wife.

He has short stories published in the Cat & Mouse Press anthology, *Beach Pulp*, the Greater Lehigh Valley Writers Group anthology, *Rewriting the Past*, and *Pilcrow and Dagger* literary magazine, *The Survivor*.

James was a finalist in the *Writer's Digest* May 2018 Your Story competition and won the Grey Wolfe Publishing's June 2018 monthly writing contest.

His short story, "Missing in Rehoboth," in *Beach Pulp*, was a semi-finalist in the 2019 ScreenCraft Short Story contest. *Beach Pulp* received second-place honors, collection of short stories by multiple authors, and honorable mention for book design at the National Federation of Press Women's annual communications awards ceremony. It also won first-place awards for book design and collection of short stories by multiple authors, and received second place for book editing by the Delaware Press Association.

James is a member of the Greater Lehigh Valley Writers Group, and the James River Writers.

Please check out his website at www.jamesgallahan.com.

www.ingramcontent.com/pod-product-compliance
Lightning Source LLC
Chambersburg PA
CBHW030919260626
47169CB00002B/318